Dear Reader:

How far will one g̲o̲?̲ ... find out as Cynthia Diane Thornton brings us *Rise of the Phoenix: Larger Than Lyfe II*, the follow-up novel to her debut featuring savvy record mogul Keshari Mitchell, leader of Larger Than Lyfe Entertainment who has ties to a sophisticated drug ring.

Keshari faked her own death and fled to Brazil where she underwent plastic surgery, transforming herself into "Darian Boudreaux." In *Rise of the Phoenix*, she daringly reappears in Los Angeles with her new identity, founding a start-up film company, Phoenix Films. An unexpected script arrives from a "mysterious source"—it's a biopic of her own life as Keshari Mitchell.

If you thrive on juicy tales from the entertainment and celebrity world, then this novel has all of the elements you crave. It also offers a behind-the-scenes look at the drug game, a timely topic with the current war on drugs at the California-Mexico border.

It's street lit with an upscale twist and I'm sure you will enjoy the next chapter in "Darian's" life. So sit back, relax and escape to the underworld with Cynthia Diane Thornton.

Thanks for supporting all of the Strebor Books authors. To find me on the web, please go to www.eroticanoir.com or join my online social network, www.planetzane.org.

Blessings,

Zane

Zane
Publisher
Strebor Books International
www.simonandschuster.com/streborbooks

ALSO BY CYNTHIA DIANE THORNTON
Larger Than Lyfe

ZANE PRESENTS

RISE
of the
PHOENIX
LARGER *than* LYFE *II*

CYNTHIA DIANE THORNTON

STREBOR BOOKS

NEW YORK LONDON TORONTO SYDNEY

SBI

Strebor Books
P.O. Box 6505
Largo, MD 20792
http://www.streborbooks.com

ISBN 978-1-59309-322-8
ISBN 978-1-4391-9850-6 (e-book)
LCCN 2011934767

First Strebor Books trade paperback edition October 2011

Cover design: www.mariondesigns.com
Cover photograph: © Keith Saunders/Marion Designs

10 9 8 7 6 5 4 3 2 1

Manufactured in the United States of America

For information regarding special discounts for bulk purchases, please contact Simon & Schuster Special Sales at 1-866-506-1949 or business@simonandschuster.com

The Simon & Schuster Speakers Bureau can bring authors to your live event. For more information or to book an event, contact the Simon & Schuster Speakers Bureau at 1-866-248-3049 or visit our website at www.simonspeakers.com.

FOR MY MOTHER, DONNA KAREN...

My biggest critic, one of my greatest irritations, the incessant voice in my head, my teacher, my confidante, and my very BEST friend.

My intellect, my independence, my strength and drive, my ability to survive and surpass even the most adverse circumstances, my creativity, my political ideologies, and the woman that I am can all be attributed to YOU.

I always took for granted that you would be here to see this project come full circle. I know that you smile down from Heaven now, having read every word of everything that I write. You're still my biggest critic. You're still coming up with great suggestions. You're still my biggest fan.

"LOVE" seems such an understatement to describe the overwhelming depth of feeling and the undying sense of gratitude I have for all that you were and all that you still are to me.

I love you infinitely, Mommie.

—CYN

ACKNOWLEDGMENTS

To the Creator, the God Consciousness, the Omniscient One from whom ALL of my blessings and life lessons flow. All that I am and all that I aspire to be is because of YOU.

Sara Camilli, my literary agent extraordinaire. Beautiful, maternal spirit, mediator when my temperamental artist side comes out, and my saving grace in contracts and negotiations. Just know that I thank you immensely always for all that you do for me, for being in my corner. My next major goal is to make movies. Be ready.

The beautiful, talented, phenomenal Miss ZANE. No matter how far or how high I go in this business, you are the woman I will always remember MOST. YOU are the person who gave me my first book deal and my professional start in the publishing industry. I am ETERNALLY grateful for the gigantic opportunity that YOU made available to me. I mean this from the bottom of my heart and I can never say this enough. Love, hugs, and a multitude of abundance, success, and blessings to you.

Charmaine Roberts Parker, the kind, accommodating, savvy sista who runs a good deal of ZANE's multifaceted publishing enterprise. As the publishing director for Strebor Books International, I honestly and truly love working with you and I wish you a multitude of blessings and success in your literary career as an author.

Keith Saunders at MARION DESIGNS. Hands down, there ain't nobody better!!! I come up with an idea, ANY rough draft of an idea, and this genius of a man can make it into the HOTTEST book cover to land on a store shelf. Can you tell that I'm one of your biggest fans?!

Timothy Ledford, my guardian angel, my knight in shining armor, my muscle-bound biker dude with the "S" on your chest. You have rescued me more times than I can count without ever requiring a single thing in return. When there was no one else to call, I called you and, the unbelievably BEAUTIFUL spirit that you are, you came to my aid EVERY TIME and you always came immediately. I shall always love you for ALL that you've been to me and I feel immensely honored to be able to sincerely call you MY FRIEND. We have had some of the most profound discussions about a little bit of everything and I never cease to be amazed by the concepts and ideas that formulate in your brilliant mind. I don't even know that I could find a woman out here in the world who is good enough for you, so, in the event that we do not find someone who is suitable to be your life partner, I'm gonna marry you. LOL!!!

Dawn "Dré" Lewis… I slapped a Post-It note that said, "MINE!" on your forehead the moment that I laid eyes on you. You've made me smile, you've made me cry, you've made me mad, and you've always made me smile again. There is a light that shines from you that is like the sun in the face of the rain. You are a TRUE FRIEND, the kind that every girl like me should have in her life. You've been in my corner in good times and in some of the absolute worst of times, cheering for me, praying for me, being present for me, particularly when I felt that no one else was, and I only hope that I can be the same friend ALWAYS to you. I'll love you forever…and that is real.

Chris Baldwin, YOU reinforced for me above all others the unbelievable amount of love and unity that survive and thrive in The Community. You were there for me at a time when I needed you most and I am so, so honored to call you FRIEND, FAMILY, MY SISTER. Love, hugs, and many, many blessings to you and your beautiful partner-for-life, Shelbie. And keep in mind that you owe me dinner!!! LMAO!

Leona Romich at URBAN REVIEWS… You gave me my first 5-star review as a professional writer, so you should already know that I could not go without mentioning you and thanking you for taking the time to read my book and the friendly communication that we had after you read it. And the fact you really enjoyed my book was like a cherry on top of it all. Much respect, girl!

To all of the authors on the Strebor imprint. We are one powerful group of African-American authors and we owe it to the African-American authors who came before us to REPRESENT and soar as high as we can soar in this literary game. At the stroke of our pens and by the keys of our computer keyboards, we have the ability to captivate, titillate, uplift, enrage, make laugh, make think, motivate, educate, and inspire generations of the masses of readers here and abroad. I love being a member of the Strebor Family. It feels like family.

To every up-and-coming author on my Facebook Friends list who aspires to be the next publishing industry superstar, LET'S KEEP GRINDIN'…cuz dreams do come true!

If I left anyone out, TRUST, I will definitely catch you the next go 'round in my next book.

Love and hugs to every single one of my supporters and readers. Without you, I could just write this shit in a journal and call it a day. **HUGE SMILE!**

FOREWORD

The following fictional account is ENTERTAIN-MENT, no different than the erotic novel or the lyrical braggadocio of the hip-hop star. The closer that I came to completion of the entire publishing process for my first novel, *Larger Than Lyfe*, and, subsequently, its sequel, *Rise of the Phoenix*, the larger the moral implications of it all became for me. I did not want readers to believe that I was attempting to glamorize drug trafficking nor the gangster's lifestyle; hence, this foreword.

My primary goal for this novel, from the very beginning, was ENTERTAINMENT. My mission is to provide readers with what so many of us LOVE…the gangster's story…because there are millions of us who are absolutely mesmerized by the danger, the intricate schemes, the unbelievable sums of money, the power, the corruption, the sex, and the bloodshed that are always associated with gangsters.

In every major city in America and in a few, not-so-major cities as well, a gangster's story exists. The gangster's story and his (or her) organized criminal affiliations and activities are as much a part of the fabric of this country as the dead presidents depicted on the currency that we exchange. Two, relatively new genres in the publishing industry called "street lit" and "true crime" were created to feed the fascination of those of us who love the gangster's story and a whole smorgasbord of authors in these two genres relish in feeding us what we love, from Nikki Turner's *Riding Dirty on I-95* to Mario Puzo's classic, *The Godfather*, to Teri Woods's series, *True to the Game*.

Scarface, *The Godfather*, *The Sopranos*, *GoodFellas*, *Belly*, *American Gangster*, *State Property*, and *Casino* are all well-known and highly successful films. The film industry has probably been the most successful at providing us with vivid, mostly fictionalized depictions of the gangster's story.

A multibillion-dollar, money-making enterprise has been created using every available form of media, from music to books to movies to videogames, to feed the overwhelming fascination that so many of us have for the gangster story. We all know that what these people do is unbelievably, heinously wrong, but, just like watching the aftermath of a horrific car crash, we cannot seem to stop watching, reading and wanting to know more, as much as we can about what gangsters do, how they live, who they are.

Once I've fully engaged my readers' attention with sex, humor, drama, danger and luxe lifestyles and landscapes transpiring in the lives of some of America's rich, famous and infamous, my mission is always to drop some knowledge, to educate, to give readers mental "food" to turn over in their minds. My desire is to provide readers with some truth, facts, provocative topics for more serious and substantive discussions and debates and, quite possibly, progressive action once they've finished reading my book. For example: some of the most ruthless and most intriguing gangsters of all are members of our own government, past and current. Powerful figures who are connected, well-connected, and very well-connected in American politics have closely protected their own dirty, little secrets of direct involvement in organized crime—from the Iran-Contra scandal to Halliburton to the alleged affiliations of "Camelot's" patriarch, Joe Kennedy, to what is taking place in the Middle Eastern areas of Iraq and Afghanistan right now. There is enough material throughout the history of the United States and American government that exposes ruthless, deceptive, and completely illegal financial schemes and enterprises committed by powerful political figures or powerful men with powerful political connections to make blockbuster, gangster page-turners for years to come. You see, real gangsters do more than run drug rings, racketeering and prostitution operations in the seedy underbellies of major cities. Real gangsters have the power to affect the policies that directly affect YOU and ME.

Enjoy *Rise of the Phoenix: Larger Than Lyfe II.*

PROLOGUE

LOS ANGELES

Palm trees, amazing weather, beautiful, silicone-and-Botox-boosted women, beautiful real estate with carefully manicured lawns, where seeing Lamborghinis, Ferraris, and Aston Martins on city streets is a fairly regular occurrence. As the theme song sings at the beginning of *The Beverly Hillbillies*, "…swimming pools, movie stars…" Los Angeles established the term "bling" and the rest of the world watches and imitates, trying to keep up.

But behind the mental and visual overload on superficiality that shall probably always prevail in Los Angeles and for which Los Angeles has probably always been well-known dwells a construct that is far more…SINISTER. It owns and controls substantial segments of Los Angeles. It doesn't care whether or not you respect it, but you damned well better fear it. From the movie industry to the finance sector, it's got the city in a chokehold and it aims to get paid…exceedingly. What is this monster, you ask, this monster that feeds voraciously on colossal sums of money and on the souls of the people in the city that it controls? This monster that operates in the seedy underbelly of Los Angeles and has for as long as Los Angeles has existed, controls some of the most respected industries that you would never imagine that it does, and has a bad reputation that it will likely never be able to shake is none other than ORGANIZED CRIME.

Have you ever wondered if some business establishment that you patronize might be a front for something else? It very well could be. Have you ever wondered how some start-up companies get their initial funding? The local bank may not be the only business entity that carefully reviewed their business plan.

They are not just the gun-wielding, dangerous-looking, lengthy rap sheet, mean-mugging, tattooed-up thugs you see when you venture toward the wrong sides of town. These are merely their soldiers.

Mafia, La Eme, Crips, Bloods, the Jamaicans, Yakuza, and others all take varying shares of the pie, and sometimes they vie with one another for larger slices.

The following is a year in the life of a few Los Angelenos.

-1-

"**D**arian, baby, come on…wake up," Mars coaxed, gently stroking Darian's hair as he sat beside her hospital bed.

Claudio Henriqué, Darian's plastic surgeon, assured Mars that she would be fine. He and his staff had kept her under close observation since completion of the surgery. She would be extremely groggy from the anesthesia, but she was expected to make a full and relatively speedy recovery.

Keshari Mitchell, now "Darian Boudreaux," had been through a total of twelve very high-risk plastic surgeries in a massive physical transformation required for her to fully assume her new identity. A team of surgeons, over the span of a year and half, employed some of the most controversial, state-of-the-art medical techniques on the planet to deliver a clean slate to the former, internationally known record label mogul. She was now…physically… a completely different person. She'd undergone four levels of skin bleaching, taking her complexion from a deep cinnamon brown to a light honey color. A team of oral surgeons dramatically altered her dental profile by breaking and resetting her upper and lower jaws and implementing dental implants so that neither dental x-rays nor impressions would ever reveal the woman she used to be. Surgical contouring made slight but noticeable changes to Keshari's almond-shaped eyes and the rest of her distinctive facial features. Chocolate brown contacts concealed her natural, hazel-green eye color. An extremely risky surgical tweaking of her vocal cords changed her voice. Painful laser surgery permanently altered her finger-prints. Her trademark raven hair was professionally colored to a vibrant auburn hue that beautifully comple-mented her new skin tone. Keshari Mitchell ceased to exist, and Darian Boudreaux was born.

From the day Keshari Mitchell and David Weisberg, her longtime attorney and friend, sat down together and privately constructed, step-by-step, the intricate scheme to fake Keshari's demise, David had formed dummy cor-porations, a wealthy familial background, an inheritance fund, and a sizeable investment portfolio to legitimize both Darian Boudreaux and her more than $100 million net worth. It had taken years to pull it all together, but REAL gangsters always had a strong exit strategy…just in case.

Before making the strategic and very expensive *Mission: IMPOSSIBLE*-style escape to Sao Paolo, Brazil, Keshari Mitchell, now Darian Boudreaux, had been one of the most powerful businesswomen in the United States. As founder and sole owner of a tremendously successful, multimillion-dollar record label, Larger Than Lyfe Entertainment, she had been the most powerful woman in the music industry. Unknown to most, there also was a far darker side to Keshari Mitchell. As second-in-command in The Consortium, one of the chief West Coast distributors of Colombian and Mexican cocaine, Keshari Mitchell had, undisputedly, been one of the most powerful women in organized crime…and she'd wanted OUT…completely…of an arrangement that was, non-negotiably, blood in–blood out.

Ironically, the more Keshari Mitchell wanted to distance herself from the criminal organization to which she belonged, the more the duality of her life that existed on both sides of the law unraveled. A DEA special task force operation mounted pressure against Keshari in an attempt to coerce her to testify before a federal grand jury. The DEA's goal, via information they hoped to acquire from Keshari Mitchell, was to take down all of the major players in The Consortium, then go after the Mexicans and Colombians who supplied The Consortium with cocaine. Keshari Mitchell knew that the only outcome for anyone in her line of business who cooperated with the law was death, and she made it clear to DEA that they would get nothing out of her. Rumors about the intensely private music mogul began to pop up on the covers of entertainment tabloids nationally. Both intimate details about her romantic life as well as careful "hints" regarding her alleged affiliation to a well-known, West Coast, criminal empire became the media's focus. An almost successful assassination attempt was made on Keshari's life. Then, when it seemed that matters could not become any worse, Keshari was framed by some unknown saboteur and arrested on murder-for-hire charges in conjunction with the prison death of Richard Tresvant, the notorious founder and head of The Consortium, who'd gone untouched for years as he mercilessly ran The Consortium, then was convicted for first-degree murder and had been awaiting a new trial on appeal.

With the deck stacked entirely against her, the ONLY way out of the colossal mess that had become Keshari Mitchell's life was by death and, in an intricate scheme planned between Keshari and her long-time attorney, she committed what authorities called "an apparent suicide," and immediately fled the United States for the anonymity of one of the most populous places on earth, São Paulo, Brazil.

Hours turned to days, days turned to weeks, and weeks turned to months as Keshari Mitchell, now Darian Boudreaux, attempted to adjust mentally to her new identity and her new home. It had taken nerves of steel to carry out her plan of escaping to Brazil. Then, from day one after her arrival, she was often consumed by the fear of someone discovering the truth of what she'd done and that she was still alive. In her chic, ultra-modern hotel suite at the InterContinental, she often snapped awake in the middle of the night in a cold sweat, having dreamt of the Mexicans torturing and then murdering her in some horrific way after having found her in Brazil. Other nights, she dreamt of the almost successful attempt that had been made on her life, a bullet having missed her head by inches as she lay sleeping in her bed, goose down everywhere, the dead stranger who'd been hired to kill her lying on the grounds of her home, taken down by her security team.

As time passed, there were days when she was ridden with depression, feeling completely out of sorts, unable to even bring herself to get out of bed, unable to eat, unable to function, unable to compose her next plans. She would be ridden with intense feelings of sadness, frustration, hopelessness. She wondered if she should simply end it all. There was no way that she could make a life out of the limbo in which she now lived. She had carefully strategized a plan to get her away from her former life, but she had not fully weighed the emotional price she'd pay once she walked away from it all and into the unknown.

On impulse one afternoon when she'd finally compelled herself to start getting out and familiarizing herself with her new city, Darian did the unthinkable. She reconnected with her former life by sending an anonymous postcard

to her former love… the former love of Keshari Mitchell…
West Coast general counsel for ASCAP, Mars Buchanan.
With the unbridled stupidity of that impulsive move,
she instantly jeopardized both her life and the life of the
man she loved. Never in a million years did she think of
what would happen next. Mars Buchanan gave up everything, resigned from his role at ASCAP, told his family
that he was taking a trip and scoured Brazil until he found
her…and married her.

—2—

Misha Tierney stared down at the seven-carat, flawless, radiant-cut, white diamond engagement ring with its matching platinum wedding band that Marcus Means had had custom-designed for her. The rings filled her with seething rage. She had no idea what had broken in her head to have caused her to wear them for as long as she had. She was clearly becoming as crazy as that motherfucker who called himself her husband. She took the rings off and hurled them across the dimly lit bedroom. They landed behind the tufted, cream-colored sectional, and she heard the clink as they hit the high-gloss bamboo floor. She truly hated that man. Today was officially their second wedding anniversary, and she would rather be dead than have to endure a third. The day before, Marcus had lovingly showed her that he had remembered their "anniversary" by having vases of premium, long-stemmed, white roses placed on every flat surface of the bedroom that Misha kept herself locked away in like a fortress. In every other room of the house that Misha walked through, there were more vases of the white roses to delight her eyes and nose. The gesture looked and felt to Misha as suffocating as a mausoleum. She quickly began organizing her affairs and making phone calls so that she could make a hasty departure from the house. She knew that if she stayed around for very much longer, Marcus would soon arrive with some other very expensive celebratory gesture for their second year of marriage, and Misha wanted to be nowhere around when he came. It was ridiculous that he even made the effort. There was no mistake whatsoever that she despised him.

Forced into a marriage to a man who made Satan appear to have some redeeming qualities, Misha Tierney's life had become a living hell. Marcus Means, her new husband, was in Larger Than Lyfe Entertainment's books, coercing her into paying The Consortium 10 points every month from Larger Than Lyfe's revenues. Marcus had even been peering into Misha's events planning firm, demanding to have his people take a look at the numbers there. Marcus and his people were following and watching Misha's every single move every day and she knew it. She also knew why. They were strategically surrounding her to make absolutely certain that no operatives of federal law enforcement came sniffing within fifty feet of her for information. They were also looking for someone, and they firmly believed that Misha knew exactly where this someone was; so they followed her, believing that, ultimately, she would slip and their target's hiding place would be revealed. Then they would eliminate this person who they had been looking for, and they would likely eliminate Misha too because she would have expended all of her usefulness.

Worst of all, Misha had been coerced out of her own home and was forced to live in the home that had previously belonged to her long-estranged biological brother, Richard Tresvant, founder and now-deceased head of The Consortium, one of the most powerful, Black organized crime rings on the West Coast and in the United States. Prior to his death, the blood had been extremely bad between Misha and Richard Tresvant for longer than she was interested in remembering and for reasons that were fairly obvious. Misha had changed her last name to ensure that no connection was ever made between her and her older gangster brother and now she was forced to suffer as a resident in the house where he'd once lived and run an extremely large criminal enterprise...with Marcus Means, no less. She was doing all of this, she believed, to protect someone she truly loved, but the cost for that protection required her to almost completely sacrifice herself, and she didn't know how much longer she was going to have the strength to do it.

Marcus Means, wealthy Los Angeles real estate investor, developer, entrepreneur, and all of the other formal, corporate-sounding business titles that he gave himself as a cover for all of the nefarious activities that he was really involved in, was America's newest nightmare, far worse, Misha believed, than her brother Richard Tresvant had ever been. Marcus Means didn't give a fuck about anything nor anyone that did not, in some way, benefit his own agenda. He took Gordon Gekko's mantra from the movie *Wall Street* and applied it on a whole different level of calculated ruthlessness to organized crime and cocaine. "GREED IS GOOD," he said with a smooth smile. "Greed is very, very good." And Misha Tierney had the grave misfortune of being married to the man for reasons, overall, in his grand scheme of psychotic plans that had yet to be revealed.

Los Angeles had no idea what they were in for in the coming months with Marcus Means. He was a whole different kind of monster, and everybody in the city had something to fear where he was concerned.

-3-

Despite the private hell that Misha Tierney's personal life had become, she dedicated herself zealously every day to the grueling job of running the major record label that had belonged to her best friend. Eighty percent ownership and controlling interest of the record label had been left to Misha in Keshari Mitchell's will and Misha did the unbelievably selfless act of putting her own successful company temporarily on the back burner to take full charge of Larger Than Lyfe.

Just prior to Keshari Mitchell's death, amidst Larger Than Lyfe Entertainment's massive nationwide talent search that traveled to ten major cities around the country, a "diamond in the rough" had been discovered during the auditions. Her name was "Ntozake," like the renowned Black poet. Larger Than Lyfe quickly signed Ntozake to a contract that started a buzz around the industry, and work commenced immediately on her debut album. Larger Than Lyfe Entertainment had been in search of a female artist they would groom to become the hottest new megastar in R & B, especially following the peculiar and mysterious circumstances under which their premier artist, Rasheed the Refugee, left the label. When they set eyes on Ntozake and heard her sing, they were willing to bet it all on her, and no one doubted LTL's hunch. Everything that Keshari Mitchell had touched since the moment she'd entered the music industry turned to platinum.

The very best producers in the industry composed tracks for Ntozake. Even Larger Than Lyfe's newest superstar producer, Mack-A-Do-Shuz, contributed two bass-laced tracks while some of the very best songwriters in the industry provided songs for her. Three tracks on the CD were written by Ntozake herself. A huge public relations campaign was launched to get the public ready for her while insiders in the industry began seeking interviews, playing her hot new single on radio stations in every major market around the country, and speculating about the future success or failure of this beautiful, new singer who Larger Than Lyfe seemed to be banking on having the star power of Beyoncé.

When her album was complete, a small listening party was thrown for the music industry's more important insiders and stories commenced to circulate immediately that "a new superstar was born." Comparisons were made to everybody from Mary J. Blige to Alicia Keys to Amerie. The album was "fiyah," Andre Harrell said. "She's HOT," megastar producer Pharrell was quoted saying.

A spectacular album release party was orchestrated by

none other than Misha Tierney herself, and no expense was spared when Larger Than Lyfe invited all of the music industry's heavy hitters, a number of Hollywood's celebrity A- and B-listers, and a few select members of media to celebrate LTL's newest and possibly greatest, guaranteed multi-platinum music project.

4

It was Saturday night and Ferraris, Range Rovers, Escalades and Porsches lined up outside the AREA Nightclub on La Cienega Boulevard in West Hollywood as only a private celebrity party thrown by Misha Tierney could bring people out. People like Paris Hilton, Leonardo DiCaprio and the infamous Lindsay Lohan were well-known for frequenting AREA. That night, AREA had been reserved for the release party celebrating Larger Than Lyfe Entertainment's new premier artist Ntozake's much-anticipated debut album, *My Love Is Complicated*. It was the album's first official week of sales and it was already in the top ten of *Billboard*'s "Hot 100." Misha was excited and happy about the overwhelmingly positive response to the project. She'd had to very quickly learn a mountain of aspects that composed the business side of the music industry when she stepped into Keshari Mitchell's shoes as the head of Larger Than Lyfe Entertainment, and she was glad to have realized success at bringing her best friend's vision in regard to Ntozake full circle.

A limousine delivered Misha Tierney, Ntozake and Marvin Shabazz, Larger Than Lyfe Entertainment's A& R director, to the main entrance of AREA at 10:30 p.m. where photographers instantly hopped forward to capture photos of the young woman who was already being compared to some of R & B's biggest names. Ntozake looked a lot like R & B artist Amerie, who happened to be one of the invited guests at the party that night, and more than a few people in the crowd of party-goers noted Ntozake's very striking resemblance to Keshari Mitchell, the fallen founder of Larger Than Lyfe Entertainment. Ntozake posed demurely for the cameras, still trying to become accustomed to the barrage of media attention that was being directed at her. She was Larger Than Lyfe Entertainment's new "it" girl, assuming the position of LTL's premier artist, the position that only been held by one other LTL artist, Rasheed the Refugee.

Chris Brown, A&R executives from Def Jam, Capitol, Interscope, and Bad Boy, Shemar Moore, hip-hop's "King of the South" T.I. and his entourage, Sean "Diddy" Combs, Keyshia Cole, Jermaine Dupri and Janet Jackson, Snoop Dogg and his entourage, Queen Latifah, the most major producer on the West Coast, Dr. Dre, the winner of Larger Than Lyfe's "Nationwide Search for a Star," and the top ten finalists from Larger Than Lyfe's nationwide talent search were all spotted and photographed in the incoming crowd. NBA star Krishawn Webb stepped out of his Bentley Continental GT with Portia Foster and photographers went crazy, practically on top of each other, trying to capture the money shots that would soon be plastered all over the tabloids.

Portia Foster, a former runway model and owner of a successful Los Angeles interior design firm, had something of a storied history. Portia Foster was the former girlfriend of Mars Buchanan and had been arrested for stalking Keshari Mitchell prior to Keshari Mitchell's death. When word got around to Misha that that crazy bitch had had the unmitigated audacity to make an appearance at her party with Misha's former fiancé, it was a wonder that AREA Nightclub didn't spontaneously go up in flames. Misha was LIVID.

She cornered Krishawn the moment that she spotted him in the crowd.

"I need to talk to you," she said, grabbing Krishawn's arm and ushering him toward the restrooms. She didn't even acknowledge Portia Foster's presence.

"What the FUCK are you doing here with that bitch?!" Misha snapped without mincing words.

"What the FUCK gives you the right to question who the fuck I date?!" Krishawn snapped back.

Krishawn's response was almost enough to shut Misha up. She had enough drama on her plate as it was, but she quickly re-grouped.

"Do you remember that bitch from the news, Kris?! Do you remember that bitch having a restraining order placed on her after she got onto Keshari's private property with cans of spray paint and a gun in a backpack, preparing to do God only knows whatever it is that crazy bitches do?! Why would you even associate yourself with someone like that?!"

Krishawn pushed Misha into the women's restroom and into one of the stalls. The women standing at the mirror applying lipstick and chattering noisily exchanged looks, and then exited the restroom.

"I miss you. Do you miss me?" Krishawn asked. "Why'd you marry that dude? Why have you fucked up my life? You know, I've heard some shit about your new husband. Are you aware that he may be caught up in the same brand of shit that the media kept hinting that your friend Keshari was involved in?"

"Kris, my life is so-o-o-o-o fucking complicated right now. I wanted to tell you to watch your back. That's all. That bitch you brought in here tonight is very bad news."

Krishawn leaned in and kissed Misha. At first, she resisted him, smacking at him and pushing him away. He kissed her again and she was quickly relenting, kissing him back, still in love with this man who was supposed to have been the one to become her husband, the one she should be celebrating second anniversaries with instead of the son of a bitch who'd coerced her into marrying him.

"Come to my hotel tonight," Krishawn said. "I have some endorsement meetings on Monday. I don't go back to New York until Wednesday. Come and see me."

"I can't," Misha responded. "You know that."

"Come anyway," Krishawn said and placed the card key to his hotel suite in Misha's hand. He held open the bathroom stall's door for her and Misha exited the bathroom.

As the album release party wound down, Misha secretly left through the back of AREA Nightclub and had her limousine drop her at the Four Seasons Hotel on Doheny, then return to the AREA to wait for Ntozake and Marvin Shabazz, who she'd rode with to the party. She took the elevator up to Krishawn's suite and relaxed on the sofa in the suite's living room to wait for him. Krishawn arrived shortly thereafter, having extricated himself from Portia Foster and delivered her back to whatever sordid little corner of hell that she belonged in.

Krishawn smiled. Misha took control. Before they knew it, they were making love.

"This cannot happen again," Misha said later as the two of them lay dozing in the king-size bed.

"I can't make you that promise," Krishawn said.

"Kris, I've got enough shit going on in my life already. So, I'm serious. This won't happen again. Let's consider tonight…what just happened here…closure and let's try to move on with the rest of our lives."

"You still love me," Krishawn said.

"I'm working to get past that," Misha said.

Krishawn sat up in bed.

"Did he force you to marry him?" Krishawn asked.

"No," Misha responded, getting out of bed and quickly starting to dress.

Her eyes were filled with tears as she leaned over and kissed Krishawn, and then got ready to leave.

"Kris, this can NEVER happen again. Don't try to contact me."

She left the key card on the bedside table and hurried out of the hotel suite.

As Misha stood at the front desk waiting for the concierge to order a car for her to drop her off at home, three, suited men with a keycard of their own rode the elevator up to Krishawn Webb's hotel suite. Krishawn never knew what was coming to him when all three of the men stealthily entered the suite and viciously attacked him in his bed.

"She's married," one of the men gruffly advised Krishawn before exiting the hotel suite. "Remember that."

Krishawn had two broken ribs, a black eye, a concussion, and a host of cuts and bruises. He'd been roughed up pretty badly. He could barely make it to the phone to call the concierge for help…private help. He made it clear that he wanted to keep the entire situation under wraps. But Krishawn should have known better than that. As soon as he was admitted into Cedars-Sinai, someone contacted the media. Eventually information reached the media that Misha Tierney had been seen at the Four Seasons, where Krishawn Webb was staying while he was in town, that same night right around the time that he was admitted into the hospital. As if Misha didn't already have enough on her hands requiring damage control, this mess was liable to be too much for any PR team to downplay.

—5—

In all of Marcus Means's unparalleled arrogance, he quickly purchased Richard Tresvant's Bel Air home the moment that it went up for auction following his murder. Marcus Means, a smooth, rich, dark chocolate dead ringer for Morris Chestnut was undeniably intelligent, charming even, but as dangerous as anyone could ever imagine. He sat now in the library of his $7 million gift to himself, having an "off the record" discussion with Devante "Big D" Johnson, leader of the R4 Crips, the set that Marcus and Richard Tresvant had been recruited into when the two boys were only twelve years old. Since taking over as the new head of The Consortium, Marcus's ambitions for the organization were all about expansion and he outlined a very controversial plan for Devante that would alter The Consortium's entire structure forever.

"Things are going to be different now that Rick is gone," Marcus said. "Rick's ultimate goal was to go completely legit. Mine is not. I LIKE being a gangster. No, I LOVE being a gangster."

"I feel you on that one," Devante said. "Keep talking."

"After Rick founded The Consortium and his paper started to get long enough for legitimate, White men in high places to take notice and want to rub elbows with him and be his friend, Rick started to cut himself off from his set. In a way, it started to feel like he thought he was better than the family who gave him his start and had his back long before his paper got long."

Devante did not respond, but Marcus knew that he was at some level of agreement with him.

"From the very beginning, our set, R4, has been The Consortium's soldiers. Our soldiers secure the interests of this whole organization. Our soldiers are the force behind The Consortium's words. Without strong soldiers, this organization would be quickly taken down. We must never forget that. My goal is to align and organize our soldiers…our family…and The Consortium…like never before. We are going to seriously reinforce our existing foundation. We will also recruit new, strong and dedicated soldiers. Our set will become an integral part of The Consortium's structure and will take on a more substantial and involved role in the organization as well as a more substantial share of The Consortium's profits. Rick did not implement the same strategies when he headed The Consortium because he felt he would somehow lose control of The Consortium if our set became too involved in The Consortium's operations. And, Rick being Rick, he somehow negotiated acceptable terms with the family that kept the peace. His ultimate goal was to go completely legit, have The Consortium be like a major corporation founded and headed by him alone, so he kept The Consortium and our set separate. He stressed "blood in–blood out" only when it was convenient for him. My goal is to make The Consortium one of the top three, most powerful, organized crime syndicates in the world, and I couldn't give a fuck about ever going legit. We are about to embark on the biggest feat ever undertaken by our family. We are going to become the Wal-Mart of the narcotics trade—marijuana, X, H, crystal and, of course, cocaine; a full product line at competitive pricing all in one place…with us. Ultimately, I intend to put The Consortium's hand on a little bit of everything…both legal and illegal enterprises. The Consortium is about to make money on a colossal level by becoming one of the top three, major players in the world's narcotics trade."

Devante snickered and shook his head.

"You are one crazy muthafucka," Devante said. "You'll have to go to war with EVERYBODY to carry off some ridiculous shit like that."

"Maybe," Marcus responded. "Maybe not. I'm thinking more along the lines of The Consortium acting as a major corporation with subsidiaries. A few hostile takeovers here and there. A few mergers and acquisitions. And whenever we do have to go to war, we will most definitely be prepared."

Devante sipped his Courvoisier and contemplated the whole scenario.

"I want you to be second-in-command in The Consortium, the position you should have held from the very beginning," Marcus said. "Let's get it straight. Keshari's heart was never truly in this. That's a bad way to be when you're in an organization of this caliber. She should never have held such a high-ranking position in this organization. You can slip one time and tear down a multi-million-dollar enterprise when your heart's not in it. I kept trying to tell Rick that, but he wasn't trying to hear me. He'd created Keshari, groomed her to be second-in-command of The Consortium when she was still a child. He trusted her. For a long time, he was fucking her. He had her carry out a couple of easy hits to prove she had what it takes to be in this game. He thought that she was "special" because he created her. He sent her to college, then graduate school, giving her corporate knowledge as well as street knowledge. Rick wanted to be CEO of a well-organized, corporate boardroom, which is why he surrounded himself with bankers and other white-collar types. I'm a gangster and I've got no confusion about that and I will die a gangster. As second-in-command, you will control our military operations. You will lose none of the power you already have as leader of our set. As a matter of fact, you will be gaining power as a member of The Consortium. You will lead our soldiers as second-in-command in this organization and you will reap all of the benefits of being a member of The Consortium. We are about to become as large as Italian mafia.

"I've been talking to Slim J from R2. I wanted to see where his head is. We have no quarrels with R2. I've tossed around thoughts of a permanent peace treaty between us as well as a possible merger. I secured background on Slim J. I've tossed around an overview of the expansion plan. He's open to meeting with us to hear more. I've also had similar sit-downs with leaders from R3 and F-Town in Compton…"

"Whoa, whoa, whoa, man!" Devante said, sitting up in his chair, his mood instantly darkening at the mention of a Bloods set. "Now, you're crossing the line…in more ways than one. I don't recall you getting with the family to get some parameters set on any of this."

"Hear me out," Marcus continued. "You know like I know that it has never been my intention to overstep my bounds…and definitely not to disrespect you. For plans of expansion on this level to be truly successful, we will need many more strong soldiers as well as more territory that solidly belongs to us. Some sets, we will form alliance with, break bread with. Other sets, we will need to take down…quickly…completely…with finality. Once we have solidified a stronghold on the West Coast with our expansion plan, I'm talking expansion in the Midwest, the South, and on the East Coast. The Consortium will become a board of directors composed of the leaders of all of the sets that we align with. I am chairman of the board. You will be second-in-command. Each additional set in the organization will be ranked based upon the number of soldiers in their set and the total revenues they come to the table with. And, yes, some members in this new collective will break the color code. Each set will continue to run their respective territories. Each set will pay monthly dues and points on the gross profits for their territory, what the Italians call 'tribute,' for membership in The Consortium as well as for the increased protection and profitability that their membership in The Consortium provide. The Consortium's board of directors will meet regularly. We will create a set if bylaws that apply to all of us. We will establish and maintain an accounting with our bankers, and determine, by vote, the direction of The Consortium's operations.

"The Italian mafia has long held power that was so strong that it could influence the government and the Roman Catholic Church. With my expansion and diversification project fully in play, that can be US...the most powerful, Black organized crime syndicate in HISTORY. This can be a beautiful, extremely lucrative thing, D... that easily rivals the Mafia...the Mexicans AND the Italians."

Devante was not at all convinced that Marcus would be able to successfully get the leaders of several, independent sets of Black gangsters, especially across long-standing color lines, to sit down together in one room and mutually agree upon terms for anything, even terms that would prove beneficial to all of them. The Crips and the Bloods had been arch-rivals since their inception. For them to come together now as allies in The Consortium based solely upon a mutual goal to make millions was a long shot indeed, but Marcus was just the crazy, ruthless, determined muthafucka to make it happen.

-6-

Six months after her very last surgery and, just as Dr. Henriqué had promised, Darian Boudreaux was absolutely STUNNING. She, miraculously, was completely free of swelling and bruising. She was a flawless honey brown with beautiful, auburn, shoulder-length curls, and a body to die for. She'd gradually taken up yoga and Brazilian tai chi as a part of her healing process. She worked out five days a week with a Brazilian trainer. She now spoke Portuguese almost fluently and she dedicated the bulk of her time to learning every facet of the film industry, from production and directing to film editing, contracts and distribution. She was blissfully in love and filled with unbridled energy and vision for the next phase of her life. She felt like the beautiful, mythical bird from the Garden of Eden, risen from the ashes of her former life and prepared to begin anew. She was the phoenix. And, with that thought in mind, Darian Boudreaux named her start-up film company, "PHOENIX FILMS."

Two days before Mars was scheduled to fly back to the United States, Darian decided that it was time to broach the subject with her husband of her returning to Los Angeles very soon to officially launch her film company. The two sat on the veranda of the beautiful little cottage Darian was leasing from Dr. Henriqué. They had dinner that Mars had prepared. Darian knew, no matter how carefully she handled the matter, Mars would be completely against her returning to the United States at any point, at any time, for any reason. It completely defied reason that she would even want to conceive of any kind of a plan to return to the very place where she had had to fake her own death to escape.

"It's time," was all Darian said quietly as the two of them sat together and Mars instantly knew what she was talking about.

"Uh-uh," Mars said, shaking his head vehemently. "That is out of the question. There is no way in hell that I'm going to let you endanger your life like that."

"There's only so long that I can sit out here in the middle of this idyllic fucking paradise doing yoga and reading. I have to DO something. I'm suffocating in 'doing nothing' out here. I've got to get back to work."

"Europe," Mars said, trying to sell what he already knew was a non-selling idea. "We could go there. London… Paris…Germany… You could certainly become fully engrossed in the film industry in any one of those regions. If anything, it would buy you some more time before you reenter the U.S. if you are still so determined that you have to go back. You'd have more time to strategize your movements. Perhaps something significant could happen with the organization with which you were once affiliated, something significant enough to ensure your safety when and if you do return to the U.S. There are tremendously active arts communities all over Europe. It could be a very exciting opportunity for you. The Europeans and the Asians love everything American. You would become major in Europe, dropping an American perspective to European subject matter or even dropping American subject matter from an American perspective."

"It's time," Darian said again, firm in her decision.

Mars was very quiet, contemplative, then worried and angry at what his wife was about to do…mainly because he knew that he would not be able to do anything to stop her. He did not understand why she was so stubborn that she would repeatedly position herself directly in the face of peril.

"I think you should give this more time," he said. "It's still too soon. I haven't even gotten to a place where I've fully wrapped my mind around the two of us here in Brazil with you undergoing this massive, physical metamorphosis. You've got to give me more consideration than what you're doing right now. I LOVE YOU and I love you most of all ALIVE."

Darian took Mars's hand and held it tight. She stared at him lovingly, wanting him not to worry, wanting him to understand.

"I'm going stir crazy here," Darian said again. "I'm accustomed to working...accomplishing things...achieving goals. You know this. I've been studying for two years. I've invested more than $2 million into physical changes so I would be able to do this. I don't know why I would do something as stupid as this, but I've GOT to. I don't know. Maybe I've lived on the edge of death for so long until I don't know how to live my life any other way. You know the woman you fell in love with. Unlike before, you now know EVERYTHING. You should have anticipated that it would come to this...me returning to the United States. Every fiber of my being is willing me to do it...no matter how dangerous it is."

Mars shook his head in disbelief. He got up from the table and had to pace around a bit before his anger got the better of him.

"The film company, the return to the United States, all of it. You're working to step right back into a very public life. All it takes is for one person to start doing some very serious prying. You'll place yourself in greater jeopardy than you were ever in before and not just with underworld crime rings. Faking your death is a federal offense. They would lock you up for the rest of your life on a whole book full of charges if your cover is ever blown."

"Mars, you remember how I took a gigantic risk and sent you that postcard?"

Mars didn't respond. He stared at his beautiful, stubborn wife solemnly and shook his head. For a moment, he allowed his mind to wonder what he had gotten himself into when he gave up everything, left the United States and came to Brazil to find Darian, then married her.

"Nothing ventured, nothing gained," she said.

-7-

The plane touched down at LAX and Darian's heart leapt into her throat. It was the first time that she had been back on American soil, in California, since… well…since she'd ended her former life to become who she now was. She was so, so nervous, and, strangely enough, even though she'd taken up Brazilian yoga and meditation during her time in Brazil, she immediately employed a technique that Richard Tresvant taught her to enable her to keep her cool.

With yet another new passport in hand that had been arranged following her surgeries shortly before she finalized plans for her return to the U.S., she came through customs without issue. With a Louis Vuitton trunk and three bags, a luggage attendant loaded the Town Car that waited for Darian curbside and she was whisked to the W Hotel in Hollywood.

Strutting into the W Hotel's lobby, Hollywood's newest "it" girl had clearly arrived. In white linen, baring bronzed legs that seemed to stretch for the sky, her striking, chocolate brown eyes, hidden behind Cartier sunglasses, took in everything with both nervousness and excitement as she headed over to the front desk to check into her suite. A few heads turned to get a better look at her, wondering if she was someone important.

As she rode the elevator with the bellman up to her suite, she looked down at her canary diamond engagement ring accompanied by its super-thin, white diamond, eternity band and smiled to herself. She couldn't wait to get her hands and all the rest of herself on her gorgeous husband. It had been more than two months since she'd seen him last. She was texting him again on her Black-Berry before she could get in the door of her suite.

The first priority on Darian's agenda upon her return to Los Angeles was to secure commercial space to open the offices of her film company. She immediately scheduled an appointment with the same agent at Coldwell Banker who she'd used to acquire the office space for Larger Than Lyfe Entertainment. She knew the agent was highly competent and would quickly arrange viewings of venues that fully met her specifications without wasting her time and the agent would quickly negotiate suitable terms on her behalf once a space had been chosen. For now, she was most interested in a small block of offices at the Capitol Records building. But she was also interested in seeing as many other upscale commercial spaces in the Hollywood/West Hollywood area as were currently available. For now, she intended to negotiate a one-year lease for space. Later, she would strongly consider purchasing a venue. She was excited and anxiously looking forward to putting her nose to the grindstone and beginning solid work on her first film projects. She was the consummate workaholic just as she'd been in her former life as founder and president of Larger Than Lyfe Entertainment.

Keshari Mitchell had never been one to waste time, and Darian Boudreaux was definitely no procrastinator either. After securing the ideal space that would become the home of Phoenix Films—she'd opted for the Capitol Records building in Hollywood—Darian quickly hired a design firm to decorate the space and, at the same time, began interviewing people to take on the very challenging role as her assistant, someone with a serious interest in the film industry but who wasn't an aspiring actress, someone who could wear many hats skillfully, was extremely proactive, and who could quickly help to lighten the ever-growing load currently on her agenda.

She had to purchase a new car. She had to find herself a house. Then she had to furnish her new home. She had to set up a website for her new company. She needed letterhead and business cards. She needed to sit down with her attorney to square away IRS and other business-related details for her new company. She needed to begin the extremely arduous task of scouting for the ideal creative projects that her film company would cultivate and launch. Of course, she was only interested in projects that would make the film industry and the public stand up and take serious notice. This would require extensive travel to the film festivals, film schools and a host of conferences and conventions. It would also entail extensive research, mountains and mountains of script reading and all of those niggling-yet-important, little details that would drive her completely insane if she attempted to tackle all of them herself. She needed an assistant as soon as YESTER-DAY, and she needed a really, really good one.

While Mars's wife was in Los Angeles preparing to make moves in the film industry, Mars Buchanan certainly did not lose step or a moment's time upon his return to the United States. He was in Palm Beach laying the groundwork for his new sports and entertainment management firm, The Buchanan Group. With $3 million from Darian's Swiss account that she called an "investment in his success" and that she had to force Mars to take, Darian carefully instructed Mars how to strategically invest and deposit the funds in his bank accounts, carefully co-mingling the funds with his personal income and holdings so that the very sizeable "gift" would not be immediately flagged by federal law enforcement. Mars sat down and dedicated a month to formulating a solid business plan. He got with business and financial advisors to crunch the numbers and to secure valuable guidance regarding the business and fiscal soundness of his plans and to make sure he had not overlooked anything significant. Then he contacted Jason Payne, Richard Bryson, and Kevin Sperrington, three good friends of his from Stanford Law School, and invited them to come out to Palm Beach for a couple of days at his expense to play some golf, hit a couple of Miami's nightclubs and discuss what he said was an "important business proposition." All three men already had careers as sports agents and entertainment attorneys. Mars was confident they would be dynamic partners at his new firm and he, thanks to his gorgeous wife, had the right leverage to make each of them offers that they could not refuse.

"I'm officially opening offices in three months at the Capitol Records Building in Hollywood," Mars said, as he, Kevin, Jason and Richard sat in the library sharing drinks and cigars at the amazing, $16 million mansion that Keshari Mitchell left to him in her will. "My business plan includes expansion to offices in Atlanta and New York within the next three years. Our focus will be full-service entertainment and athletic management. We will progress into large-scale sports- and entertainment-based production and development projects on the same timeline as the opening of new offices. That equates to movies, music, endorsement deals, real estate... We are only limited by the scope of what our minds and drive can cultivate."

"My first two officially signed clients are none other than Krishawn Webb and Rasheed the Refugee. You all know Rasheed is a multi-platinum hip-hop artist, formerly with Larger Than Lyfe Entertainment. He currently owns his own record label with two certified platinum artists on his roster and he releases his own music through his label. He has a serious interest in venturing into the field of acting, and I'm going to help him to secure the right projects. Krishawn Webb is a free agent and is being seriously courted by the Lakers as well as Gatorade and Nike. So, as you can see, the moves have already started, and they are major ones. We're talking multimillion-dollar projects and endorsements and I'm working to do more…much more. Imagine what can be accomplished with all of us working together along with a team of driven associates working under our direction."

Jason Payne LOVED the idea of joining his best friend as a partner in their own management firm. The business plan for the firm was amazing.

"I've got to discuss this with Brynn," Jason said, referring to his wife. "This is a major life change and I've got step back from the excitement of it all to evaluate this from every side myself. I've got my family to consider."

The same was true for Kevin Sperrington. He needed to discuss the move into a partnership position at The Buchanan Group with his wife. He was already a partner at the very prestigious law firm where he currently worked, but he loved the idea of being part of a ground-breaking major Black management firm in Los Angeles. Until now, it was very much a rarity. And, like Jason and Mars, he had dreamed of one day having his own firm ever since law school.

Richard Bryson was the only one who was somewhat dubious of Mars's plans.

"You got William Morris, Endeavor, EXCEL, Eileen Koch and Company. These are major firms with established client lists of heavy hitters. In this economy, especially, the competition is ferocious. I'm merely questioning the overall viability of these plans for a start-up at this time."

"I considered ALL of that as well," Mars responded. "Take my business plan home with you. Review it carefully. I've had both attorneys and financial advisors go over the business plan with a fine-toothed comb. I'm prepared to make The Buchanan Group a significant force in the entertainment and athletic industries in spite of the current economy. Now, how does a $150,000 signing bonus for each of you help to influence your decision-making?"

"Well, it certainly doesn't fuckin' hurt, man." Kevin Sperrington laughed.

The other men laughed too.

"Are you serious?" Jason asked.

"I need you all to understand how important this endeavor is to me," Mars said. "Since law school, we have all discussed starting our own firm. When Keshari died, it compelled me to seriously consider my own mortality. I asked myself if I was doing what I really wanted to be doing professionally and if I was where I really and truly wanted to be in my life. I did a lot of traveling when I left ASCAP. I took a lot of time to think, meditate, pray and formulate plans. The Buchanan Group is the answer to all of those questions I asked myself."

"Okay," Mars continued, "I'm giving you guys two weeks from today to assess whether or not you would like to accept my offer. Talk to your wives, discuss it with your business and legal advisors, carefully review the business plan for yourselves, and carefully think about where you want to be professionally in the next five years. Perhaps The Buchanan Group can take you there."

"Misha Tierney's firm is doing an 'inception party' for me in two months to celebrate the official launch of The Buchanan Group. Some of everybody who's anybody in sports, music and film will be there. It will be a huge opportunity to do some networking, establish some new relationships. Imagine what can be accomplished if the three of us, as partners in The Buchanan Group, are working the room together."

While the interior design work for the offices of Phoenix Films was being completed, Darian decided to pay her husband a surprise visit in Palm Beach. He'd wrapped his meeting with his three long-time friends from law school and he told Darian he believed that all three men would accept his offer to come aboard as partners at The Buchanan Group. He sounded so excited. Before they finished their two-hour call, he told Darian how much he missed her.

While Darian dozed in her first-class seat out of LAX,

headed for Miami, she thought about her wedding. It had been an unbelievable private affair, just her and Mars and a full staff at their service on Turtle Island in Fiji. Barefoot on the sand, wearing a Vera Wang Platinum Collection gown and Mars in Armani Privé, Darian Boudreaux vowed, with every fiber of her being, to share the rest of her breathing life loving this very, very special man. And Mars Buchanan promised Darian Boudreaux with all of his heart and his soul that he would love her and protect her and share and dream with her as long as God gave him the honor and the privilege to do it.

They honeymooned by making love on the sand outside their grand buré for seven nights straight. They hiked and swam during the day. They had dinner by candlelight on a mountaintop at night, drinking Australian wines and talking, laughing, planning, dreaming. Amazing was an absolute understatement for what the two of them experienced in that ultra-exclusive, exotic paradise. Darian would remember that week that she'd spent alone with her beloved husband for the rest of her life.

"Oh, my God, I have missed you so much." Mars smiled, planting a huge kiss on his wife's lips and picking her up from the floor.

Darian wrapped her arms around his neck and planted a kiss on top of his bald head. They held onto each other for what seemed like forever, the love emanating between the two of them.

The housekeepers busied themselves with Darian's luggage, carrying the multiple bags from the limousine upstairs to the master suite. Mars and Darian went out onto the terrace and sat underneath the shaded pergola to have drinks and catch up. Mars was still very excited about the proposal he'd made to his three law school friends and the opening of his management company. He talked at length about upcoming meetings with potential new clients. He talked about the upcoming party that Misha's event planning firm was throwing for him, and they talked about some of the pivotal people on his guest list. Then Mars wanted to know everything about his beautiful wife's progress.

Darian talked about starting the arduous task of finding an assistant who could help her to accomplish the multitude of tasks ahead of her as she stepped fully into her new life in the United States and her role as head of a start-up film company. She talked about ideas she was composing for Phoenix Films' new website. She talked about the grueling schedule she was about to have as she began scouring the country for worthwhile scripts. She wanted Phoenix Films' first impression on the film industry to be a powerful one. She wanted to hit the industry out of nowhere and have the same indomitable impact creatively and from a business standpoint that Larger Than Lyfe Entertainment quickly had. She knew this would require some very, very special concepts and scripts. She had been brainstorming over the past few weeks and had come up with a few very good ideas. She was most seriously entertaining the idea for a highly controversial topic, one she wasn't quite ready to broach with Mars. He would be livid once he heard what she wanted to do, and he would fight her every step of the way to keep her from carrying it out. So she stayed mum about it for the time being and curled up in his lap, loving the masculine feel of him that she'd missed so much, loving the smell of his aftershave, loving the touch of his fingertips on her.

"Mr. Buchanan," Darian whispered into Mars's neck.

"Yes, Mrs. Buchanan?"

"I'd like you to make love to me right now."

Mars smiled.

"I can do that," he responded.

The following evening, Darian took Mars to see Ledisi, Maxwell, and Ntozake, who'd just been added to the headliner line-up, in concert at the American Airlines Arena in Miami. Darian had managed to acquire VIP seating, backstage passes, and passes to the after-party that was being held at the Viceroy Hotel that night. The concert was unbelievable. Both Mars and Darian LOVED Maxwell and Ledisi. Then Ntozake and her band took the stage and the entire audience grooved together, swaying and singing the words with Ntozake to her just certified double-platinum debut song, "If It's Not Me." Mars was positively blown away by how talented she was. He failed to even recognize the fact that he had once had a one-night stand with this blossoming, young superstar when he believed Keshari Mitchell, the love of his life, had committed suicide. Watching Ntozake perform was bittersweet for Darian. Keshari Mitchell had seen a spark in Ntozake during the auditions of Larger Than Lyfe Entertainment's "Nationwide Search for a Star" and she immediately offered Ntozake a recording contract. Watching this woman now becoming the superstar that Keshari had firmly believed that she would become was something else. She literally had butterflies as she watched her. Her hunches about talented artists had always been eerily accurate and had turned Larger Than Lyfe Entertainment into a goldmine. Darian hoped those hunches were equally as good in terms of the upcoming creative projects she would be cultivating at Phoenix Films.

Darian and Mars skipped the after-party, preferring the company of each other alone together instead. They rode the chauffeured Maybach back to the Palm Beach house and made love in the infinity pool and under the pergola all night until the sun began to rise. Later that morning, the two of them had breakfast in bed together that Mars made himself—cheese omelet, freshly ground coffee, turkey sausages, fresh strawberries, and the red dragon fruit that Darian liked so much. The two were still extremely talkative. They were two newlyweds who truly, truly enjoyed being together again after months apart. They admired one another's intelligence, business acumen and drive. They were hopelessly attracted to one another. They were FRIENDS, and they loved sharing themselves with each other via their lengthy conversations. That was the part about Darian that Mars loved most, this new openness that he could not fully get from Keshari Mitchell for reasons that he now far better understood.

Darian carefully began to tell Mars about the project she was strongly considering developing as the premier project for Phoenix Films. She wanted to do a big-budget biopic of Keshari Mitchell's life with emphasis on her long-rumored affiliations with The Consortium.

Mars was jarred abruptly into silence by the excitement in Darian's voice as she talked in detail about what she wanted to do. The air between the two of them grew icy cold.

"Why the fuck do you keep trying to put your life in jeopardy in this way?!" Mars finally snapped at her. "What the fuck is wrong with you?! What the fuck is wrong with ME?!"

He hopped out of bed and almost toppled the breakfast tray onto the floor. He paced back and forth at the foot of the bed.

"You're trying hard to act as if the last three years of your life have been relatively 'normal' when 'normal' could not be farther away from what the two of us have. This shit is UNREAL!!! You orchestrated a plan and faked your own death, Darian! You've had these unbelievable surgeries done to completely alter your physical identity. You believe that the change of identity makes you safe. And now you've made this return to the United States, you're starting a film company, which will CLEARLY become a major player as long as you have anything to do with it, and the two of us are here working together as a 'power couple' while at the same time having to hide our marriage. I can't even digest this shit right here before you come up with some new shit more outlandish than the shit before! You haven't been back in the United States for six months and already you're strategizing to get a new price put on your head?! You, better than anyone, know what these people from your past are about. They do NOT do publicity campaigns, they don't want any inferences made about them in the public eye, and they would off you to keep this movie you're talking about producing from making it to theaters. And I am NOT going to allow you to do it! I was completely against you coming back into the United States in the first place, but I am trying…with everything in me…to make the best of it…because I love you…and I know your life will never be anything close to normal, but I'm putting my foot down now. I am NOT going to allow you to endanger your life with the kind of film project that you are talking about."

"Not going to 'allow' me?" Darian asked him challeng-ingly.

This was the very first time since the two of them had

gotten married that they had really argued, and it was about to get very ugly.

"You know what? I don't want to talk about this anymore, because I don't want to say something right now that I later regret. Why don't we talk about this when both of us are back in L.A.?" Mars said seriously. "I'm going to go down to the office and get some work done."

He paused in the doorway before heading downstairs.

"I gave up my life…my entire life…because of how much I love you. I just want some reciprocation."

=9=

A caravan of limousines containing the Who's Who of the Black organized criminal underworld filed into the gates of Marcus Means's Bel Air home. For those in the know, it was a very auspicious night, a night on which history would be made.

Marcus had taken every possible precaution and had been mostly successful at keeping his plans for expansion of The Consortium as well as the meeting that night below the radar of the very watchful eyes of law enforcement and other criminal organizations. The library, the very same location where the murder weapon had been found that had killed prominent, Los Angeles corporate attorney, Phinnaeus Bernard III, when Richard Tresvant owned the ten thousand-square-foot home, was where the leaders of several of the largest and most notorious Black gangs in Los Angeles County sat down to hash out the details of one of the most powerful alliances ever formulated in organized crime.

There were Cuban cigars and $500 bottles of cognac and platinum money clips that Marcus had had custom-made, engraved with The Consortium logo and individually engraved with each set leader's initials. It was the caliber of finesse that surpassed *The Godfather* and *Scarface* and Marcus had carefully orchestrated every single detail.

"Gentlemen," Marcus said magnanimously, "tonight marks an event that will change all of our lives…for the better. Welcome to The Consortium."

The men all took seats around the luxurious library. All the men had come accompanied by their lieutenants. Marcus's attorney was also present.

"Each of us comes to the table tonight, bringing with us a unique set of resources and assets," Marcus said. "Individually, each of our sets is powerful. Collectively, we are most powerful. Collectively, we control more territory, we become more liquid, we possess more leverage, our ambitions and our goals collectively and individually can be conceived on a MUCH, MUCH larger scale.

"When I began to assess and compose the plans for this expansion project, I had absolutely no reservations about crossing color lines."

"It would be foolish of you not to," Leon "Big Bree-Z" Poussant of Compton's F-Town said, still not thoroughly convinced that a merger between Crips and Bloods sets would work out. "Some of us in this room right now have unresolved beefs with one another."

The other set leaders nodded in agreement.

"We are 'big boys' now," Marcus answered confidently. "We all rep and respect the colors and the sets that helped to get us to where we are, but we are now MORE than just repping colors, holding down street corners and pulling off drive-bys against our enemies. Each of our sets independently generates well over $500,000 a month EASILY. Each of us diversifies our money into legitimate business enterprises. Collectively, we…The Consortium… will become powerful and organized enough to easily compete with any Fortune 500 company. And whatever beefs any of us have with anyone else who is present here tonight are surely smaller than THAT."

"I hear that," Big Bree-Z responded.

"Suppose you've got beef with other people out here in these streets?" Slim J from R2 Crips asked.

"When you've got beef with other sets, your organization is behind you," Marcus answered. "We are a unit. We meet, we discuss the issue, we vote, we eliminate the problem. And we always outnumber and outgun our enemies."

All of the set leaders liked the idea of the increased muscle to support and defend their agendas.

"What about accounting and distribution of profits?" Slim J of R2 Crips asked.

"There are a group of accountants who manage the books of The Consortium who shall continue to maintain the books of The Consortium," Marcus said. "Each of you can bring your own accountants to the table to review the books once a month for your assurance. Profits are split equally with each of the heads of the sets who are present here tonight. There is still honor at the top with us. I'm not running a hustle here and looking to go to war with any of you over financial differences.

"We will meet weekly to establish bylaws for the organization and to discuss such issues as bringing new members into the organization, legitimate business enterprises to allocate money into, expansion of territory, and any other issues that are associated with the operations of The Consortium. With our collective resources, we can invest in major, legitimate real estate development projects, retail franchises, the stock market, sports, entertainment, the works. Everything we undertake as a unit will go to vote. We will pay monthly tribute to the organization. There will be monthly distribution of profits beginning three months from tonight. Members of The Consortium can even take out loans from The Consortium to fund your individual endeavors and these loans shall be repaid at ten points annually above and beyond tribute.

"Now, since I've met individually with each of you to discuss the proposal of you joining The Consortium, each of you understands that we each must come to the table tonight with an initial offering to the organization of $1.5 million…"

There was an instant rustling around the room as lieutenants came forward with duffle bags and briefcases. Marcus's lieutenants and enforcers came forward as well and began to collect and make an accounting of the contents of all of the briefcases and duffle bags. Marcus's attorney busied himself by making notations on a legal pad of the sizeable receivables. Seven set leaders bringing $1.5 million to the table at the same time equated to $10.5 million in about one hour's time and Marcus was making the guarantee to each of these set leaders that they would quadruple this tribute in one year's time. It was a risky investment, hinging largely on Marcus Means's street credibility, that, clearly, none of them could say no to.

"Finally," Marcus said magnanimously, "I have one more, shall we say, 'appetizer' to prove to you that membership in The Consortium does have its privileges."

"Oh, yeah?" "Dread," set leader of R3 Crips said. "And what is that?"

"Larger Than Lyfe Entertainment," Marcus responded.

"WHAT?!" Dread exclaimed and immediately sat up in his chair with interest.

"That company is completely legit," Big Bree-Z stated. "I checked. Rick Tresvant helped to fund that company when it started, but he had no involvement in it at all. Keshari Mitchell was determined to keep that entire operation clean and she did. What are you talking here? A hostile takeover?"

Some of the other set leaders chuckled.

"Larger Than Lyfe is currently a $425 million record label and growing. Ten points per month from that record label equates to some nice bread to break among us. That's what The Consortium is taking off their books right now."

"Quit fuckin' around," Big Bree-Z said.

"I never joke about money," Marcus said seriously. "The new Consortium is a win-win situation for us all. We are about to get richer than any of us ever imagined possible. We will be the most powerful Black gangsters in history."

"To The Consortium," Marcus said, lifting his snifter in a toast.

"To The Consortium," the other men responded, lifting their glasses.

Thomas Hencken pulled his car as close as he possibly could to Marcus Means's mansion without alerting Marcus's security team, got out of the car, walked the half block it took to get closer and quickly snapped photos of the limousines arriving at the house that night as if there were some sort of party. With the powerful zoom lens, he captured the faces of some of the men as they stepped from the cars and entered the house. Thomas Hencken had been watching Marcus Means's movements off and on for many months, ever since the very questionable prison murder of Richard Lawrence Tresvant while he awaited a new trial on appeal for the murder of prominent Los Angeles attorney Phinnaeus Bernard III.

Marcus Means was an extremely busy man, and he had his hands, eyes, and mind wrapped around every piece of dirty business currently transpiring in Los Angeles County. Over the past few weeks, it had become clear that Marcus Means was working on something major. He had been conducting meetings with leaders of other Crips sets as well as Bloods sets all around Los Angeles and sometimes he flew out of the state for meetings in other parts of the country.

Sometimes Thomas Hencken had been able to safely follow Marcus and capture bits and pieces of what he was doing. Other times, Marcus's security force, which included police officers who were on his payroll, was simply too heavy and Thomas Hencken had been forced to back off.

Thomas Hencken was engaged in what could easily be called a suicide mission. His wife had called him crazy, said he clearly had a death wish, that he was placing his own family in danger, that he needed to get some help, and then she packed up their children and left him.

Ever since being forced to resign from his career at the Drug Enforcement Agency, Thomas Hencken had been single-handedly continuing the compilation of evidence against The Consortium, the powerful organization Marcus Means now headed. He was bound and determined to take Marcus Means down and all of the other members of the infamous Consortium, and he was not going to stop until he did.

After all that had happened to him and with all of the corruption, cover-ups and lies that seemed to be so prevalent all around him, Thomas Hencken still possessed what seemed to be so sorely lacking in today's society. He had an unshakeable code of ethics. He could not be bought nor intimidated by any criminal, and he believed what was right always, ultimately, triumphed over wrong. In Thomas Hencken's mind, it was beyond time that someone cared enough about the nation in which they lived to commit themselves, no matter the risk, to bringing down vile, vicious criminals like the ones in The Consortium, and on his own time, energy, and money, he was continuing exactly where he'd been forced to leave off when he had been unceremoniously ousted from the DEA.

People like Marcus Means, Richard Tresvant and countless other high-ranking, organized criminals possessed such a willful and ruthless disregard for the law and community that they maimed and killed and got away with it, they trafficked their drugs, placed law enforcement officers on their payroll, and bribed judges with money that didn't even make a dent in their deep pockets. Left unchecked, the lives and safety of most average American citizens would be grossly compromised if men like Marcus Means and those in other highly sophisticated crime rings were just allowed free reign to go about their business working and expanding their criminal enterprises and amassing vast sums of money doing so, and it would take many men like Thomas Hencken to ensure that that was NEVER allowed to happen, no matter how futile the effort seemed to be. Thomas Hencken was a one-man sort of vigilante, attempting to secure justice against a construct far greater and far more dangerous than he could possibly know.

-10-

While Marcus Means was machinating a new level of trouble in organized crime at the meeting he was conducting that night at his Bel Air home, Misha Tierney, his extremely reluctant bride, had a meeting of her own. She took a first-class flight into New York, had a car waiting curbside for her, and went directly from LaGuardia into Manhattan.

Krishawn Webb had an amazing loft apartment on West Broadway in SoHo. Her keys still worked, and she let herself in. She had not seen Krishawn since that fateful night when the two of them got together and he was violently attacked by some of Marcus's employed thugs. She had called all around the country looking for him, and he had completely removed himself from the map, avoiding her and the press like the plague for weeks. Finally, Krishawn's personal assistant revealed to Misha that morning that Krishawn was going to be home all week prior to flying to Los Angeles for business meetings.

Krishawn was on his computer in his office. She stood in the doorway watching him silently until he looked up.

"Hi," was all that she could muster.

"You shouldn't be here," Krishawn said. "Does anyone know you're here? Does your husband know you're here?"

"My 'husband' is very busy tonight. He does not know that I'm here."

"What do you want?" Krishawn asked.

"I wanted to see how you were. I haven't seen you since that night. I've called everywhere for you. I am SO, SO sorry."

"This is some deep, crazy shit you've gotten yourself into, Misha. You're still in love with me. He knows you're still in love with me. What is he holding over your head that would force you to have married him? And WHY did he force you to marry him?"

Misha shook her head.

"I couldn't even begin to explain it to you…"

"What is it?" Krishawn asked again.

"I can't tell you," Misha said. "I cannot place you in any more danger than I already have."

"What about cooperating with the feds? Have you considered that? Has anyone approached you?" Krishawn asked.

"I'm not cooperating with any federal law enforcement. Marcus has more than a few of them on his payroll. He would kill me without hesitation if he even thought I was thinking about going to the feds."

Krishawn was quiet.

"I've missed you," Misha said, changing the subject.

"Yeah, me, too," Krishawn responded seriously. "But THIS…this right here…you sneaking here to see me… this can't continue. I'm not playing this game."

Krishawn got up and hugged Misha. He held her for what seemed like a very long time, wanting to protect her, keep her away from shit like Marcus Means, and then feeling so powerless because he knew who Marcus Means was and what he was said to be capable of. He'd personally experienced some of what Marcus Means was capable of.

Before the two of them knew it, they were shedding their clothes. Misha ached for Krishawn. She so missed being with him. Probably one of the only fortunate things about her sham of a marriage to Marcus Means was that Marcus had made no sexual advances toward her…yet. His motivations where Misha was concerned appeared to be almost solely based upon The Consortium's interests, locating Keshari Mitchell and building his financial empire. Misha didn't know if his sadistic ass even had sex.

Tears streamed down Misha's face as Krishawn kissed her, and Krishawn kissed her tears. NBA players were constantly given a bad rap as bling-swinging, arrogant whores with kids all over the country that most of them failed to take proper care of. Krishawn Webb was the diametric opposite of all of that. He was handsome and strong and intelligent and funny and sensitive and caring, an astute businessman and he ADORED Misha. She was wracked with sobs as she wrapped her arms around

Krishawn's neck and he carried her upstairs. He made love to her, and then kept her wrapped in his arms while the two of them lay in his huge bed in the amazing loft that overlooked much of the first floor of the apartment. The following evening, in his black Maserati, he drove her to the airport while, somewhere in the distance, someone with a high-powered camera captured every moment of it.

-11-

Darian arrived back in Los Angeles after her trip to Palm Beach and plowed right back into work. She was breaking in the new car she'd ordered, a special edition carbon black Aston Martin DBS Volante, and she absolutely loved it. With the top down, she sped up La Cienega, capturing stares as she passed by. The interior design work for the offices of Phoenix Films over at the Capitol Records Building had just been completed and she would be moving in in the next few days. Darian was also ready to move herself out of the W Hotel and into a home, and she hired a residential real estate broker to begin looking for a house for her in the Hollywood Hills.

Mars would soon be returning to Los Angeles from Palm Beach, and he was looking forward to moving into his new offices. The industry, thanks to Mars's PR team, was getting full saturation regarding the news of his new management firm, The Buchanan Group, and the three partners who would be joining him. All three men had accepted Mars's offer.

In Darian's search for a new assistant, she had turned up the unbelievable through a headhunter agency in Downtown Los Angeles—Terrence Henderson, who had been Keshari Mitchell's assistant at Larger Than Lyfe Entertainment. Terrence Henderson had been left with $2 million cash in Keshari Mitchell's last will and testament, and he had eventually quit his job at Larger Than Lyfe Entertainment, believing that he could live on the money he had been bequeathed. Terrence's partner, though, had quickly run through most of the money and then ran off with some other man with what was left. Terrence was heartbroken and embarrassed and was unceremoniously thrown back into the workforce. The fortunate thing was Terrence had possessed enough presence of mind to purchase a two-bedroom loft when he first received the money from the will. It was the one stylish asset, a foreclosure, in a trendy, upscale neighborhood of West Hollywood that he still managed to hold on to to show he had not completely squandered the large sum of money that had been left to him.

Terrence interviewed with Darian at the W Hotel. He was highly professional and charming as he had always been, and Darian could tell he had done extensive reading on the film industry prior to his interview. He referenced important names of insiders and immediately began to tell Darian some of the things that could be done to quickly accomplish some of the tasks that lay ahead of her. She was so impressed, just as she had been in her former life with him, that she hired Terrence Henderson on the spot.

After wrapping up the interview in one of the W Hotel's smaller conference rooms, Darian walked Terrence to the lobby and continued to chat with him. Sitting on one of the sofas across the room was a familiar face that caught Darian's eye. It was Marcus Means and he was staring directly at her. Darian quickly averted her gaze back to Terrence. Her heart thumped as if it was about to pound right out of her chest and she felt certain that every drop of blood had drained from her face as her legs grew rubbery and seemed very much on the verge of crumpling underneath her. Darian could not be sure if Marcus Means was watching her out of some sort of recognition or if he was watching her merely because she was a very attractive woman. He soon got up and exited the busy hotel lobby with a group of men with whom he'd obviously been waiting to meet.

"Are you okay?" Terrence asked with some concern, noticing the abrupt change in her talkative, amiable mood.

"Yes, yes," Darian said, quickly regrouping. "I haven't eaten anything today. I think my body was attempting to send me a STRONG message."

"Go eat right now, girl," Terrence advised her sternly with a smile in his typical, semi-paternal way.

"Yes, sir," Darian responded. She scribbled down her e-mail address and phone numbers and handed them to Terrence.

"I will see you back here tomorrow morning at seven o'clock SHARP."

-12-

Right after she hired an assistant to help her get completely settled in Los Angeles and to work at her side at Phoenix Films, Darian's real estate broker called her and told her he had located what he believed was a residential property she would not want to miss. It was a $6 million architectural jewel on Haslam Terrace with breathtaking views of Los Angeles all the way to the Pacific Ocean. Darian drove up to the house a few hours after the broker's call and was instantly blown away.

"How much?" she asked.

"Thirteen thousand dollars per month with an option to buy," the broker responded. "They had prior tenants who resided here for a year and then their jobs transferred them to New York City. It's been vacant for only a month."

"Why aren't the owners living in the residence?"

"Believe it or not, they purchased it solely as a flip. They brought in one of the nation's top architects, renovated the house from bottom to top, and then...well... the real estate market took a nosedive."

"What's the asking price for purchase?" Darian asked quickly, looking around her again. "I LOVE it!"

"The owners are asking $5 million," the broker said. "Due to the current real estate market, they recently were forced to cut the price more than $900,000. The original asking price was $5.95 million. It's been on the market for just over a year."

"I'd like to make an offer," Darian said. "I'm thinking more along the lines of $4 million. Why don't you run comps right now and see if I'm in the right ballpark."

"Not a problem," the broker responded and went out to his Range Rover to grab his laptop.

Meanwhile, Darian contacted the printer to determine if her business cards and business and personal stationery were ready for pick-up. Terrence Henderson sent a text message to her BlackBerry to let her know he had touched bases with a very good website designer who had done the website for Larger Than Lyfe Entertainment and Def Jam. The website designer was available to meet with Darian at nine the next morning if she was available to take the meeting.

"Book it," Darian quickly typed back on her Black-Berry.

Darian would be meeting with the interior designer to complete the formal walk-through of her newly finished office space later that afternoon. Then she would be moving into her offices and getting situated all the rest of the week as well as the following week.

She had initially entered into her search for a home looking for something to lease until she and Mars fully discussed and came up with alternate plans. But after seeing the home on Haslam Terrace, she could not pass up making an offer to buy it. Once the real estate market truly picked back up, the house would be a phenomenal investment.

Darian's real estate broker sat down at the table in the contemporary house's glass-walled dining room and pulled up comp prices for other similar homes that had recently sold in the area.

"You're low-balling it more than a bit, but let's give it a whirl."

"They've been listed for more than a year," Darian said. "If they purchased it solely as a flip, I feel certain they are more than ready to entertain any serious offer. Why don't you give their broker a call now? I don't want to wait on this. I've got a lot of other work to do."

Darian strode back and forth across the bamboo floor, admiring the huge, spectacular, pop art piece on the wall behind the real estate broker's chair. The longer she stood in this unbelievable Hollywood Hills living space, the more she fell in love with it.

The broker hung up a moment later and told Darian the buyers had turned down the offer of $4 million. Darian chuckled.

"Okay," Darian said. "Four point three million, final offer and then I walk."

The broker got back on the phone. He haggled aggressively for several minutes, a tournament Ping-Pong match between Darian's broker, the sellers' broker and the sellers themselves. He chuckled himself once he finally hung up.

"I really like you," he said. "You are making my commissions for the month look really, really nice. Offer accepted."

"YES!" Darian grinned, pumping her fist. Her hunch had been right. "Fax the paperwork to me at the hotel. Arrange the inspections. Let's move to close this thing. I've gotta run. I've got a meeting in less than an hour with the interior designer for my office space. My assistant and I are getting ready to move in!"

Even though the W was a beautiful hotel and the staff took amazing care of her, Darian was looking forward to packing up and moving out of it and, if all transacted smoothly at her bank and with the closing, she would be moving very soon.

-13-

Misha returned from her impromptu trip to New York and felt rejuvenated. Krishawn had been exactly what she needed in more ways than one. She so regretted how she had hurt him by not marrying him, but Marcus had insisted she break things off with Krishawn and marry him, and he had given her an ultimatum she couldn't even take the time to think about.

Marcus watched Misha now as she moved about the kitchen getting coffee and scones as she prepared to head into the office. He thought for a moment he'd actually heard her humming some love song. He was both amused and a bit perplexed by the joyous way she was flitting about. She had operated on an emotional scale between sulking and fury ever since the day he had gone into her townhouse with a couple of his employees without her authorization, removed all of her personal belongings, and moved them into his mansion, stating that he needed to be able to keep an eye on his "wife."

"You look happy," he said. "Perhaps you have a better outlook on our marriage."

"Fuck you!" she snapped and walked out of the kitchen.

"I've been meaning to talk to you about exactly that," Marcus said, always thoroughly entertained by how much Misha despised him. "That might be just what is needed to get our marriage on the right track."

Misha arrived at the offices of Larger Than Lyfe Entertainment and the first meeting on her agenda was Ntozake. The meeting was a casual one. Misha simply wanted to sit down and touch base with Ntozake, who had just returned to Los Angeles after wrapping her concert tour date with Maxwell and Ledisi in New York City at Madison Square Garden. Ntozake was positively basking in her new success, but she was physically and mentally exhausted from numerous nonstop show dates that had begun almost as soon as her debut album dropped. She talked about what a cool person Ledisi was and how absolutely sexy Maxwell was, but he was also quite shy, she thought. She then told Misha that, more than anything, she'd like to have a couple of weeks to just lie in bed and veg out by the pool.

"You're only as hot as your last successful CD," Misha reminded Ntozake. "When my sister chose you to represent this record label, she chose you to assume Rasheed the Refugee's position as the premier artist of this record label. We want to saturate the industry with very best you have to offer. I've got you booked to head into the studio next Saturday to start work on the new album. There've already been whispers around the industry about Grammy nominations for you."

"WHAT?!" Ntozake exclaimed, beaming.

"Girl, STOP!" Misha said, laughing. "You know your shit is hot. You are an amazing talent and you're only starting to come into the superstardom that my sister foresaw for you."

And Larger Than Lyfe was putting everything they had into making Ntozake's second album even hotter than her debut. LTL's super-producer, Mack-A-Do-Shuz, was laying tracks for her. So were Timbaland, Kanye West, and Raphael Saadiq. Misha was also giving Ntozake creative license to do some more writing this second time around. Two of the three singles Ntozake had written for her first album were now double platinum.

Ntozake had a photo shoot and interview for a feature spread and the cover of *Essence* magazine the following month, and she and Misha chatted a bit about that. Ntozake was flying to New York to make an appearance on BET's *106 & Park* the next day. VIBE magazine had been calling, wanting to do an interview and photo shoot with Ntozake. Ntozake was scheduled for two video shoots for two new singles on her album. LTL's management and PR team couldn't seem to coordinate all the things that were steadily coming Ntozake's way fast enough so that she could get all that she needed to get done accomplished. Ntozake was going to need a more personalized, professional management team to handle the ever-growing amount of things she had on her plate. Misha wanted her to have a sit-down with The Buchanan Group soon.

Misha hugged Ntozake and told her to shut her phone off the moment she wrapped her appearance on *106 & Park* and not to turn it back on until the following Saturday when she went into the studio. Ntozake laughed and told her that that was a promise she could easily keep.

People truly had no idea the inhuman amount of work involved in creating a superstar in the music industry. Ntozake had to be both strong and focused and have an above-average work ethic when she came to the table and signed a recording contract with Larger Than Lyfe Entertainment. If she hadn't possessed these traits, she would never be able to cut it; the music industry would eat her alive without apology, particularly when one considers the months and months of sleepless nights, show dates, interviews, studio time, and artist promotion required to take someone like Ntozake to the very top. She was incredibly talented and Misha intended to work with her in every way that she could. A lot of people came and went in the music industry. Mainly, it was because many of them had grown up watching BET, fantasizing and thinking that the life of a hip-hop or R&B star would be easy when they had no earthly idea what truly went on behind the scenes and was involved in making an artist into a superstar.

Next on Misha's agenda was a meeting with the three A & R executives who were working on development of the new jazz genre at Larger Than Lyfe. When Misha stepped into Keshari's shoes as the head of Larger Than Lyfe Entertainment, she had been completely determined to continue to accomplish every facet of Keshari's overall vision for her very successful record label. Everything they had discussed as friends, everything that had been carefully outlined in her will were tasks Misha had been diligently working to complete and she was succeeding.

The jazz genre was something Keshari had very seriously talked about that was near and dear to her heart, and she had started to work on it prior to her death. Misha was just finishing what her sister had started.

The A & R execs each appeared at the meeting that morning with demo CDs in hand and video footage of shows they'd caught, promising talent they believed Misha should consider. Misha immediately turned the music and video footage over to Andre DeJesus and Sharonda Richards, the other two shareholders of the record company. She had enough on her plate already and they both were thoroughly seasoned players within the company. She trusted whatever they decided.

Misha had signed a highly talented female artist with the vocal range of Rachelle Ferrell and the young, eclectic style of Floetry. With blonde dreadlocks piled on top of her head and a stage presence that rivaled Erykah Badu, the woman was sumthin' else. They would finalize her album budget that week and schedule studio time for her, then let the magic begin. The artist already had something of a following, and Larger Than Lyfe intended to blow jazz lovers' minds with her new album.

She'd also signed a very talented saxophonist who would easily rival Gerald Albright and Najee. He was already in the studio recording and the A & R execs laid out a tentative timeline as to when they would completely wrap recording on his amazing debut album. Budgets and crews needed to be arranged for two videos that would soon be scheduled for shooting for two singles soon set to drop off the artist's new album and Misha quickly jotted down a note to take care of that.

Misha was also hoping to, one day in the near future, sign Me'shell N'Degeocello. She'd recently had the opportunity to talk to her for a few minutes following a show she did in Hollywood, and Misha was as in love with her overwhelming talent and the music that she made just as Keshari had been. Her work likely would not fall under the jazz genre, but it would be an awesome feat to sign her on as a Larger Than Lyfe artist. Lalah Hathaway was another very talented artist who Misha had her eye on.

Last on the agenda for the first half of the day was a meeting with Larger Than Lyfe Entertainment's general counsel. He sat down with Misha in her office over coffee and pastries and up-dated her on a pair of lawsuits that had been launched against two of Larger Than Lyfe Entertainment's music producers. Court dates had recently been set for both of the cases.

Not uncommon in hip-hop music are lawsuits seeking compensatory damages on behalf of older and lesser known artists and producers alleging sampling violations of their music. New and hot or major and established artists and producers who create music tracks, the background music, looping, and hooks that singers and/or rappers drop their lyrics on and perform over often "dig through the crates" and utilize elements or very similar beat sequences of popular songs from back in the day— think of Queen Latifah's remake of "Hello Stranger" or the many tracks on which Snoop Dogg raps that have elements from popular songs from the 1970's. When the newly created music track has beat sequences that are so similar to the older song version and the artist/producer has not secured proper legal permissions to utilize portions of the older song, it is no different than plagiarizing a writer's intellectual property and making it your own, and it is considered a sampling violation. Everyone from Dr. Dre to Jermaine Dupri have been hit with sampling violations suits, and they either settled their cases quietly out of court or battled it out, depending upon the merits of the cases against them. Overall, the more famous a producer becomes and the more longevity said producer has in the music game, the more likely his/her chances are of being hit with a sampling violations suit. The mega-producers at Larger Than Lyfe Entertainment were not exempt.

"So, what do you think? Are these claims legitimate? Can these cases be settled or do you think we're justified in having our day in court?" Misha asked the general counsel.

"Yes, I've listened to both of the tracks as well as the two songs for which the plaintiffs are alleging sampling violations. I met with both producers and checked with our people to confirm that all of the required paperwork had been filed. Both were definite slips on our part. I think that both of these cases can be settled out of court for a fair amount. Then I would suggest you have a meeting with the two producers as well as the production department to ensure this does not repeat itself. They absolutely MUST follow every single step of the record label's protocol to prevent allegations and litigation in regard to sampling."

"Then, let's do what needs to be done to get these cases settled," Misha said. "No reason to rack up court time and legal fees if it can be avoided."

It was payroll time, and someone from the accounting department stopped by with the forms that needed to be signed for the Larger Than Lyfe staff's payroll checks to be run. Misha quickly looked over the documents, and then scrawled her signature on the signature line before the rep rushed back over to accounting. Keshari had set her company up in such a way that not a single thing moved within the company that involved the transacting of her/the company's money without securing her authorizing signature of first. Keshari Mitchell had been an extremely shrewd businesswoman and Misha now employed the same habit, requiring at her event planning firm that every single item that required the transacting of Misha Tierney money also required her signature of authorization.

Running a major record label was more work than Misha ever imagined. There were some days when Misha barely got in three hours of sleep because she also had to make the time to keep an eye on the running of her own company, MISHA TIERNEY. But, for the moment, she was not complaining. She would do practically anything and did to avoid the physical presence of the sick fuck she had been forced to marry.

Just as Misha made her way out of the office, headed to the offices of her event planning firm to oversee the final touches of The Buchanan Group's upcoming launch party, Thomas Hencken called her on her iPhone. It had taken a favor from a friend at the FBI to secure the phone number, as it had changed multiple times since Thomas Hencken's last contact with Misha. Misha was silent, very much on the verge of simply hanging up, when he announced who he was.

"Hello???" Thomas Hencken said.

"Yeah, I'm here," Misha responded. "You shouldn't be calling me. I have no information I can give to you. Trust me on that. I don't even understand why you continue contacting me. Last I checked, you're no longer even an agent for the DEA. You're gonna go and get yourself killed."

"You do realize that Marcus Means is most likely responsible for the death of your brother. I also have evidence that leads me to believe he may have been responsible for the execution-style murder of corporate attorney Phinnaeus Bernard III…the murder for which your brother was so adamant he had been set up. Marcus Means does not possess anything resembling a conscience and he will kill you, too, once you have expended your purpose to him and his motivations. There is no telling what was operating in his scheme of plans when he coerced you into marrying him, but a couple of reasons are certainly obvious."

Misha was silent.

"Misha, I need your help," Thomas Hencken said. "As his wife, you are around him almost every day. You live with him. I know you have seen or heard something that might be useful to me. Sometimes even the most minute details can turn out to be very significant farther down the line. Marcus Means is ten times worse than your brother ever was. He needs to be taken down…before it's too late."

"If you know how very dangerous Marcus is, if I had to marry him to save my life, if you can't even offer me protcction in cxchangc for any information that I might be able to provide to you, what would possibly make you think I'm going to help you?" Misha asked.

"I have some alliances with both the DEA and FBI who will get you the protection you need if you agree to co-operate."

Misha completely dismissed that statement.

"There are some very, very dangerous people who believe Keshari Mitchell is still alive," Thomas Hencken said. "If Marcus Means is keeping close tabs on you because he believes you are covering for Keshari Mitchell, these other people are doing the very same thing. You are in grave danger and you know it."

"And offering up information to an ex-DEA agent is going to reduce the hazard levels in my life?" Misha responded. "Look, I can't do this. I can't talk to you. Please do not call me again. If you call me again, I'm going to change my number. Better yet, if you call me again, I'm going to contact the police. Because you are no longer with the DEA, you are no longer operating under the line of duty."

The call was terminated.

As Misha dropped her phone on the car seat beside her, she wondered for a moment where Keshari was and what she was doing and if she had any idea what Misha was going through or if she even cared.

A FEW FACTS ABOUT COCAINE:

☞ Did you know that, prior to President Barack Obama signing the *Fair Sentencing Act* into law in 2010, a person convicted for simple possession of only five grams of crack cocaine received a five-year minimum sentence, the same sentence applied to a person convicted for trafficking 500 grams of powder cocaine? The *Fair Sentencing Act of 2010* is helping to reduce the gross disparities (which have ultimately equated to gross racial disparities) between powder cocaine and crack cocaine convictions.

☞ Did you know that, of all of the cocaine consumed throughout the entire world, the United States by itself consumes half of this amount?

☞ Did you know that most cocaine enters the United States at the border between the United States and Mexico?

☞ Organized crime rings in Colombia continue to maintain full control of the worldwide cocaine trade.

Mexican crime rings control wholesale distribution of cocaine in the West and Southwest regions of the United States and Dominican crime rings control street-level distribution of cocaine along the East Coast.

☛ Pharmaceutical giant Parke-Davis once said that cocaine "could make the coward brave, the silent eloquent, and render the sufferer insensitive to pain."

☛ Did you know that up until about 1916 a person could buy cocaine over-the-counter?

☛ While Southern California was once held as the main hub for Mexican wholesale cocaine distribution activities, did you know that Chicago and Atlanta are now two major hubs where Mexican organized crime rings control their Mexican wholesale cocaine distribution operations?

☛ Did you know that the very troubled nation of Haiti is currently one of the most major Caribbean shipment points for Colombian cocaine?

☛ Street gangs like the Crips and the Bloods continue to control the sale of cocaine at the retail level across the United States.

☛ Women have played a role in cocaine trafficking since the very beginning. Today women have a steadily increasing role in cocaine trafficking. As women begin to play a larger and larger role in top positions in corporate America, women are also playing larger and larger roles in the trafficking of cocaine. Women are gaining respect from some of the top players in cocaine trafficking for their shrewdness in finance and money laundering.

☛ A fairly recent trend in regard to women in cocaine trafficking is the use of "beauty queen" types for the transport of large quantities of cocaine. The belief is that the way these women look, particularly when you place these women in very expensive clothes and jewelry, places them above the suspicion of federal agents, police and narcotics officers. Per Gerardo Reyes of the *El Nuevo Herald:* "Sexy and daring women appear on 'Most Wanted' lists in the United States, Mexico and Colombia or are awaiting trial on charges of trafficking large quantities of cocaine."

☛ Did you know that, because of the deaths or arrests of their husbands, boyfriends, or family members, several key women have taken over as head and successfully controlled several major cocaine operations? For example, Enedina Arellano Felix of the very powerful Tijuana cartel took control of the drug ring's operations when her brother was killed. In an article written by Gerardo Reyes for the *El Nuevo Herald*: "According to analysts, she modernized the organization, making it more like a [legitimate] business, and she is considered the financial brains behind the family clan." The Tijuana cartel has long been one of the most powerful criminal organizations in Mexico, transporting massive quantities of cocaine into the U.S. and distributing it at the wholesale level throughout California, the Northwest and Midwest states.

☛ Per *FRONTLINE: PBS Online News Source*, "The DEA and Colombian National police believe there are more than 300 active drug smuggling organizations in Colombia today. Cocaine is shipped to every industrialized nation in the world and profits remain incredibly high."

-15-

Before the prison murder of Richard Lawrence Tresvant, founder and former head of The Consortium, The Consortium and Machaca were growing a very solid business relationship and alliance together. The "big boss" of Machaca respected Richard Tresvant and the way he ran his business. Richard Tresvant respected the "big boss" and the way he ran his business. When Richard Tresvant was charged with the first-degree murder of a prominent White attorney, Machaca severed all ties with The Consortium, having no desire to be caught anywhere in the fray of a federal law enforcement investigation. Now that the murder case was past, and Richard Lawrence Tresvant was past as well, Marcus Means wanted The Consortium to re-establish its relationship with Machaca. Machaca was one of the most powerful criminal organizations in the world, and they produced and distributed cocaine as pure as The Consortium required and at prices that the Consortium was far more amenable to paying.

Marcus Means and all of the new Consortium members had a meeting in Mexico with the heads of Machaca to discuss renegotiation. Marcus and the other members agreed it was best for all of them to attend the meeting together as a show of solidarity for the new Consortium. In a private jet chartered for the group, the men flew into Mexico City and arrived as the sun began to set. Three cars awaited them to drive them to Lomas, the most exclusive residential area in Mexico City and one of the most affluent residential areas of the entire Mexican nation. The men were meeting that evening at the house of the "big boss" of Machaca and that in and of itself was a significant event. The "big boss" rarely met with anyone. It would be Marcus Means's first time meeting him. When Richard Tresvant was alive, the "big boss" would only take meetings with Rick or his "protégé," Keshari. Now that both of them were gone, all of that had changed and the "big boss" was meeting with him. Javier Sandovar arrived at the airstrip to meet the Consortium members. Javier rode in the car with Marcus Means to Lomas.

The "big boss" was a very short man, but he was almost as wide as he was short. He was built like a small, fat hand grenade, and, as much as he looked like a jovial Mexican "abuelo" (meaning "grandfather" in Spanish), he had a renowned reputation for ruling his organization with an iron fist. It was said that he had ordered more murders in Mexico, Texas, and California than almost any other criminal organization operating in the United States. He had absolutely no compunction about taking out anyone, from judges to political officials to law enforcement officers, and he would take out members of his own organization if they even thought about betraying him.

The Mexicans, for the most part, dismissed the new alliance among the Black set leaders that formed the new Consortium, but they kept The Consortium's movements under close scrutiny nonetheless.

"They are like crabs in a barrel," the "big boss" had said after hearing of the auspicious meeting that had taken place at Marcus Means's home. "They do not understand nor respect the concepts of loyalty nor unity. They will betray one another and kill each other in no time."

Other organizations agreed, but, as much as they felt the way they did regarding The Consortium's expansion, there was money to be made, and Machaca was certainly willing to sit down and hear them out.

"Welcome to my home," the "big boss" said in Spanish, and Javier Sandovar translated for him. "What can I do for you?"

"The Consortium, via the acceptance of our newest members, has tripled its territory. We intend to quadruple it by the end of the year," Marcus Means said carefully.

Javier Sandovar translated for the big boss.

"This means our demand for product has very quickly and substantially increased," Marcus continued. "This certainly places our organization in a unique bargaining position for far more advantageous pricing in regard to our product, I believe. When Richard Tresvant was indicted for murder, our business relationship with your family was unfortunately yet understandably severed, and we would like to reestablish that relationship with you. The Consortium would like you to be our exclusive supplier. This relationship could be an extremely lucrative one for both of us."

The "big boss" sat back in his chair. His expression was very pensive.

If Machaca did not agree to re-establish a business relationship with The Consortium as their exclusive supplier, The Consortium would have to continue purchasing its cocaine from several suppliers and not always at the same high level of purity that could be guaranteed to them by Machaca. This was a sign of weakness, and, for Marcus Means, this was not acceptable.

"Keshari Mitchell is still alive," the "big boss" said through Javier Sandovar. "For us, that is a problem. For Machaca to do business with The Consortium, you will have to eliminate that woman without giving her the opportunity to carefully plan another escape."

Marcus nodded.

"It's done," he said. "I'll let you know as soon as that situation has been taken care of so that we can move forward with our business."

"We shall see," the "big boss" responded.

-16-

Mars, Jason Payne, Kevin Sperrington and Richard Bryson were all getting their files, furniture and other personal effects situated in the new offices of The Buchanan Group. They were all laughing, happy, excited as they moved about among the movers, issuing instructions and fielding calls on their BlackBerrys and iPhones.

"Man, did you get a look at the babe who owns Phoenix Films downstairs?" Jason Payne, Mars's best friend, said. "DAMN! The girl is BAD…super bad."

Mars smiled to himself.

"Yeah, she's alright." He chuckled. "I exchanged a few words with her on the elevator when I was meeting with execs in the leasing office a couple of weeks back."

"Well, don't you think it's time for you to get your feet back in the dating pool? We're gonna have to revoke your player's card if you continue to try to uphold this vow of celibacy you've been keeping."

"You mean get back into the dating pool by asking out the new tenant who owns the film company downstairs?"

"Hell yeah!" Jason said. "The girl is FIONE!"

Mars chuckled again.

"I'll give it some thought," he said.

"Well, you better not think for too long. I don't think that one is gonna have to wait around long at all for a date in this town."

The new offices for Phoenix Films were amazing. The interior designer's vision had all been brought together with Mediterranean and Moroccan influences in a modern setting. Cream-colored sectionals and seating were strategically situated all about the huge, open office space, and they served almost as a backdrop for bold splashes of color and the intricately carved woodwork that were traditional to Moroccan design and culture. There was a 1,000-gallon fish tank that covered an entire wall outside Darien's office near the reception area. Darian's desk had been shipped directly from Morocco. "Phoenix Films" largely and boldly welcomed visitors into the tastefully decorated offices as it was the first thing that could be seen when anyone entered the double glass doors and walked down the short hallway into the office suite.

"Girlfriend, you did not spare expense when you had this office done," Terrence complimented her on his first day at work with her in the new space. "These are some substantial pieces here. Trust me, honey, I know."

Darian smiled in appreciation at the overall quality of the outcome of the interior designer's work, and the two of them quickly began opening boxes of books and electronics, organizing things in a way that would work most efficiently for both of them.

There was MUCH work for them to do, a multitude of contacts that needed to be made. Darian Boudreaux and Phoenix Films were complete unknowns in the film industry and it was time to take her company public. Darian got on the phone that day and hired top Los Angeles PR firm, Eileen Koch & Co., to represent Phoenix Films. She wanted Eileen Koch to quickly solidify interviews and write-ups in all of the major Los Angeles trade magazines and other media for her to introduce herself and announce the opening of Phoenix Films.

Two days later, Darian sat with an interviewer from the Los Angeles Business Journal in Phoenix Films' offices and discussed her vision for the future in filmmaking at Phoenix Films.

"So, tell me, what kind of motion pictures would you like to depict for the masses?"

"GOOD ones," Darian quipped saucily, making the interviewer smile.

"I figured as much," the interviewer said. "Foremost, what subject matter would you like to cover to make your impact on the film industry?"

"I intend to make movies that give powerful voice to WOMEN, women in general, Black women in particular.

Not in secondary roles as the eye candy or victim, but in leading roles consistently. My desire is to empower women, and, at the same time, smash a multitude of the stereotypes about women, especially Black women."

"So, can the public and the industry expect that Phoenix Films will dedicate itself to films that are typically classified as 'chick flicks'?"

"Absolutely not," Darian responded. "I will do GOOD movies. My goal is to make blockbuster movies, and women can hold the leading role in these movies without ever having to come close to relegating and limiting the film to 'chick flick' status. Heroine, villain, teacher, mother, lover, corporate raider, trailblazer...there are many extraordinary, powerful and empowering motion pictures just waiting to be made with women in the leading roles, and I'm going to make them."

"Is there anything else you'd like the public to know about your film company?" the interviewer asked.

"Yes." Darian smiled. "I am currently seeking and accepting scripts from very talented writers."

The next day, Darian Boudreaux had write-ups announcing the opening of Phoenix Films in *Variety*, *Hollywood Reporter*, *Script* magazine and *Creative Screenwriting*. A huge black and platinum billboard was raised on Sunset Boulevard and also on Pico Boulevard on the Westside announcing the opening of Phoenix Films. The closely knit film sector of Los Angeles now had its first glimpse of the strategic handiwork of the new "hot girl" in town.

-17-

Amazing jazz music, premium liquors, tapas tables throughout—The Buchanan Group launch party at the world-renowned Beverly Hills Hotel was like a really amazing, upscale networking function filled with executives, athletes, producers, writers and other elite members of the NBA, NFL, music, and film industries. Even Los Angeles's mayor and several members of the Los Angeles Chamber of Commerce had made an appearance to put their stamp of approval on the new, much-talked-about entertainment and athletic management firm.

Although Misha spent the greater part of her days at the helm of Larger Than Lyfe Entertainment running the successful record label, she had personally overseen every facet of The Buchanan Group's event that night through the event planning firm she still owned to make sure it was PERFECT. She even made a point of having the DJ drop three, yet-to-be-released tracks from two of Larger Than Lyfe Entertainment's new jazz genre artists into the music selections to give the event that evening something no one else could claim, something truly exclusive, and there were more than a few listeners around the packed room who either asked "who the artist was" or "what the song was" when the DJ interspersed the smoky, sexy jazz tracks into the music mix.

"How are you doing?" Mars smiled, kissing Misha on the cheek as he looked around him at the typical, top-notch work she did as a high-profile events planner.

"I'm good…as well as can be expected," Misha said carefully, not wanting to ruin his upbeat mood with her true feelings. "How are YOU doing?"

"Really good." Mars smiled, looking across the room at Darian. "Everything is falling very nicely into place."

"I'm glad," Misha said. "If anyone deserves that, you do."

"Likewise, Misha," Mars said to her seriously.

Mars knew Misha was completely unaware that Darian Boudreaux was Keshari Mitchell. While they were in Brazil, Darian had carefully broken down the details to Mars about how much Misha did know about Keshari Mitchell's "suicide." Misha knew that Keshari had not really committed suicide, but she knew nothing about what had happened once the ambulance took Keshari away from her Palos Verdes home. Misha knew nothing about Keshari Mitchell leaving the country, she knew nothing about Brazil and she knew nothing about the very radical surgeries that Keshari had undergone to alter her physical identity. That was upsetting to Mars, more than he ever let on to Darian. Again and again since arriving back in the United States, he was being forced to confront the fact that there were a lot of things that he still needed time to wrap his mind around since going to Brazil in search of the love of his life and finding her.

"We need to get together soon to talk," Mars said.

"No, we don't," Misha said matter-of-factly. "And you know why. We need to keep as much distance between the two of us as we can, and we need to make a point of keeping it that way…to keep things from getting any more complicated than they already are."

"Okay," Mars said a little sadly, but he was abundantly aware that Misha was most likely right. He kissed Misha on the cheek again and walked away.

A huge, double chocolate cake in the shape of The Buchanan Group logo with lit sparklers all across the top of it was rolled out into the middle of the room. Waiters were at the ready to serve. Magnums of Cristal were popped by each of the four new partners of The Buchanan Group. There were cheers and applause from the huge crowd of attractive and upwardly mobile party-goers and potential clients. Mars was absolutely ecstatic and he beamed at his beautiful wife across the room as she raised her glass of champagne to him in salute.

Mustafah Ahmad was not your typical, young, Black man. He was a genius. He had a 170 I.Q. and a penchant for the sciences. For two years, he'd majored in Chemistry at UCLA with plans for going into medical research, and, while he was there, he had singlehandedly developed a process for manufacturing "ecstasy" in less time and at a cheaper price than traditional methods of manufacture. While the essential oils required to manufacture "ecstasy" were relatively inexpensive, the overall process for the manufacture itself was not, and Mustafah refined the overall process, by creating and using cheaper, more mobile equipment, and by eliminating some of the steps in the overall synthesis process that cut the manufacture time almost in half. He'd played around with the entire process like a hobbyist tinkering with a model car, and the result was a potential goldmine.

"Ecstasy," scientifically named methylenedioxymeth-amphetamine or MDMA, was a highly popular drug on the nightclub scene and among many college students and the twenty-something crowd. It produced a euphoric state in its users, diminished anxiety and depression, and was supposed to dramatically enhance intimacy, taking sex to a whole other level. Mustafah took to dealing his concoction of "X" around campus until information about it somehow made it to the offices of the undergraduate dean, who quickly and unceremoniously initiated the necessary proceedings to eject Mustafah, accompanied by campus police escort, permanently from UCLA's campus. It was a wonder he had not had to face criminal charges, but the school could prove nothing against him beyond some very small-time, school drug dealing, which was certainly not unheard of on most college campuses. The school wanted to quietly be rid of the entire situation, and, although Mustafah's family was furious and heartbroken, Mustafah didn't even seem to care. He had other plans for himself and his future.

It has often been said that there is a very thin line between genius and insanity, and the young genius Mustafah Ahmad knew somebody who knew somebody who introduced him to none other than Big Bree-Z, one of the new members of The Consortium. Mustafah had come to the conclusion that he wanted to become independently wealthy, become an entrepreneur, since his future in medical research was now null and void. Mustafah wanted to take his innovative concept for the manufacture of ecstasy and turn it into a lucrative enterprise for himself. A meeting was arranged with Big Bree-Z. Considering The Consortium's plan to expand its wares in all facets of the drug game, Big Bree-Z loved the idea. Now he simply needed to take the idea before Marcus Means and the rest of The Consortium. They were going to take over the Los Angeles nightclub scene and, ultimately, take full command of Los Angeles' ecstasy game…by whatever means necessary.

When they met later that week at Marcus Means's Bel Air mansion, Mustafah was extremely impressed as he looked around at the paneled library with its cathedral ceilings and black marble floors. It was like he was meeting the Black "Don Corleone." Marcus Means was gangster FOR REAL. And Marcus Means and the other Consortium members were definitely enthused about the idea of taking over Los Angeles' "X" game.

-18-

There was a large credit card fraud scheme The Consortium was carrying out in ten states. There were the two, well-known, Los Angeles art galleries that had been owned by The Consortium well before Richard Tresvant's death to which The Consortium sometimes transported portions of its cocaine shipments and through which The Consortium laundered some of its cocaine money. The NEW Consortium members acted as suppliers/distributors of all the cocaine sold to and by their respective sets. Each of these sets then trafficked and distributed their cocaine supplies to an out-of-state client base via traveling members of their sets or by members of their sets who temporarily or permanently moved out of Los Angeles County to other major cities all around the country. There were more than twelve fast food franchises, drug dealing operations throughout the California prison system, very substantial, legitimate investments in the Wall Street stock market and in several emerging markets overseas, and highly sophisticated chop shops with DMV employees on The Consortium payroll to help legitimize the sale of stolen cars at several used car dealerships around Los Angeles and in at least three other cities in Southern states. It was absolutely true that Marcus Means and The NEW Consortium had their hands on every piece of filthy business going down in Los Angeles County, and, still, they wanted MORE.

Marcus and the members of the new Consortium sat around the Olympic-sized, black-bottom pool at Marcus's Bel Air mansion. Their meeting was a casual one. They'd come together to toss around ideas and to discuss any immediate concerns that needed to be addressed within the organization. The meeting in Mexico had gone as they had anticipated. Marcus assured them all that Keshari Mitchell would most definitely be located…and, somehow, they didn't doubt it where he was concerned.

"So," Marcus said, with a smooth smile. "What is something that each of you have fantasized about doing?"

"I've wanted to put a price on the head of that fucking mayor and have it fully carried out," "Dread," leader of R3 Crips, said.

"I'd like to bend over that rap star Trina and bang her out, then brand her fine ass with my name," Big Bree-Z said.

"Nah, man, not like that." Marcus chuckled. "What have you wanted to do as one of the most powerful gangsters in Los Angeles that you have not done already?"

"I'd like to own an NBA team," "Slim J," leader of R2 Crips, said seriously.

"I've always said that same thing," "Big D," leader of R4 Crips, said.

"Now, we're talking." Marcus smiled. "How 'bout we do that?"

"Buy an NBA franchise?" Big Bree-Z said. "The feds would be all over that shit. The entire NBA would never be the same."

"There are some folks in the game who are already NBA owners. I've got dummy corporations that go deep enough that the feds could dig for years and they would never be able to trace a thing to us."

"I like that shit right there," Big Bree-Z said. "Let's do it."

Marcus Means flew to Miami to meet with "The Colombian." Keshari Mitchell had established the business relationship with The Colombian immediately prior to her "death" when Machaca severed their dealings with The Consortium during Richard Tresvant's criminal charges and trial for the first-degree murder of prominent Los Angeles corporate and anti-trust attorney Phinnaeus Bernard III. The Colombian had respected Keshari. He'd said that she was "ballsy" and "smart." Before the enactment of the NEW Consortium, The Consortium had been dealing with The Colombian almost exclusively for their cocaine supply because transport was simpler, and The Colombian could provide the same high level of purity in the product that Machaca had always provided. But The Colombian had recently indicated that some changes would have to be made and it was pretty obvious by his tone when he contacted Marcus that there would be no room for negotiation in the matter. When The Colombian and Marcus rode out on The Colombian's yacht that afternoon shortly after one of The Colombian's cars picked Marcus up at the airport, The Colombian did not mince words. He kicked up the price per kilo for the cocaine that he was supplying to The Consortium. Then he kicked up the price for transport by another 10 percent.

The Colombian, like the prudent head of any criminal organization, had been doing his research, keeping his ear to the underground grapevine to know what was transpiring around him. He knew about The Consortium's meeting with Machaca's "big boss" in Mexico. He knew the outcome of the meeting. He knew that The Consortium was in a difficult position in terms of leverage because of a niggling little problem that had yet to be resolved. The fact that people in high and low places a little bit of everywhere believed that Keshari Mitchell was still alive was becoming an expensive problem for The Consortium and it was positively making Marcus Means LIVID.

Marcus returned to Los Angeles the very next day and immediately called a meeting with all of the other Consortium members. They hashed out their options late into the night. They compared all of their connections to determine if they could quickly locate a new main supplier. If not, they were going to have to bend to this new higher pricing that The Colombian was essentially strong-arming their organization into accepting.

It was very, very clear. They were going to have to find Keshari Mitchell as soon as possible and eliminate her.

-19-

Darian firmly decided that the only way that she would be able to get the right depiction of the story that she wanted to tell about Keshari Mitchell's life and The Consortium was to write the movie script herself. She was giving herself two months to complete the script. Then she would immediately begin orchestrating the rest of the production for the film.

Escrow for the Hollywood Hills home would close in a couple more weeks and Darian was extremely excited about it. Via text messages and during some of the private telephone calls made during stolen moments in their extremely busy schedules, Darian had told Mars all about the house. She told him she couldn't wait for him to see it. Darian and Mars also seriously discussed selling the Palm Beach mansion as soon as the economy picked up. The upkeep for the palatial home was exorbitant, and neither of them spent any real amount of time there anyway. With both of their start-up companies based in Los Angeles, there would be little time for them to spend in Palm Beach.

Theirs was the ultimate in unorthodox relationships. Since their return from Brazil, both of them had promptly thrown themselves into their respective career projects, and no one in the United States had any idea of their marriage or even of the fact that they knew each other. Mars had traveled to New York to visit his family and Darian had remained in Los Angeles. Besides the short visit they had with each other in Palm Beach, the two had barely even gotten the opportunity to see and spend time with each other. There had been a couple of brief and very secret occasions when they had gotten away from work for just long enough to connect, but, because of who Darian Boudreaux really was and for the overall safety of all concerned, Darian and Mars were going to have to strategically ease into any public displays of them being a couple. Both of them knew that, just as Marcus Means kept a close eye on Misha at all times in hopes that she'd slip and reveal Keshari Mitchell's where-abouts, they were surely keeping a close eye on Mars's movements too. Darian and Mars had even discussed whether or not Marcus Means or anyone else had found out about Mars's trip to Brazil and tracked his move-ments there, particularly since he'd quit his job and left the country for nearly two years. Now that both of them were back Stateside, only time would tell.

On the evening after escrow closed on the Hollywood Hills house, Mars went up and carried with him a gigantic bouquet of three dozen, long-stemmed, pink roses and a bottle of pinot grigio. Darian did something she absolutely NEVER did and cooked dinner for him, and she made something for him that he almost never got and LOVED... soul food. Mars pretended he was looking around for the housekeeper who'd prepared the delicious meal while Darian rolled her eyes at him. She made stuffed chicken breasts and collard greens and candied yams and macaroni and cheese from scratch and homemade Parker House rolls. It was so, so good that Mars said, "I love you, Mrs. Buchanan," and then he planted a single kiss on her forehead.

Darian took him on a tour of the entire house and Mars fell in love with it in the same way Darian had. Darian had negotiated the purchase of many of the furnishings inside the home as well as some of the artwork from the staging firm that had prepped and decorated the house for the sale. She would, of course, hire her own decorator at some point in the near future to truly add all of the very special touches to the house to truly make it her own, but there was no rush. The house was perfect.

Darian and Mars curled up by the fire pit with a bottle of wine on the spectacular terrace with its incredible, panoramic views of Los Angeles, and Darian carefully began to revisit the discussion that she'd initiated in Palm Beach about doing a biopic of Keshari Mitchell's life. She felt compelled to discuss the issue with her husband because she had firmly decided she was moving full steam ahead with the project. The woman had serious control issues, and these issues stemmed from owning and running a major record label and from running one of the most powerful crime rings on the West Coast as well as having to fend for herself early on in life following the death of her mother. Her problem was that she could not bring this same level of control she wielded in business into her marriage if she wanted her marriage to survive. There had to be COMPROMISE. She and Mars Buchanan were engaged in a partnership.

An evening that had started so beautifully almost immediately took a negative turn. Darian was not bending and Mars absolutely was not bending either. "You could get yourself killed over this movie project!" Mars told her again. "You could get the people who work with you killed over this movie project! You could get me killed over this movie project! Is that what you want?!"

They argued about it. They argued heatedly. They went to sleep in anger. Mars lay as far away from Darian in their huge bed as he could get. Darian was surprised Mars had not hopped into his Porsche and sped back down the hill, headed back to his condo in Marina del Rey after the way they had argued.

Darian lay awake for hours after their fight thinking. She smoked a cigar and lay back in the candlelit darkness contemplating so, so much. It was funny how a major fight made you intensely think about things that were completely unrelated to the fight. Her thoughts immediately drifted to Misha. Darian missed her best friend so, so much. Keshari and Misha had been through EVERYTHING together. There was not a day that went by when Darian did not think of Misha. Sometimes Darian reminisced about the amazingly good times she and Misha had had, the parties they'd thrown, the dreams they'd shared, and the many dreams the two of them had worked their asses off, side by side, and accomplished. Other times, Darian was overwhelmed by intense feelings of guilt about having dragged her best friend into the dangerous mess of Keshari Mitchell's life in the first place. Misha had NEVER been involved in any way at all with The Consortium, and now she was. Keshari had completely left her former life behind, left Misha with the humongous task of running, without any formal training, one of the largest, most successful record labels in the United States, and then left Misha to fend for herself in her current nightmare of a marriage to Marcus Means. All the while, Misha's only motives had been to love and protect her best friend. Misha was sacrificing everything to protect the sister she loved, and Darian felt like she was sacrificing nothing in return for all Misha had done and was doing now for her. That absolutely broke Darian's heart.

Misha Tierney had been the one person in the entire world who knew FULLY about Keshari Mitchell's involvement in "the game," and still loved her unconditionally.

Some nights, when Darian was not snapping awake in a cold sweat from one of the many nightmares of after having been found, captured and tortured to death by The Consortium, she had nightmares of that blood-curdling scream of Misha's on the day of Keshari Mitchell's "suicide." The sound would reside vividly in Darian's memory for the rest of her life…because, in those moments before Misha thought about the situation and remembered what Keshari had once told her, Misha had actually believed Keshari was really dead.

Darian quickly shoved those painful thoughts out of the forefront of her mind and looked over at Mars as he slept. People always said that he was Boris Kodjoe's dead ringer. He was super-fine and oh-so-sexy and kind and funny and very successful and monogamous and he absolutely, undeniably ADORED her. Why in all fuck did she have to repeatedly go and test the limits of his love for her? She was going to wind up losing the very thing millions of women prayed about and dreamed about having.

Mars rolled over onto his back. His mouth was slightly open. His breathing was relaxed. He threw his arm over into Darian's lap. She smiled both lovingly and sadly at his sleeping form. Then, with a feline-like movement, she slid under the sheets and got between her gorgeous husband's long, hairy legs and sensuously caressed his perfect penis with her tongue from the base to the tip. Mars stirred as his caramel-colored member began to show signs of life. When Mars finally opened his eyes,

Darian was going down on him and he was very, very aroused, and as much as he wanted to fight it, he just couldn't bring himself to fight it.

Mars loved Darian so much, but he positively hated the predicaments she seemed to almost intentionally wind herself up in. He hated some of the outlandish and dangerous decisions she made, particularly in regard to this film, and he hated more how fucking stubborn she was about it all. When her mind was made up, not even he could get her to bend. He hated how consumed in her he was, most times at the expense of himself. And now, while he had been sleeping, she had started working this slow seduction, ready to try to make amends for their ferocious disagreement…all on her own terms, still moving full steam ahead with the plans to make this dangerous movie about the life and times of Keshari Mitchell, prodigy, music mogul, multimillionaire and gangster. She was so goddamned beautiful as she crawled back up the bed to him, having rendered him as hard as he could get…and even that made him angry.

"Good morning." She smiled as he lifted his head from the pillows.

A look of total surprise registered on her face when he flipped her onto her stomach and, without uttering a word, entered her roughly from the rear and fucked her until he climaxed, a move that was clearly filled with his anger at her, how dangerously in love he was with her and his need for some of the control that she always seemed to have.

—20—

Ecstasy is typically sold at anywhere from $20–$40 a pill inside and on the parking lots of nightclubs, at raves, and at concerts in most major cities across the United States. Marcus Means had been carefully casing the "ins" and "outs" of the "X" industry and how ecstasy moved on a typical busy night. The money was not as good as cocaine, particularly when cocaine was converted to crack, but "X" most definitely turned a very nice profit. The Consortium was all about profits.

With Mustafah's ingenious new process, The Consortium would manufacture premium quality ecstasy pills for less than 25 cents per pill, and then sell the pills on the street at $10 each, a significant discount to the average "per pill" sale price on the street, instantly rendering them very heavy competitors in this industry that was completely new to them. Using a large stash house in the San Fernando Valley that he owned, Marcus Means and the other Consortium members assembled a "work" crew. The "work" crew, under Marcus Means's close supervision, put all of the equipment and needed supplies into place, and, with The Consortium's logo embossed on each pill, the first batch of "X" was run and was a success. They would continuously increase the overall efficiency of their process as they went. The Consortium very quickly set a production and earnings goal for itself. At 375,000 pills per week, 1.5 million pills per month, they could easily net nearly $8 million per month on ecstasy.

A little more than a week later following four successful runs of ecstasy pills, The Consortium strategically assembled three different "work" crews. The first crew was assigned to hit every nightclub in Hollywood. After casing the club scene in Miami and New York and getting a full grasp of how the "X" game worked in those two cities, The Consortium sent the other two work crews to move "X" on the nightclub scene there. The members of all of these work crews were mostly composed of folks who could easily fit into the nightclub scene in each of the areas that the Consortium had carefully pinpointed to sell ecstasy. Most of the members of these work crews were not even gang-affiliated. They were White girls, White boys, Latin boys, Latin girls, some gay, some straight. They were all professional anglers there to work the "X" game and earn some fast money, and each of them were fully aware of the deadly repercussions of fucking with The Consortium's "work" or their money or cooperating in any way with law enforcement.

The Consortium booked airfares into New York City and Miami respectively, booked cheap hotel rooms, supplied the work crews with enough "product" to work the clubs for a month, and then sent them on their way. The work crews would move all the product, then fly home to settle up and pick up new product, and then do it all again. A pair of lieutenants from Marcus's and Big Bree-Z's sets flew with each of the crews to Miami and New York to keep a watchful eye on the money and the product. Meanwhile, The Consortium's crew who had been assigned to work Hollywood were starting to move product quickly and turn money over to lieutenants who reported directly to The Consortium.

The "X" game in the West Hollywood area was mainly dominated by Asian crews. It didn't take long for a few members of these Asian crews to take notice of the fact that their sales were dropping more and more substantially over roughly a week's time. When the Asian crews began to pinpoint who had begun dealing in their territory, the BlackBerrys came out, texting started, and phone calls were made. One member of The Consortium's work crew was beaten viciously in the parking lot at AREA Nightclub and left near death in the back seat of his car. When Marcus Means received the call of what had happened, three members of the Asian crew were killed over the next three days. Pretty soon, a turf war broke out. One of ours, two of yours. You shoot my dog, I'll kill your cat. You hurt one of my crew and I'll take out your whole fucking family. The Consortium was quickly and firmly establishing its position in the "X" game.

As it turned out, the Asian crew who The Consortium muscled in on in Hollywood was connected, quite well-connected, to Yakuza. One of the "big bosses" of Yakuza requested a meeting with Marcus Means. Marcus Means obliged. When the big boss of Yakuza attempted diplomacy and informed Marcus Means he had probably intercepted their territory and business inadvertently and he would permit a "pass" to allow The Consortium's crew to completely remove themselves from their territory, Marcus Means acted as if he had no idea what the big boss was talking about.

"None of my men have been working your territory," Marcus Means said, "and I take offense to you insinuating that we would."

The meeting accomplished absolutely nothing. If anything, it provided the big boss of Yakuza the opportunity to see the arrogant, ruthless man who now headed The Consortium and had, basically, thumbed his nose at the attempt for compromise and civility that had been extended to him by Yakuza. The Consortium's crew further expanded their "X" enterprise into more West Hollywood and Los Angeles nightclubs and venues and then began acting as supplier to other smaller, Los Angeles dealers. A much more serious power struggle was about to start.

-21-

Chris Winters had just entered her third year at UCLA's School of Law. She was smart, she was savvy to the management game, she was very organized, and she was proactive. She'd worked her entire first year of law school in the law library. She'd done an internship working doing legal research for the paralegal team in the media and entertainment division at Latham & Watkins. She interviewed with Mars Buchanan and he was thoroughly impressed. She expressed that she planned to enter into entertainment management after graduating from law school and passing the California bar. She'd done an internship with the Los Angeles Lakers management office during undergrad. Mars did some routine reference and background checks on her, he ran a check of her undergraduate and law school transcripts, and then he offered her the position as his executive assistant. Chris Winters happily accepted.

Jason Payne, Kevin Sperrington, and Richard Bryson, The Buchanan Group partners, had recently hired assistants as well. Jason, Mars's best friend, noted the strong resemblance of Chris Winters to Mars's former girl-friend, Keshari Mitchell. He almost made a joke about it, but caught himself immediately, knowing that the joke would be in poor taste.

Since Mars's return from Brazil, Jason hadn't had time to sit down and talk to him seriously. Mars had taken Keshari Mitchell's death very, very badly. Although he seemed okay and had thrown himself completely into his work and into the vision for a highly successful enter-tainment and athletic management firm, conscientious attention to detail in career did not necessarily mean that he WAS okay. Mars had been deeply in love with that Keshari Mitchell woman and he had an almost complete mental breakdown when she died. When Mars started to come around, he immediately quit his job at ASCAP and flew to Brazil. Only the people closest to him knew he had gone to Brazil and Jason still wondered why he had gone there and stayed for two years. Jason also won-dered about the fact that Mars still did not have a new girlfriend. He seemed to have absolutely no interest in women whatsoever, which was a vast change from the best friend Jason Payne had always known.

When Krishawn Webb's contract with EXCEL Athletic Management was about to expire and a few whispers from reliable sources had it that Krishawn would not be re-signing with EXCEL, Mars Buchanan quickly and aggressively courted Krishawn Webb and convinced him to allow The Buchanan Group to represent him. There'd been a press conference in Los Angeles, then Mars Buchanan had immediately gone to work to show Krishawn Webb that all of the promises and assurances he'd made to gain him as a client had not been mere lip service. This was all before The Buchanan Group had partners who'd left careers at prestigious Los Angeles firms to join The Buchanan Group. This was before The Buchanan Group moved into plush offices in the Capitol Records building or had gained any name recognition whatsoever. That's how determined Mars Buchanan had been about having The Buchanan Group taken very, very seriously.

Krishawn Webb was at the height of his career. At 17 points and 10 rebounds per game and with an 85 percent free throw average, he was still a hot commodity. He was ready to leave the Knicks in New York. The Sixers as well as the Lakers wanted him.

Now Krishawn was back in Los Angeles preparing to accept an offer from the Los Angeles Lakers. Mars Buchanan was still at the bargaining table with Jerry Buss. There was much media coverage of the event and discussion of how Krishawn Webb would fare in meshing with Kobe Bryant. There'd been talk in the media that the finalized deal would net Krishawn Webb $20 million over the next three years. Krishawn was in it to win a championship ring. Then he would retire and dedicate his time to his charities, endorsements, and other business enterprises.

After three days of numbers crunching, Krishawn finally sat down with Mars Buchanan, the Los Angeles Lakers general manager, Lakers owner, and Lakers coach to sign his contract. In black Armani, he was smooth, confident, with a $20 million smile on his face. He walked out of the Lakers management offices and fielded questions in a televised press conference regarding his move to Los Angeles. Then, instead of heading to a huge party thrown in his honor to celebrate, Krishawn was whisked quickly and secretly away and back to his hotel. Misha met him at the door of his luxurious suite, and Krishawn promptly peeled her out of her clothes. She'd dedicated the entire day to prepping for this moment. Her hair was a perfectly coiffed tumble of Tiffany & Co.-scented curls. She'd gotten a full body massage and head-to-toe brown sugar scrub. Fingers and toes had been pampered and polished in her favorite Cappuccino Sheer.

Krishawn poured Cristal all over her and tried to lick every single drop of it off. He wanted her all night in every way and he intended to get what he wanted. This was the celebration of his contract signing he had been thinking about all week. The two of them were danger-ously making love again as if the violent attack that had occurred when the two of them connected following Ntozake's album release party had never happened. Misha was all over him and Krishawn was all over her. For an entire week, the two had been secretly planning their meeting for that night.

A week and a half after Krishawn Webb signed to come to L.A. and play with the Lakers, the media captured their first photographs of Krishawn and Misha together. As they waited for the valet to bring them their car at Mr. Chow's in Beverly Hills, Krishawn Webb leaned down and playfully planted a kiss on Misha Tierney's lips. She smiled and smacked him. The two were casually dressed, the epitome of the young, rich, beautiful and famous, and they definitely looked like a couple. They both climbed into Krishawn's rented Maserati and sped off, and paparazzi ate up every single millisecond of it. When the photographs and video footage were released a few days later on the cover of the *National Enquirer* as well as in several other entertainment tabloids, on several entertainment websites, and on *TMZ* and *E! News* on television, the whole situation had been blown up and out of proportion in more ways than one and the public loved every single moment of it.

Misha had seemingly refused to even think about the potential meltdown that would follow. Here she was in what was clearly a very bizarre concoction of a marriage to a man, many whispered, was one of the worst reputed gangsters on the West Coast, and now she was cozied up in public with none other than her ex-fiancé, the newest "hot boy" in the L.A. Lakers line-up, Krishawn Webb. It was like Misha Tierney and Krishawn Webb had some sort of a death wish.

Only in L.A. was that brand of drama allowed.

=22=

Marcus Means, for the most part, had been giving Misha free reign to come and go as she pleased as his reluctant new wife. Most people thought there was something peculiar and unsettling about their relationship anyway. Marcus Means, real estate developer, entrepreneur, or whatever he was calling himself these days, had a reputation that was undeniably, unquestionably…"gangster." All over Los Angeles, people knew about him, whispered about him, spread rumors about him, and hated him. He and Misha Tierney had never, ever been publicly connected as a couple prior to their out-of-the-blue nuptials. There did not appear to be a romantic notion that had ever once entered Misha Tierney's mind about any part of Marcus Means nor anything in his immediate proximity. It had been said by the folks around her "in the know" that Misha had disowned her very own brother for his organized crime affiliations. It made absolutely no sense that she would condone what Marcus Means did. The two as a couple just seemed as ill-matched and as uncomfortable as it could get. Misha always had a distracted or disgusted look on her face and in her body language whenever the two were photographed together. Some people thought Marcus Means might be trying to strong-arm his way into ownership of Larger Than Lyfe Entertainment, or he must have been holding something else very significant over Misha's head to force her into marrying him… like, perhaps, the rumor of Keshari Mitchell not being dead. Overall, the matrimony between Misha Tierney and Marcus Means seemed to everyone to be a marriage that was nothing more than a technicality, a loveless predicament that was solidified by a license on paper and by whatever it was Marcus Means was holding over Misha's head.

When Marcus saw the photograph of NBA star Krishawn Webb playfully stealing a kiss from a casual, happy, smiling Misha Tierney on the cover of *National Enquirer*, regardless of what people thought about his marriage to Misha and regardless of the fact that, for all intents and purposes, it wasn't really a marriage, he confronted her immediately, and he was mad as hell when he did. Clearly, that motherfucker needed a refresher course of what he'd gotten not so long ago at the Four Seasons.

The media coverage of the newest Los Angeles Lakers player and his former fiancé, Misha Tierney, together was more a blow to Marcus Means's colossal ego than anything else. Misha had grossly disrespected him directly in front of the press when he had been, for the most part, magnanimous to her. If Marcus Means could not control his own wife, Marcus thought others would believe, how could he possibly have a strong grip on a very major criminal enterprise?

Never in a zillion years would Misha have ever even partially fathomed the slightest possibility this motherfucker of an asshole would haul off and hit her. Marcus backhanded her so hard across her honey brown face she now fully understood the expression about "seeing stars." She tilted like a pinball machine, and then stood there for a moment, dazed and in complete shock. When she finally came to, her first instinct had been to take off her Giuseppe Zanotti heel and take out his eye and it was like Marcus read her mind as she got that fire-filled, dangerous look in her eyes, letting him know she was about to attack.

"You son of a bitch!" she screamed.

Marcus had to grab her and hold her as she started viciously swinging her fists, one blow catching him across the brow and drawing blood.

Never in Misha's entire life had any man ever hit her or even thought about hitting her, to the best of her knowledge, and she would be damned if this bastard got away with it. Misha was well aware of Marcus's dangerous reputation and she was just as aware of what could happen to her if she pushed Marcus too far. Hell, she had grown up with the man. He'd been her brother's best friend. And even back then, he had not been quite right. Her mother had once called Marcus Means a "classic sociopath," slick as a can of oil and as evil as the devil. Before her passing, Misha's mother wouldn't even allow him into her house.

While Richard Tresvant had been alive, Misha, even though she worked diligently to stay away from her brother and to keep him far away from any connection to her, had always taken for granted that there was an invisible line that Marcus knew that he had better not cross because, regardless of her feelings for Rick and for what he did for a living, as her brother, he would always protect her. With Rick now out of the way, Marcus had finally gone and crossed that line. Well, in actuality, Marcus had crossed the line when he forced Misha to marry him.

Little did Misha know that Marcus had a helluva lot on his plate and he was in no mood to deal with her shit. He was smack dab in the middle of what was a growing turf war over both cocaine and ecstasy. He had been willfully and strategically muscling into the territory of several groups and they were not taking it lying down. He was also dealing with major cocaine suppliers who were trying to strong-arm The Consortium into paying ridiculously higher prices for product until Marcus found and killed Keshari Mitchell, who they all firmly believed was still alive. So, when Misha blatantly disrespected him by publicly hooking up with her former fiancé, with all the pressure that he was currently under, she was very, very lucky that a slap in the face was all that she got. It could have been much worse.

Media quickly reported the "trouble in paradise" as it pertained to the very strange marriage of Misha Tierney and Marcus Means when a neighbor made an anonymous contact with an television entertainment news show and outlined the details of what had happened on the night that Misha finally had enough and left Marcus. The public quickly lapped up every bit of the story when it was released on the internet and immediately wanted more. It's funny how the public is intoxicated by the troubles and the scandals of the rich and famous. They can't seem to get enough of reading and watching as the young, beautiful, hip, famous, and paid completely melt down or unravel in an ugly way right before their eyes. Perhaps it enables them to deflect away, at least for a moment, from the day-to-day problems in their own, far more average existences.

The neighbor of Marcus Means who wished to remain anonymous reported hearing a woman's scream and very loud arguing coming from the terrace at the rear of Marcus Means's Bel Air home late, possibly as late as 1 a.m. The neighbor stated that he was just about to call the police when, a short time later, possibly little more than half an hour, the automatic security lights on Marcus Means's property went on and Misha Tierney's Mercedes con-vertible was seen pulling out of the gates and speeding away from the mansion on the quiet, palm tree-lined street. "As fast as she was driving, she seemed to be 'fleeing' from the scene," the neighbor embellished. "I've heard stories about that Marcus Means, you know."

Misha had, in fact, packed every single thing she could fit into her car that night and she left Marcus Means's sadistic, gilded cage of a house for good and didn't give a FUCK what threat he came up with to try to make her come back and she felt that it was the most liberating thing that she had done all year.

She was so fired up with rage that night after he hit her that Marcus knew it would turn into a major police matter if he even tried to make her stay. He was actually surprised she hadn't called the police on him at all after what had happened. It was probably because her mind was so rabidly focused on one thing…LEAVING… and she was not wasting one second to do it.

-23-

There was an angry, red, swollen bruise across Misha's cheek where Marcus Means had struck her, but Misha was still so, so damned mad, wanting to positively KILL that motherfucker, that she couldn't even find it in herself to be embarrassed about it when she rushed into the office early the next morning for a couple of meetings. She hadn't even given a single thought to what Marcus was going to do to her and, for once, she was just enough of herself again to absolutely not care.

The water cooler whispers were rampant. Everyone at Larger Than Lyfe Entertainment had wondered from the very beginning what in the world Misha had gotten herself into to have gotten mixed up with Marcus Means in the first place. They just knew that the very obvious outline of a glaringly red handprint across her face had come from him. A couple gossipers around the water cooler wondered if Misha might have some involvement in Marcus Means's criminal activities, even if this involvement was by force. They wondered if their jobs might be in danger. Suppose the feds came in, seized files, and shut the whole company down? It was only a matter of time before this very strange relationship blew up in all of their faces. Others who had their ears and ideas invested in the current gossip knew Misha and her brother Richard Tresvant had been estranged for many years specifically because of his organized crime affiliations. Misha had legally changed her last name to ensure that people did not link her with her brother in any way. She had wanted nothing to do with her very own brother, even after he had been murdered in prison, so they knew for sure she had nothing to do Marcus Means's criminal affairs. Marcus Means had obviously blackmailed Misha into marrying him with the threat of doing something very bad to her or to someone else important to her if she didn't marry him. But what did all of that have to do with his recent turn to violence against her? What had driven him to hit her? Then, as if all of them had gazed into a crystal ball at the very same time, they all suddenly knew.

KRISHAWN WEBB.

All of them headed back to their respective offices and lay in wait for the next dramatic episode…and they knew without a doubt that there would be one.

Before her first meeting that morning, Misha quickly sat down with "Sheri," her makeup artist, who she'd called on her BlackBerry on the way into the office. The makeup artist worked a miracle and took already flawless beauty to the next level. You would never even know that an asshole whose days were numbered had hauled off and hit Misha once the makeup artist had done her magic. Misha smiled as she stared at the makeup artist's work in the lighted mirror. Misha was determined that she was not going to lose a step because of what had happened the night before. If anything, it made her more steadfast in her resolve that she was going to get her fucking life back regardless of any threats from Marcus Means or anything that he did. She also had to figure out how to get Marcus's hands off Larger Than Lyfe Entertainment, and off its profits. She was not going to allow that bastard to fuck up a thriving major enterprise by, eventually, laundering Consortium money through it when her sister had managed to keep the record label completely legitimate for all of the years that she'd owned it.

Despite all of Misha's current personal turmoil, Larger Than Lyfe Entertainment was realizing the same caliber of success it had always realized when Keshari Mitchell was at the helm. Ntozake, LTL's new premier artist, the woman who had stepped into the seriously large shoes of multi-platinum hip-hop artist Rasheed the Refugee when he left the label, was receiving accolades from some of the best in the business, and there was much industry talk that Ntozake would be nominated for a Grammy Award as Best New Artist of the Year for her debut album, *My Love Is Complicated*. She was also a shoo-in for nominations at the American Music Awards, Soul Train Music Awards, BET Music Awards and MTV Video Music Awards for the same album. *My Love Is Complicated* was now almost triple platinum, four of her singles had now hit number one on the *Billboard* Pop and R & B charts, and much of the album was in heavy rotation on most of the playlists at radio stations around the country. Every major music magazine from *Rolling Stone* to *VIBE* wanted interviews and photo shoots with exotically beautiful Ntozake. Her weekly work schedule was becoming more and more demanding of her time and energy, even after signing a contract with The Buchanan Group for management services and, since their last meeting, it all was beginning to take its toll on Ntozake. She'd begun showing up late for studio sessions, and sometimes she missed her scheduled studio sessions altogether. She'd even missed her scheduled interview with a writer from *Essence* magazine, the interview they'd excitedly discussed that would have accompanied a featured cover spread on Ntozake had she made the effort to reschedule or show some indication she cared when she missed the appointment. With the level of money and major music names involved in Ntozake's highly anticipated second album, and with Larger Than Lyfe Entertainment's name and reputation riding heavily on this new artist and her talent, the matter of her starting to slip needed to be addressed immediately. Misha arranged a meeting with Ntozake for ten o'clock that morning, her very first meeting of the day, and told Ntozake that it would be in her best interest not to be a minute late. It was far too soon for her to start trying to do a self-destruct on her career.

Ntozake arrived at Larger Than Lyfe Entertainment dressed to kill and on time. The meeting with Ntozake and Kevin Sperrington, Ntozake's manager from The Buchanan Group, went well. The air had been cleared. Misha had decided to handle the situation with diplomacy instead of entering into attack mode and issuing threats that would likely make the matter worse.

Ntozake was committed to getting back on track, staying there, and keeping an open line of communication with Misha when she was becoming overwhelmed. A lot of major things were happening very fast for Ntozake, and she was still getting acclimated to a professional career in the music industry, stardom, and all that came with all of it. Misha wanted to help her make the full transition into superstardom and the public eye as painless and drama-free as possible.

Some recording artists who were not prepared for the fast stardom they gained quickly did a complete downward spiral when the rigors of stardom began to pull them in too many different directions at once. Often their own record labels failed to step in until it was too late, even when all the signs that something was wrong were present all over the place. Misha, as daunting a task as it was, refused to allow that to happen to any artists on the LTL label.

The group—Misha, Ntozake, Kevin Sperrington, and Marvin Shabazz, director of artists and repertoire—went to lunch at "Crustacean" in Beverly Hills after their meeting that morning. They were all animated since the meeting had gone so well, they were all chatting and enjoying themselves, and had certainly not expected the Kenya Moore-looking "whirlwind" that made an uninvited appearance at their table.

"First it was your deceased friend…what was her name… Keshari Mitchell. Now it's you. What's with you bitches not being able to find your own men?!" Portia Foster snapped.

"I told Kris not to get mixed up with this crazy bitch," Misha said under her breath.

She shook her head and rolled her eyes in exasperation.

"Look, I know you are not wrapped too tight," Misha said, "but I guarantee you, you're fucking with the WRONG ONE. I don't know whether or not you recall, but Krishawn Webb and I were ENGAGED. Not that it is any of your business, Kris is my FRIEND and I will see him any fucking time that I damned well please, and if you so much as make the mistake of stepping to me in this way again, the next media coverage I receive will be me whipping your crazy ass…and THEN getting a permanent restraining order against you. Now, get the fuck away from my table. I'm trying to have lunch here."

"The two of you are no longer 'engaged,'" Portia Foster responded. "You're married now…to someone else…a rather storied 'someone else,' I might add. You should make more of an effort to move on with your life and marriage with THAT person."

Restaurant patrons who'd been in the immediate vicinity to catch the exchange between Misha and Portia swiveled their heads to watch Portia as she turned on her Gucci stilettos and made her melodramatic exit from the up-scale restaurant. Ntozake, Kevin Sperrington and Marvin Shabazz shook their heads and laughed at the ridiculous scene that had just gone down. After that brand of non-sense, they ordered another round of drinks.

-24-

Misha put an early wrap on her workday after lunch with Ntozake and her manager and Marvin Shabazz and headed home to her upscale, three-bedroom townhouse in Beverly Hills. She was going to take a bit of time to herself to regroup for the rest of the day from the asshole she'd had to deal with the night before. She was going to return Kris's calls because he had been absolutely blowing up her phone that day, probably having gotten wind in one way or another that something had happened to her. She also needed to try to get her home back into order since moving abruptly back into it after that asshole had abruptly moved her out of it. She got the shock of her life, though, when she entered her den, flicked on the lights and found that Marcus Means had been sitting there in the dark waiting for her. There were three neat stitches at his brow where she had landed a blow in response to him slapping her. At any other time, seeing him literally in stitches would have been funny as hell, but, because this asshole had unceremoniously let himself into her residence AGAIN without her authorization, the only things that came into her thoughts were the most vile, negative, and murderous things her mind could conceive. It had not been twenty-four hours since she'd left "Hell in Bel-Air," and here Satan was again, determined to torment her some more.

"What the FUCK are you doing in my house?!" Misha snapped.

That had been a rhetorical question for sure. It would never cease to boggle Misha's mind how men like Marcus and her deceased brother believed they could do whatever they wanted to do whenever they wanted and wherever they wanted without a single moment's regard to whoever they trampled over in the process. She had no idea how he managed to bypass her security system and get into her home or what it was in his mind that made it seem perfectly okay for him to do so. "I came to check on my pretty wife," Marcus said with a smile.

"FUCK YOU!" Misha glared. "Oh, my God, I hate you!"

"Look, I wanted to apologize for hitting you. That was completely out of line. I will never do it again."

"Give me a fucking break!" Misha snapped. "And get the fuck out of my house!"

Marcus changed the subject.

"I want to know where Keshari is," he said without mincing words. "This is serious now, and I can't keep fucking around with you about this anymore."

"Keshari is dead!" Misha responded icily.

"I'm gonna ask you one last time. I want to know where Keshari is. I NEED to know where she is…and I know like you know that she is still alive. You really are very, very foolish to put yourself completely on the line by covering for her. You do realize that I am not the only one who is looking for her. "

"You have all of the connections in the world. You're privy to more confidential information than the FBI. Shit, you've got half of the FBI on your payroll! Why in the hell would you come to me…break into my house in search of information I don't have…if you already know beyond a shadow of doubt that Keshari is still alive?! Why don't you just pay some of your people to find her?!"

"WHERE IS SHE?!" Marcus yelled, getting up and grabbing Misha by the arm.

"You motherfucker!" Misha growled at him. "Take your goddamned hands off me!"

"I've been pretty patient with you, Misha," Marcus said in a deadly calm voice. "Do you remember how I convinced you to marry me in the first place? I got someone who'd been directly involved to confirm my suspicions about your girl. A dirty EMT who was involved in Keshari's intricate, little ruse had loose lips… for a price, of course. EVERYBODY has a price, and, if you name the right price, they'll do anything you want, tell you anything you want. That EMT told me about his part in Keshari's faked death scheme. He told me that Keshari was absolutely not dead when they took her away from her Palos Verdes home in that ambulance. He said that a particular pathologist at the coroner's office had likely helped her for a price and had falsified her death certificate, then provided a Jane Doe to represent Keshari's remains. This dirty EMT told me how much he was paid. He gave me the names of the other emergency workers who were in on it. He told me enough to take a whole lot of people down…with a little more work, of course, but that was never my objective. When I brought all of this information and carefully laid it out to you along with a few other details, you started to see things my way. The look on your face that day…it was almost like your girl's caper had been blown wide open."

Misha didn't respond. With hands on her hips, she rolled her eyes and waited impatiently for Marcus to make some movement to leave her goddamned house.

"Keshari, I'm sure, told you that one day 'the game' might get too deep and she would have to implement an escape plan. Because the two of you were so close, she most likely shared with you her plans to fake her death. It's not so uncommon, you know, the whole faked death scheme. Wealthy, white businessmen who wind up deeply in the red from bad business decisions have, on more than a few occasions, faked their deaths because their sizeable life in-surance policies made them financially worth far more dead than alive.

"Your girl is definitely a smart one. She worked on this scheme FOR YEARS, slowly and painstakingly setting things in place, and I've been relaxed about searching for her until now because it was not as much of a priority, but I'm about to start to get others talking just like I got that EMT to talk because I've got a business to run and

Keshari, wherever the fuck she is, is causing problems in my business. Keshari rose too far on the ladder of this game to just decide one day to resign; she knows too much and that does not sit well with anyone right now. One way or the other, I am going to get what I need… and you already know, my beautiful bride, I've got all sorts of tactics to make it happen. Perhaps, like I told you before we were married, I can share what I know with a few prosecutors in high places and let the chips fall wherever they may. Perhaps you'll get charged for collusion in Keshari's scheme. Maybe you'll do some prison time. One thing's for sure, it would open up an international law enforcement manhunt for Keshari, and, ultimately, she would be shaken from whatever tree she's currently hiding in. Or perhaps having our newest Los Angeles Laker meet with some tragic circumstance might make you more agreeable to supplying me with the information that I need. You think about that. But you better start thinking fast."

For a moment, Marcus's last words threw Misha off balance. She quickly regrouped.

"I truly don't give a fuck about you threatening me, Marcus. Not anymore. Keshari is dead…DEAD," Misha said as calmly as she could. "She committed suicide. She's gone. If you believe she is still alive, I'm sure you will set out to find her…with or without any information you receive from me. Please leave me alone. Get out of my life. Whatever reason caused you to force me to marry you doesn't matter to me anymore. I don't care what you do to me, but I cannot suffer your ass another second. Now, GET THE FUCK OUT OF MY HOUSE!"

Marcus clearly had something of a soft spot for Misha or he was still toying with her dangerously as he had done with so many others before he pounced on them unexpectedly and did his real damage because he left her home without incident. He didn't have some of his thugs come in and ransack the place to torment her. He didn't put his hands on her again. He didn't argue or issue another threat. He came with nothing and left with nothing. Before Misha shut the door and locked it behind Marcus, she said, "The very next time you let yourself into my house without my permission or invitation, I WILL get the police involved."

He smiled, slid behind the wheel of his Bentley and was gone.

What Misha didn't know was Marcus had something of an epiphany as he sat there in her den. Maybe Misha didn't know where Keshari was. Maybe she had been let in on the fact that Keshari might one day fake her death, but Keshari never revealed to Misha when she would do it or where she would go once it was done. Yes, indeed, Keshari Mitchell was a smart one…but not quite smart enough.

The next week, after a lengthy meeting with her attorney, Misha filed for divorce from Marcus Means at Los Angeles Superior Court in Downtown Los Angeles.

=25=

The Buchanan Group hit the ground running the day the three partners opened the firm's doors. The firm was extremely busy. They had a growing line of A-listers in their client base, and they were zealously working to make sure that all of these clients were satisfied. The Buchanan Group was already well on its way to fiercely competing with the other far more established management and PR firms around Los Angeles.

Darian Boudreaux had hit the ground running as well ever since stepping foot onto American soil under her new identity. Her start-up company, Phoenix Films, now had posh offices in a landmark Hollywood location. Darian had used a well-known PR firm to let the industry know of the launch of her new film company. And she was getting ready to provide Phoenix Films with its first major film project by writing the controversial script herself.

In the face of all that, Mars and Darian were fortunate when they were able to spend time together as man and wife, face-to-face, without interruption, two days out of the week. If both of them had taken a moment from their hectic schedules to think about it all seriously, as much as they proclaimed their love for each other, both of them had wasted no time at all after they returned to the United States to place their marriage on a back burner, in second position to their respective careers and their start-up companies. Was this an arrangement the two of them had mutually agreed upon in advance? Partially. Partially not.

While Darian worked zealously to bring her film company's first movie project full circle, Mars had been handling the heavy workload of his high-profile personal client list. First, he had been working to get Krishawn Webb, his biggest client, situated in Los Angeles. There had been the typical orientation-type meetings to get him better acclimated with his new family, the Los Angeles Lakers. There were more contracts he'd had to sign. He'd had to complete a physical exam with L.A. Lakers' doctors. There had been endorsement meetings to finalize deals with both Gatorade and Nike. The Nike deal alone stood to gross Krishawn more than $5 million, 15 percent of which would go to The Buchanan Group, and they were set to sign the contracts within the next week.

Krishawn was also interested in purchasing a new home in L.A. Since he was geographically grounded in Los Angeles, at least, for the next three years, he wanted something a bit more permanent residentially. He'd indicated to Mars that he was not interested in purchasing another "bachelor" pad; he needed something more substantial. Mars raised an eyebrow at that one. Nevertheless, he set Krishawn up with the very same high-end real estate broker Darian used to purchase her Hollywood Hills home. The broker would show Krishawn multimillion-dollar properties in tune with his style and tastes whenever Krishawn's schedule allowed.

Mars had been following the news stories and he'd heard a few things from a few people in the industry who were personal friends of Krishawn. Mars was particularly aware of the very recent news of Misha Tierney filing for divorce from Marcus Means. Mars also knew that Krishawn was seriously involved with Misha again, and he'd heard the stories of the vicious physical attack that Krishawn had suffered before he promptly went into hiding for several weeks, supposedly, at the hands of Marcus Means's hired thugs when he and Misha had secretly connected one night prior to him signing his contract with the Lakers.

Mars just hoped that Krishawn didn't allow his re-involvement in Misha's complicated life to become career damaging…or deadly. But, then again, Mars certainly was in no position to judge. Just look at the decisions he'd made and the lengths he'd gone to in his own life when it came to the love he had for a woman who was in a dangerous predicament.

On a different note, The Buchanan Group was also

engaged in discussions with Hugo Boss about Krishawn doing an ad campaign for the following year's spring and summer collection of men's suits. This contract, once finalized, stood to gross well over one million dollars for Krishawn, 15 percent of which would go to The Buchanan Group. That September, Krishawn would be starting basketball camp with the Lakers before the season officially tipped off with him in the starting line-up. Then *GQ* magazine had Krishawn booked to do their December cover, accompanied by an interview with a *GQ* staff writer to discuss Krishawn's career move to the Los Angeles Lakers and all of the other details that made many call him "one of the sexiest, smartest men in basketball."

Yes, indeed, Krishawn Webb was a gold mine for The Buchanan Group, and Mars Buchanan made certain that every single employee at The Buchanan Group treated Krishawn Webb that way.

Next in priority on Mars's personal client roster was Rasheed the Refugee. Rasheed had been taking acting classes, both privately and with a group. He was very serious about stretching himself creatively into acting. His instructors were praising his growth, and he was beginning to read scripts in hopes of auditioning for and securing his first acting role. Mars knew of one script Rasheed had not yet read, and Mars wasn't exactly anxious for Rasheed to read the script either. Mars had a strong hunch Rasheed was going to get the opportunity very soon to take on his first, professional acting job. He would more than likely get to play himself in Darian's upcoming biopic on the life of Keshari Mitchell, and Mars would make this happen for his client regardless of his continued resistance to the film project himself.

Rasheed was also preparing to release his first, much-anticipated album since his mysterious break from Larger Than Lyfe Entertainment. After leaving Larger Than Lyfe right before Keshari Mitchell's death, Rasheed launched his own record label and purchased the masters to all of the music he'd made at Larger Than Lyfe. He then signed and began working with some talented, underground, hip hop groups, helping to better cultivate them to take them mainstream. Both groups released mildly successful albums, but neither of the two groups, despite their tremendous talent, had been able to catch and keep the spotlight in the gigantic way that Rasheed did whenever he took the stage. Rasheed was going to continue working with the groups. He knew how fickle the music industry was, and he was confident in the skills of both groups. He was working with them on their second albums while he traveled back and forth, mainly to New York, New Jersey and Atlanta, checking out other groups and solo artists to potentially sign them to his label. Mars and The Buchanan Group worked in the meanwhile to bring more and more focus to Rasheed's record label, masterminding and launching a major PR campaign and making sure that solid, serious promotion of the record label was popping up everywhere, from billboards to nightclubs to the top hip-hop radio stations around the country, particularly with the new album about to drop. The intent was to capture the attention of music industry insiders, MC's, and aficionados of hip-hop like never before. As a result, more and more demos of hungry hip-hop artists wanting record deals began to land in the mailroom at Rasheed the Refugee's record company. For their services, The Buchanan Group charged Rasheed, in some instances, at a single "per project" rate and, in other instances, at an hourly legal fee/management fee. Because of the many money-making and philanthropic enterprises in which Rasheed was involved, The Buchanan Group did notably well financially from their representation and management of him.

It had been three years and Rasheed had not done any new music under his own moniker. He hadn't even set up a new concert tour schedule as he went to work exclusively on the business side of his record label with The Buchanan Group assisting him. Rasheed's new album, titled *New World Order*, was bound to be a hip-hop extravaganza. Rasheed had teamed up with everyone from Eminem to Mos Def to Jay-Z to create what many were already proclaiming was one of the "greatest hip-hop productions of all times." The Buchanan Group had already begun to arrange his press schedule, photo shoots for publicity and posters, and video shoots for the first singles. He'd just completed an interview with *Rolling Stone*, whose reporters positively LOVED sitting down and chopping it up with the super-intelligent hip-hop star whenever he felt like talking to them.

Ultimately, Rasheed the Refugee's work ethic was a lot like Keshari Mitchell's. He worked inhumanly grueling hours in order to hone his craft and accomplish his many goals.

Jason Payne, Mars's best friend and one of the partners at The Buchanan Group, had just signed Branden Mechel, a seventeen-year-old, extremely talented pop singer with a bit of a hip-hop and R & B edge to him, who had just signed a sizeable contract with J Records. He was new to the industry, and the talk and media attention surrounding him were steadily growing. Industry insiders were excited and they were already anticipating he would be a superstar on the Justin Timberlake level or greater. A & R executives at J Records said "he was a White cross between Usher and Chris Brown." Teenage girls around the country were going to flock to auditoriums and stadiums to see him, and Clive Davis was putting a power punch behind him in terms of the production budget for his debut album as well as public relations and promotion. The Buchanan Group was handling Branden Mechel's portfolio to make sure he was promoted everywhere and in every way optimally. From MTV's *TRL* to *Seventeen* magazine and *Rolling Stone*, the music industry and the public were about to get to know and become hopelessly obsessed with Branden Mechel. He was going to be a mega-star, and The Buchanan Group was getting in on the ground floor. All of the partners had recently gone to see Branden at the Staples Center in Downtown Los Angeles. Watching him perform his first single as a show opener for Ne-Yo had been a high-energy, adrenaline-rushing experience and a half. Some folks left the concert that night saying his performance had upstaged Ne-Yo's.

Richard Bryson, the fourth partner at The Buchanan Group and an experienced sports manager, had just signed 6-foot-9-inch Andreas Spivey, who the NCAA and the NBA were calling the next Kobe Bryant. He was bound to become The Buchanan Group's next major money-maker. He was tall, extremely good-looking, an extremely talented athlete who would soon make everything from cellular phones to fast food to tennis shoes seem like the hottest product on the market and compel the public to want to go out and buy. After making the decision to forego his first year at Duke University to enter the NBA draft, The Buchanan Group immediately got to work to secure major endorsements for him. He would soon be doing a block of television commercials for McDonald's. Chevrolet wanted him for television and magazine advertising for the redesigned Camaro. And, of course, Nike wanted a piece of him, too.

Ever since Misha Tierney made the referral, Kevin Sperrington, as a partner of The Buchanan Group, had been personally handling Larger Than Lyfe artist Ntozake's increasingly heavy schedule and the steadily growing number of demands and projects that were coming her way. There had, most recently, been serious discussions of making a mini-movie/music video for Ntozake's soon-to-be-released, sophomore album, *Life and Times of a Superstar*. Snoop Dogg had done it with *Murder Was the Case*. R. Kelly had done it with *Trapped in the Closet*. No female artist had ever done it and Larger than Lyfe Entertainment believed the time had come for this to change.

Keshari Mitchell had been a trailblazer for WOMEN. She had always believed and firmly lived by the motto that "she could do anything any man could do…better." She consistently worked and accomplished milestones throughout her career as "the first woman to have done it," and many of the records in the music industry she set prior to her death had yet to be broken. Doing a mini-movie music video for Ntozake's new album, *Life and Times of a Superstar* would exemplify the true essence of

Keshari Mitchell and the vision...HER vision...that continued to be maintained at Larger Than Lyfe Entertainment. Only she would have come up with a plan so extravagant and so ingenious that it would instantly break a new barrier and continued to make Larger than Lyfe Entertainment one of the most talked-about and most successful record companies in the country. They wanted to do the shoot for the mini-movie in Los Angeles, Las Vegas, New York, and Miami. It was going to be so, so hot.

Misha Tierney, CEO of Larger Than Lyfe Entertainment, had already given the project the "go-ahead." She'd sat down with LTL staff and accountants and given the project a rough budget to start with. The record label now needed to get with a film company to develop a storyline for the mini-movie, cast the project and shoot it. When Kevin Sperrington told Mars about the project, Mars instantly thought of his wife's film company, Phoenix Films. It would be an excellent opportunity to help her build up her name for her new company. Mars immediately sent text messages to Darian's BlackBerry as soon as he got the details about the music video project. Mars told Kevin to hold off for a day or two on helping Larger Than Lyfe to secure a film company to develop and shoot the project. There was a film company he'd like to recommend. Perhaps the mini-movie project would enable Mars to redeem himself a bit after the stance that he'd taken in regard to the Keshari Mitchell movie project his wife was producing.

Chris Winters, Mars's executive assistant, had been instrumental in accomplishing so much of the legwork for the very lucrative projects connected to Mars's personal clients. She had stretched her "legal" legs and was helping to move the firm closer to a finalized agreement on the numbers with the Hugo Boss project as well as the Gatorade project for Krishawn Webb while not losing step in her regular, day-to-day duties as Mars's executive assistant. Mars was thoroughly impressed at how quickly she was learning the game and he realized he was not going to be able to keep her on as his executive assistant once she passed the California bar. She was going to want to manage and recruit new accounts herself and she would definitely deserve the opportunity.

Mars was meshing very nicely with Chris Winters. He liked her a lot, and it was evident that she liked him too. Whenever he was in town and in the office, she always made a point of bringing him lunch when she went to get her own lunch. He never asked her to do this, but she always did. She was attentive to so many little things that were in no way responsibilities directly associated with her job. Jason Payne, Mars's best friend and business partner, had joked and said she had a little crush on Mars. Mars had chuckled to himself, not reading a single thing into it. His and Chris Winters' relationship was a professional one exclusively.

-26-

Marcus Means, using expansion of The Consortium as his excuse, had been stomping on toes all over town. The turf wars that The Consortium had been contending with were growing. There was blood shed by rival Crips and Bloods gangs as The Consortium inched into their territory to sell cocaine and marijuana. Some of The Consortium's soldiers shed blood, too. There were powerful, well-established organizations having to endure the wide range of Marcus Means's ego, and they were not going to take it lying down. Marcus Means was extremely smart, yet he was even more ruthless. When he'd said he wanted to take over the whole narcotics game, he seriously wanted to take over the WHOLE game. Ultimately, he probably even had ideas about taking down the Mexicans, "La Eme" as the Mexican Mafia was called, and that would be the bloodiest mistake he ever made.

In retaliation for the continuing battle over "X" territory, one of the chief members of The Consortium, Slim J of R2 Crips, was taken hostage by Yakuza. Yakuza, for the most part, was a highly respected family. They did not deal in violence until it was absolutely necessary. Their organization was one of the oldest, tracing all the way back to Japan. Marcus didn't give a fuck who they were. He'd studied them only to know what he was up against, and then he had continued with his plans for expansion.

A single phone call was made to Marcus Means in the middle of the night as he lay in his bed.

"There is a price for disrespect." Then the line went dead.

At 6 a.m., breaking news on all of the local television stations reported details of a high-profile murder that had caused an entire block of Downtown Los Angeles's business district to be blocked off. Reputed gang member Jermaine "Slim J" Jackson, leader of R2 Crips, had been thrown naked from the top of a high-rise building located at 300 South Grand, the very same location where corporate attorney Phinnaeus Bernard III had been murdered. Slim J had landed in the middle of South Grand Street, his body completely pulverized by the fall from the forty two-story building. News helicopters were in the air. News vans were on the street.

Marcus Means was lying in bed at his Bel Air home watching the story unfold on television. Moments later, his phone was ringing. Other Consortium members wanted a meeting immediately.

-27-

In 2010, how much closer are we to winning America's "war on drugs" since Richard Nixon coined the phrase more than forty years ago? Numerous academicians, politicians, law enforcement officers, judges, and average, law-abiding citizens believe that the American "war on drugs" has been one colossal FAILURE and that there is as much, if not more, to do now in 2010 as there was to do when the "war on drugs" started.

Since its inception forty years ago, $1 trillion have been spent on the "war on drugs." The face of the "drug game" has certainly changed, but there has been markedly little, real improvement in the trafficking and sale of illicit drugs and ending the detrimental effects of the illicit drug trade on this nation. In 2010, illicit drugs are "cheaper, purer, and easier to get than ever before." "For every drug dealer you put in jail or kill, there's a line to replace him because the money is just so good." As long as there is a hefty demand for illicit drugs…and there definitely IS, there has been and will continue to be a non-ending supply of them. This certainly does not indicate any notable progress made in the "war on drugs."

One of the chief reasons that the war on drugs has been a mostly fruitless venture is because the United States and other nations' governments have, for years, maintained a direct and covert involvement in the illicit drug trade and are profiting from it. There are some academicians who assess that America's involvement in the illicit drug trade, ultimately, goes to bolster its true desire for global domination and that, until the United States has accomplished its goal of global domination, the "war on drugs" shall continue to be one huge, empty, extremely expensive, political machine to assuage the minds of American citizens and taxpayers while American government secretly continues to profit from the illicit drug trade and to fuel its true agenda.

Per the Office of National Drug Control Policy, "about 330 tons of cocaine, 20 tons of heroin and 110 tons of methamphetamine are sold in the United States every year—almost all of it brought in across the borders. Even more marijuana is sold, but it's hard to know how much of that is grown domestically, including vast fields run by Mexican drug cartels in U.S. national parks."

Martha Mendoza writes for the *Huffington Post* that "the $320 billion annual global drug industry now accounts for 1 percent of all commerce on the planet. A full 10 percent of Mexico's economy is built on drug proceeds— $25 billion smuggled in from the United States every year, of which 25 cents of each $100 smuggled is seized at the border. Thus, there's no incentive for the kind of financial reform that could tame the drug cartels."

Per *Wikipedia, the Free Encyclopedia:* "The United States Central Intelligence Agency (CIA) has been involved in several drug trafficking operations. Often, the CIA worked with groups which it knew were involved in drug trafficking, so that these groups would provide them with useful intelligence and material support, in exchange for allowing their criminal activities to continue, and impeding or preventing their arrest, indictment, and imprisonment by U.S. law enforcement agencies. According to Peter Dale Scott, the Dirección Federal de Seguridad was in part a CIA creation, and 'the CIA's closest government allies were for years in the DFS'. DFS badges, 'handed out to top-level Mexican drug-traffickers, have been labeled by DEA agents a virtual 'license to traffic.' Scott says that The Guadalajara Cartel, Mexico's most powerful drug-trafficking network in the early 1980s, prospered largely because it enjoyed the protection of the DFS, under its chief Miguel Nassar (or Nazar) Haro, a CIA asset."

"The CIA—in spite of objections from the Drug Enforcement Administration, allowed at least one ton of nearly pure cocaine to be shipped into Miami International Airport. The CIA claimed to have done this as a way of gathering information about Colombian drug cartels. But the cocaine ended up being sold on the street."

In short, the United States and other nations have been making it relatively easy for dangerous drug traffickers and dealers to do about doing their work. There are entirely too many very powerful figures here in the United States and beyond who benefit greatly from NOT winning the war on drugs. They take big pay-offs from the bad guys and then hide their hands so that the rest of us cannot detect the corruption, then continue to issue up the empty lip service and propaganda about the winning the "war on drugs" while, if we are to rely upon statistical data and what we watch every day going on all around us, this war, overall, seems to have done more harm than good.

"The dealers who are caught selling illicit drugs have overwhelmed justice systems in the United States and elsewhere. U.S. prosecutors declined to file charges in 7,482 drug cases last year, most because they simply didn't have the time. That's about one out of every four drug cases."

Per the Drug Policy Alliance, "Roughly 1.5 million people are arrested each year on drug law violations—40 percent of them just for marijuana possession. Nearly half a million people are currently behind bars here in the United States on drugs charges and this is more than ALL of the incarcerations in Western Europe for ALL of their criminal offenses combined and Western Europe has a much bigger population than the United States."

Per the Drug Policy Alliance, "public health problems like HIV and Hepatitis C are all exacerbated by zero tolerance laws created by the war on drugs that restrict access to clean needles."

"People suffering from cancer, AIDS and other debilitating illnesses are regularly denied access to their medicine or even arrested and prosecuted for using medical marijuana."

Incarceration rates for drug offenses remain grossly disproportionate along racial lines while the mostly White "major power players" in the illicit drug trafficking game never see one day behind bars.

Drugs destroy entire communities and drugs destroy the initiative and ambition of a community's people. Families and homes can be wrenched apart when a drug addict is involved. Babies are born with expensive and devastating medical problems and birth defects when these infants are born to mothers who are abusing drugs. Drug addicts burglarize homes, snatch purses, pick pockets, break into cars, do whatever needs to be done to get enough money to buy their next "fix" and any one of us could easily be their next victim. For every crack and heroin addict and every crack and heroin dealer, ultimately, their dirty work winds up tagging the average taxpayer's pockets, and for every dollar that continues to be spent fighting empty battles in the "war on drugs," tax dollars are taken away from other, very necessary social programs as well as from the public school system. Funding the empty battles in the war on drugs leads to the scrapping of valuable social programs for individuals and families, typically adversely affecting disenfranchised people in disadvantaged communities that cannot stomach another failure, loss or program cut.

Nonetheless, with all of that said, why do ALL American citizens still need to be continuously focused on and aimed at triumphing in the "war on drugs?" Despite what a ridiculously futile effort the war on drugs seems to be, especially after all of the years and money spent since the so-called war began, despite the high levels of corruption and the multitude of other problems that render the "war on drugs" an entirely uphill battle, NOT continuing to fight the good fight in the war on drugs shall, in one way or another, have a detrimental impact on EVERY SINGLE ONE OF US. ALL of us have a moral obligation to continue the fight for as many small triumphs as we can garner in order to maintain the safety, order and growth for the next generation as well as for the current generation. Turning a blind eye on the war on drugs is like having cancer and doing nothing at all to treat and eradicate the disease. Ultimately, it will metastasize and destroy the entire body.

Overall, we shall never completely eliminate drug trafficking nor the illicit drug market except through legalization and we shall never, ever completely win any "war on drugs" even after legalization. We must establish and maintain social programs that WORK. We must not only put the dealers and the traffickers in jail; we must also work to put the government officials, judges, politicians, and law enforcement officers in jail who work to help the traffickers and the dealers. We must work to end addiction to illicit drugs. We must continue to educate our youth early on to completely steer them away from the decision-making processes that lead them to use and abuse drugs in the first place. We must say a resounding "FUCK YOU!" to the empty lip service of politicians and vote accordingly in elections.

-28-

Darian and Mars never spoke again about the film project that she was about to proceed with, but the silence about the subject was far worse than the two of them fighting about it. As Darian got prepared to start writing the script, the film project was fast becoming the central focus of her days and nights and Mars wanted absolutely no part of it. She thought about various elements, segments from Keshari Mitchell's life, that she wanted to include in the film. She thought of music. She thought of casting. She wanted to talk about it, exchange ideas, get her husband's advice, but couldn't. Every time the two of them stole a few moments to be together, Darian could feel a piece of their very strong connection missing as her excitement grew and she had to keep that bubbling excitement to herself where Mars was concerned. She was hurt by it. She couldn't deny that. She had no idea how she was going to get Mars be okay about her making this movie. He firmly believed the film was too dangerous and that she should promptly dismiss all ideas about it entirely. There'd only been one other time when the two of them had been in such bitter disagreement about anything and that was when Mars had found out about Keshari's "double" life.

Deep down, Darian had always known that Mars more than likely kept a lot bottled up inside him; he would talk to her frankly, intimately, revealing all, except for those deepest, darkest, most troubling thoughts and feelings he held that he didn't want to hurt Darian with and that he could not even handle himself. Mars had probably been privately fighting an internal battle with his conflicted feelings about her and being with her for nearly the entire duration of their relationship, from the moment he'd found out who she really was up until he'd found her in Brazil and married her…and then now.

There was no doubt that Mars loved her completely, but all of the love in the world could not fully and indefinitely withstand all that constantly weighed up against the two of them. Theirs was a CRAZY life. Mars had led a normal life until the night he'd literally run into her and, from that day forward, he would never be the same nor see normal again. There was so, so much about Darian's former life, so many decisions that she had made upon assuming her new identity, so many decisions she was making now, and so many reckless decisions that Mars had made himself, decisions all directly linked to her until, more and more, Darian found herself confronting the fact that all of it might eventually explode like a bomb and pull the two of them irreparably apart, no matter how much Mars loved her.

Nevertheless, Darian set eight weeks aside to write, refine, and finalize the script for her movie. Regardless of what it might ultimately do to her marriage, she had determined in her mind that she was moving forward with the project, and would not stop until it had been released in theaters everywhere. She completely moved all of her things out of the W Hotel and into her new Hollywood Hills home. She shut herself away in the quiet luxury of her architectural masterpiece overlooking Hollywood and immediately got down to work.

The backdrop of the Downtown Los Angeles skyline and the "Hollywood" sign spelled out on the hill in the distance provided the ideal ambiance for what she was creating. She moved from the terrace, to the living room, to the dining room to her bed with her laptop, free-writing and then refining the script. She slept, she ate, she worked out, she wrote. She meditated, she did yoga, she worked out, she wrote. Nearly every night during the first couple of weeks, Mars came up to the house and she set aside small blocks of time when he came to give her full attention to him. The two of them often curled up on the terrace together with a fire in the fire pit, a bottle of wine, and close, intimate conversation late into the night. They never once discussed the script. When Mars left in the mornings, Darian immediately got right back to work. The entire time, she was determined that she would make a major impact with this movie.

At the same time that Darian began work on completing the script for the movie, the very first batches of scripts, treatments, and short film submissions began to arrive at Phoenix Films' offices. Phoenix Films, through Eileen Koch's PR firm, had put out a mass request for film submissions on Phoenix Films' website, in most of the major industry publications, and on the campuses of all of the major film schools around the country. Darian had no idea that Phoenix Films would receive such rapid and heavy response to the film company's mass call for scripts, but mailroom baskets full of treatments and full scripts and short film reels were arriving every day in the mail room at the Capitol Records building.

Fortunately, Terrence Henderson, Darian's assistant, was a dynamo and he had been working overtime, an indispensable force, in helping Darian accomplish her goals for her new film company. When Darian shut herself away in the new Hollywood Hills home to begin work on the script for the biopic of Keshari Mitchell's life, she left Terrence to run the office, and was completely confident that he would be more than capable of managing all that needed to be done while she was away. Just as he had been when he had worked for her at Larger Than Lyfe Entertainment, he was constantly coming forth with valuable ideas, sometimes, before they could even formulate in Darian's head. He touched bases with her every day and began to organize the scripts and treatments that were coming in, taking scripts home on some nights to read them and separating the "garbage," scripts and treatments that he knew were in no way in tune with Darian Boudreaux's vision for Phoenix Films, from the scripts that showed definite promise. A couple of times, he drove up to Darian's Hollywood Hills home and had lunch with her, discussing what he had managed to accomplish, enjoying shrimp lo mein and spring rolls from Chin Chin, bottles of Pellegrino, and plenty of sunshine as the two sat outside together on the terrace, talking and laughing like old friends. Terrence told Darian about a couple of scripts he thought she should read as soon as she wrapped her current work, and Darian assured him that she would. She actually trusted Terrence's eye for picking out quality pieces. The two also discussed her need to immediately hire at least two associate producers to help her accomplish the arduous task of completing production of Phoenix Films' first film project. These associate producers would also be responsible for helping Darian select and set into production subsequent film projects that would come after the release of the biopic of Keshari Mitchell's life.

Darian was abundantly aware of what a diamond Terrence Henderson was to have in her corner and she paid him quite handsomely for all that he did. Terrence had instantly taken a liking to Darian Boudreaux from the day the two of them met and he carefully began to weed out little tidbits about her personally that he'd been overwhelmingly curious to know. But, overall, Darian Boudreaux was as deeply mysterious as his former boss had been, so he did not to pry too much all at one time. If Darian Boudreaux was as much like Keshari Mitchell as Terrence had been noticing that she was over the short time the two had been working together, she would instantly and permanently shut down if anyone overstepped their bounds and attempted to delve too deeply into her private affairs…into her personal life.

Creating the script for the biopic of the life of Keshari Mitchell quickly revealed itself to be an unbelievable, life-altering experience for Darian. It was both therapeutic and challenging at the same time. She was forced to confront things she had never dealt with internally during her life as Keshari Mitchell. She was forced to confront things she had not wanted to fully contemplate even after she assumed her new identity.

Peeling off all of the layers as she honestly and freely wrote about her extremely complicated life was a mental and spiritual release for her. There was guilt, sadness, stress, fear and anger within herself that she'd kept bottled up for so long that she was now able to bring to the surface and let go. On some days, she cried and cried and cried. She thought a lot about Misha and the awful predicament she had selfishly placed her very best friend, her sister, into. There wasn't a day that went by when she didn't think about how much she missed Misha and how much she worried about her and her safety and, even though the two were now in the very same city once again, they may as well have been a million miles apart. At the launch party for The Buchanan Group, Misha had actually brushed up against her as she moved through the room, exchanging pleasantries with some of the party's guests. Darian had stared across the room at her friend until her eyes burned as Misha hugged Mars, talked to him briefly, and then walked away.

Misha had no idea that Mars even knew that Keshari was still alive. She certainly had no idea that Mars had traveled to Brazil specifically to find Keshari and had married her. Ultimately, Keshari Mitchell, now known as Darian Boudreaux, had terminated one mess of a life to create and live out a new mess that was as dangerous and over-the-top as the one before.

As Darian continued to compose and refine the script, she had to acknowledge that Keshari Mitchell had done some unbelievably heinous things and gotten away with them in the course of her life…including murder. Darian wondered once again if there was redemption after the life she'd led, after all of the things she'd done, even after the way she had so selfishly taken advantage of her friendship with Misha and brought her into this intricate, dangerous ruse, causing Misha to place her very own life in grave danger. Perhaps this film would be the first step at setting things right.

Darian realized the serious dangers associated with what she was undertaking, especially since she would be exposing the edgy dark side of Keshari Mitchell's double life and her long-rumored affiliations to major organized crime. On some levels, Darian would be "naming names" and providing the details with this movie, and it would surely capture the full attention of some of the most dangerous men in the country, men with whom Keshari Mitchell had once done business as second-in-command of The Consortium. But Darian had been walking on a razor blade edge for the greater part of her life; so, as much as Mars wanted her to feel the fear of what could potentially happen to her and the people around her in the course of making her movie, the fear simply would not come. Darian decided to title the controversial film *LARGE*. It was a play on words, giving reference to the name of Keshari Mitchell's record label as well as to the decadent, over-the-top, and dangerous double life that the powerful, wealthy woman at the helm of that well-known and highly successful record label had led.

-29-

Cars quickly arrived at Marcus Means's Bel Air home and all of the members of The Consortium, with the exception of Jermaine "Slim J" Jackson, assembled in the library where Marcus awaited them. The two housekeepers brought in rolling trays of coffee as the men quickly situated themselves, some of them accompanied by their lieutenants. There was seriousness and anger all around the room. A massive war was starting that involved more than one organization, all of them against The Consortium. It had been many years since most gangs in Los Angeles had seen bloody retaliations play out on the level that were beginning to develop against The Consortium under full media coverage and increasing scrutiny of both federal and local law enforcement. When The Consortium was under Ricky Tresvant's control, The Consortium had never gone to war nor stirred the level of recklessness in the streets that Marcus Means had managed to stir up in a few short months. Rick Tresvant had a reputation that preceded him, he established and maintained alliances, and he had demanded and had gotten a certain level of RESPECT from all other organizations. Marcus Means was a whole other ball game.

Each set leader present that morning could attest to having recently lost some of their soldiers in murders directly linked to the expansion plans of the new Consortium, and none of them were happy about it. Perhaps the relative quiet on the streets over the past few years had squashed some of the gang leaders' ambition, Marcus Means thought to himself as he silently watched all of them. They had accusatory looks on their faces and tense words on the tips of their tongues like a band of junior high school bitches. For the past ten years, most of them had been on their respective grinds, making enough money to fuel their enterprises, pay their debts and break bread with their sets, with only minor skirmishes that had to be dealt with here and there. They'd seemingly gotten too comfortable and complacent in what they'd been doing to acknowledge what would be required of them to realize success in a far more major grind like the one that Marcus had outlined for them when they all agreed to align with him as members of The Consortium. The Consortium "expansion project" would make all of the men present in the room that morning…all of them who managed to survive, that is…some of the wealthiest, most powerful, Black criminals in the world. It seemed patently ridiculous to Marcus that none of them truly wanted to embrace the fact that there would be substantial bloodshed and struggle in order for them to reach that level of power. When had a Black man ever had it easy getting to the top of the game…any game??? And once a Black man did get to the top of whatever game he was engaged in, there was always somebody or a group of "somebodies" orchestrating that Black man's quick removal from the top. What happened to Slim J was an occupational hazard, one of the consequences of The Consortium's rise to a higher power. It wasn't personal. That was the nature of the business. And they could not allow what had happened to throw them off course. The Consortium was on the verge of a major breakthrough. Marcus could feel it.

The men each paid tribute to Slim J, the just-slain leader of R2 Crips. What happened was horrible, it was overkill, and it was clearly meant to send a message. It hadn't slipped past any of them that Slim J was murdered at the same location where that attorney Phinnaeus Bernard III had been murdered. But that point was a whole other matter. Slim J had been one of them, having committed himself to a lifetime membership in The Consortium. Each of the Consortium members solemnly acknowledged it could have been any one of them to have met with the same fate that Slim J had met. Marcus Means was the only exception. He firmly believed that his mind constantly calculated on a level that would never allow what had just happened to Slim J to happen to him. Not once since receiving the details regarding Slim J's murder had he allowed himself to wrap his mind around the very real possibility that he could be taken out too.

As they all sat there, some of the top Black gang leaders on the streets of Los Angeles, they tossed around ideas about how to proceed. First, they would need to put their noses to the streets and find out who was behind Slim J's murder. They would, of course, find out before the police did. All of them firmly believed the murder was directly associated with The Consortium's expansion project, particularly after the phone call Marcus told them he had received in the wee hours of the morning right before he turned his television on and saw the aftermath of the murder as the breaking news story. Bree-Z wondered out loud if the hit had been carried out by Yakuza. Marcus also believed that the culprits were likely to be Yakuza. Marcus told the assembled group that the head of Yakuza despised him. The meeting they'd had regarding The Consortium moving into their "X" territory had definitely not gone as the head of Yakuza had planned.

The others all turned this information over in their minds for a few moments. They would take a couple of days to confirm their suspicions and then they were going to need to act quickly before somebody else got taken out. Retaliation was always the very first option. They'd already gone a couple of rounds with one of the Asian gangs affiliated with Yakuza and could certainly do it again. A couple of the members expressed that they wanted to make an attempt to enter into talks again with the head of Yakuza or with whatever organization had orchestrated the hit, in the event they found out that Slim J had not been murdered by Yakuza. They wanted to try and reach some sort of compromise or a temporary truce.

WHAT THE FUCK?!

Marcus Means did not believe in compromises. Wanting to sit down and talk now with the organizations whose toes The Consortium had pretty flagrantly stepped on was not only a sign of weakness but of complete and total stupidity, and Marcus was not having that now or ever. He verbalized all of his feelings to the group in regard to this. He also emphasized that they needed to strategically align the troops of all of their sets so they could initiate the "take down" of their rivals who they had been battling with over the past few weeks. They needed to hurry up and stabilize operations in the areas they'd recently moved into, the hostile territories that had very recently belonged to other organizations, so they could continue their expansion, taking over still more new territory and then expanding in other states.

Nonetheless, the rules of the organization dictated that the matter of how to proceed with the Slim J situation go to vote. Before they voted, Devante "Big D" Johnson, second-in command of The Consortium and leader of R4 Crips, the set to which Marcus Means belonged, took a moment to say a few words.

"This shit is getting too deep," he said in his raspy voice. "We are not young G's on the corners anymore. We can't act like young, dumb hotheads tryin' to take out everybody. There is more than one way to handle this shit without shooting it out, and we still get to profit from it. I joined The Consortium to make money. I didn't join this shit to die. I been in this game too long for that. One of the primary members of this organization is already dead, and we haven't been involved with this new set-up for even a year. Marcus, you are a reckless, ruthless muthafucka. In some ways, that is a good thing, not so much in other ways. We need to slow this thing down. Most of us got involved in this thing to make our paper longer. None of us are lookin' to put our lives on the line any more than they already are. We all knew the history of The Consortium and have heard the kind of numbers that Rick was bringin' in…the kinda weight he was pushin'…and we all wanted to be a part of THAT caliber of shit. Rick made his paper…a LOT of paper… and he never had to go to war with NOBODY to do it. We need to take this expansion project down a notch and reconsider some of our strategies before we get in way over our heads against other organizations. It's getting REAL HOT out here in these streets because of us. Our sets are losing lives in these streets. The soldiers who are dying have families. We need to make things right with these other organizations. We can expand operations without shit gettin' this deep this fast."

A couple of the other Consortium members nodded their heads in agreement.

Marcus was livid as he listened to the words of Big D going against him. He was especially livid at the references Big D made to Rick Tresvant. But no one would ever have known how absolutely furious Marcus Means was by looking at him. His calculating exterior remained completely calm. He made a mental note and started the vote.

All of the members of The Consortium, with the exception of Marcus Means, voted against retaliation for the time being. All of them were in favor of Devante "Big D" Johnson's idea that they slow things down a bit, revise strategy and work to meet, at least, a small level of accord with the other organizations around Los Angeles that they had been feuding with in order to end some of the bloodshed.

There was no telling what was truly simmering underneath the surface of Marcus's cool demeanor as he conceded to the decision of the other members. The death of Slim J was no longer even the priority…not that it ever really had been.

-30-

Just before Jermaine "Slim J" Jackson, reputed leader of Los Angeles-based street gang, R2 Crips, was murdered, Thomas Hencken had decided to make some changes. He was stepping away from his very dangerous surveillance work, following Marcus Means and the men in his employ all over the city of Los Angeles. Instead, he was going to begin to go through the mountain of information and evidence that he already had—all of the notes, the logs, the court transcripts, police reports, legal documents and other classified information he had managed to photocopy and smuggle out of the offices of the Drug Enforcement Agency immediately prior to his forced resignation, and all of the photographic and video-taped evidence he'd taken over the past several weeks and that DEA had taken over the many, many months that the agency carefully tracked the movements of The Consortium. Thomas Hencken began to reorganize and rework EVERYTHING so he could bring finality to what had become a sad and destructive obsession for him. It was time, once and for all, to make something significant happen where The Consortium was concerned or let it all go, take all of the boxes of evidence, what he'd come to call "futile effort," out to his trash cans, do like everyone around him seemed to be doing and not give another moment's thought to people like Marcus Means, and make a sincere attempt to resume some semblance of a normal life. Enough was enough.

With the recent scourge of gang-related murders that had occurred in Los Angeles, Thomas Hencken was confident Marcus Means's hands were all over that blood-soaked mess. More likely than not, Marcus Means was primarily responsible for ALL of those gang-related murders, particularly the recent murder of Jermaine "Slim J" Jackson, who Thomas Hencken had discovered, through one of his contacts/informants, had been a member of what was being called "The NEW Consortium," the latest brainchild of Marcus Means and what had been the cause of all of his movement, travel and meetings over the past several weeks.

Thomas Hencken, more than anybody else in Los Angeles, firmly believed Marcus Means was responsible for the execution-style murder of corporate attorney, Phinnaeus Bernard III. Of all the far-fetched possibilities, it was crystal clear in Thomas Hencken's mind that Marcus Means had the most motive. Regardless of the courtroom conviction, it certainly had not been Richard Tresvant who had murdered that attorney. Despite the personal vendetta of the Los Angeles district attorney against

Richard Tresvant and a mountain of mostly circumstantial evidence, Richard Tresvant had had the LEAST amount of motive for that murder.

There was also not a single doubt in Thomas Hencken's mind that Marcus Means had single-handedly orchestrated the prison murder of Richard Lawrence Tresvant, the founder and former head of The Consortium, after he'd set him up for the first-degree murder of corporate attorney Phinnaeus Bernard III. What was Marcus Means's chief motivation for all of this bloodshed? The answer was extremely obvious when you had been tracking The Consortium for as long as Thomas Hencken had. Marcus Means had been very tired of operating in the background, tired of being third in command in the infamous Consortium organization almost for the entire duration of The Consortium's existence. Marcus Means had been half-patiently biding his time for years, carefully orchestrating to take both Richard Tresvant and Keshari Mitchell permanently out of the picture so he could take full control of The Consortium. Once Marcus Means did have control of The Consortium, in all of his murderous ambition, he had to strategically take out other people to accomplish his goals of becoming one of the single, most major players in the entire game. He didn't care who stood in his way and had to be removed. He didn't care who knew about the murders he'd carried out. Marcus Means had become like a monster on the loose in the city of Los Angeles. No law enforcement agency had yet come up with a single thing to even bring him into one of their precincts for questioning or to make a legitimate criminal charge stick against him.

Where was the missing videotape that had been taken from the security offices of 300 South Grand on the night that Phinnaeus Bernard III was murdered? Who had possessed the capability to hack into the office of the building's computer system to strategically delete all security camera footage for the entire day of the date Phinnaeus Bernard III was murdered in the subterranean garage of 300 South Grand as well as the security office's video coverage of all of the other public sectors of the upscale, high-rise building in Downtown Los Angeles where Phinnaeus Bernard III had been murdered? While most were confident they had put Phinnaeus Bernard III's murderer away when they convicted Richard Lawrence Tresvant, surely there was somebody besides Thomas Hencken who thought that it was more than a little suspect that Richard Tresvant was murdered in prison very soon after his conviction.

And what about his brutal murder inside a high security prison? Richard Tresvant was not just anybody. He had people on the inside as well as on the outside protecting him. Somebody with a lot of money and a lot of clout who could call some shots and call in more than a few favors inside the walls of a high-security prison was the only kind of person who could have arranged to have Richard Lawrence Tresvant killed. Yet, to date, no one was being held responsible for his murder and the case, for the most part, had gone cold, seemingly swept under the carpet by prison officials who may have been paid off, too.

None of it made sense.

Who was the anonymous caller who'd provided LAPD with enough tips to lead to the arrest, indictment and conviction of Richard Lawrence Tresvant for the first-degree murder of Phinnaeus Bernard III? Why would someone be that willing to cooperate with the law in that way? What was their motivation? How had they known where to tell police to go to find the murder weapon... inside Richard Tresvant's house, no less...that had led to Richard Tresvant's indictment and conviction? What did they have to gain from it? How had police gone without locating this very important figure?

Next, there was the kilogram of cocaine and a substantial amount of money that had been found in Phinnaeus Bernard's car on the night of his murder. What was the explanation for it being there? Phinnaeus Bernard was not a dealer. And why would someone who murdered him leave property of that level of value behind? It had to have been a plant. But why? Was someone trying to send a message? The trial for the murder of Phinnaeus Bernard III had given almost no attention to these details, neither on the prosecution side nor on the side of the defense. These details, in Thomas Hencken's mind, were very significant. And clearly the details pointed to someone who was in the cocaine business. You did not come across that much money and that large a quantity of cocaine at one time under any other circumstances without there being a sizeable inside connection to an organized cocaine enterprise.

Thomas Hencken knew the DEA had begun to question Phinnaeus Bernard III shortly prior to his murder. Thomas Hencken orchestrated much of the questioning himself. DEA wanted to know about several corporations that Richard Tresvant headed as CEO and had majority share holdings. Marcus Means was also on the board of directors of each of these corporations. Keshari Mitchell had been on the board of directors of a couple of these corporations prior to her death. Each of these corporations had been set up by corporate attorney Phinnaeus Bernard III at the law firm where he worked. Following Richard Tresvant's murder, Marcus Means became the new CEO and majority shareholder in each of these corporations. It was the belief of the DEA that The Consortium was laundering millions and millions of dollars made from the trafficking and sale of cocaine through these corporations. The DEA had approached Phinnaeus Bernard III because he had been involved in the set-up of most of these corporations. The DEA also believed that Phinnaeus Bernard III had specific information regarding several, major, U.S. banks that were knowingly assisting Richard Tresvant and The Consortium to launder The Consortium's drug money. The DEA believed several executives at each of these major U.S. banks were the "silent" members of The Consortium, benefitting financially on a personal level from The Consortium's criminal enterprises. These bank executives, who held positions ranging from senior vice president to CEO, assisted in many ways and made it possible for The Consortium to diversify their massive holdings into such major, legitimate, American enterprises as residential and corporate real estate developments, telecommunications, biotechnology, which was truly where the money was in today's markets, franchise operations from fast food to shipping services, and art. Phinnaeus Bernard was most likely killed because he knew too much about something that was going down behind the scenes in The Consortium. Perhaps Phinnaeus Bernard III had had knowledge that a "coup" was in progress.

How had litigators and prosecutors managed to get through such a high-profile trial with so many unanswered questions, so many strings left untied, so many holes that were directly related to the case? Then, almost immediately after the murder trial, while Richard Tresvant awaited a new trial on appeal, he was murdered in a high-security prison and his murderer had not been caught. There had not even been a list of adequate suspects or witnesses to question.

There was much, much more to this story than met the eye. There was certainly far more to the story than what had been revealed in Phinnaeus Bernard III's murder trial. Thomas Hencken intended to reveal who had murdered Phinnaeus Bernard III. He intended to determine WHY Phinnaeus Bernard III had been murdered. He intended to reveal who had orchestrated and carried out the murder of Richard Lawrence Tresvant. He intended to reveal how the recent murder of Jermaine "Slim J" Jackson was directly connected to The Consortium. And, in his heart of hearts, to the very core of his soul, every gut instinct that he had said that Marcus Means was responsible for it ALL.

Thomas Hencken woke up that morning with a very strong hunch, an epiphany, and he could not let it go, and he was going to pore over every single thing that he had again and again and again until he was able to fully organize the answers that would nail Marcus Means's ass to the wall. Thomas Hencken felt sure Los Angeles's crime rate would show an immediate and drastic decrease if Marcus Means was either behind bars for the rest of his life or dead.

Both Phinnaeus Bernard III's murder and Richard Lawrence Tresvant's murder were directly connected. Of that, Thomas Hencken was sure. And when attempting to come up with answers to many of the questions Thomas Hencken had in regard to both of these murders, all roads seemed to lead to Marcus Means every time.

Two months passed from the last contact that Thomas Hencken made with Misha Tierney. When he heard from her again, Misha Tierney contacted him herself and she was ready to cooperate...to a certain degree. She told Thomas Hencken that she needed to keep her communications with him to an absolute minimum. She told Thomas Hencken she had something that might be of help to him. She told him that she would call him again to arrange a meeting place very soon. Then she quickly hung up.

Misha's hands shook as she unlocked the safety deposit box at City National Bank in Century City. It had been years since she'd opened the box, nearly twelve years to the day since her mother's home in Leimert Park, a predominantly Black, middle-class section of Los Angeles, had been raided and ransacked by LAPD and DEA officers. Until now, Misha had had no reason to open the safety deposit box and view its contents. In fact, she had avoided doing so. Despite everything her biological brother had done to cause damage to her family, she had never considered nor held any serious desire to endanger her life by cooperating with either federal or local law enforcement. She knew the kind of man her brother had been. She knew the kind of men he did business with. She wasn't stupid. At least, she hadn't been until now.

Inside the safety deposit box that Misha had been closely protecting was a bundle of nondescript-looking 3.5" floppy diskettes, an antiquated oddity in the current new age of advanced computer technology featuring memory cards, flash drives and such. The diskettes and what was on them had no real importance whatsoever to her, but they were of tremendous importance to The Consortium and to most local and federal law enforcement as well if they had any idea of the diskettes' existence. On the diskettes was vivid information on some of the dummy corporations that had been owned and headed by, Richard Tresvant and The Consortium while Richard Tresvant was still alive. There were significant financial figures on the diskettes. There was even a $1 million allocation that had been strategically given to Keshari Mitchell for the start-up of Larger Than Lyfe Entertainment. The corporations noted on the diskettes still existed, and several of them currently had a number of legitimate, non-criminal shareholders. These corporations were operating and, doing business with other completely legitimate enterprises around the United States, and these corporations were showing a profit in their quarterly earnings reports that were also part of the saved information on some of the diskettes. These corporations were also doing business with several large and well-known banks that were all named on the diskettes, including the names of the specific bank executives who were managing The Consortium's accounts. These major banks were based in both Los Angeles and New York and these banks, from the financial figures on the diskettes, were holding, laundering and investing close to $175 million of The Consortium's money during the time period years ago when the diskettes had been made.

Richard Tresvant didn't even reside in his mother's Leimert Park home, but he had hidden his dangerous shit there, placing his own mother in harm's way. Misha's and Ricky's mother lived a normal, uncomplicated life. She worked and went to church. Richard Tresvant, her son, had aspired to and now ran a multimillion-dollar criminal enterprise. The police or the DEA or the FBI were always watching his movements, trying to apprehend him on a whole host of criminal charges, but they were never able to until right before his death. Ricky's mother had absolutely no connection to his business affairs and deeply despised all of the bad things she knew that her son did. Ricky had placed the bundle of diskettes where he believed no one who actually knew the significance of the information on them would ever go to look for them; more than $100 million worth of incriminating evidence had been stashed away in his mother's unassuming little house on a tree-lined street in a very regular neighborhood.

To some degree, Ricky had been correct. When LAPD and DEA had gone through his mother's home like bulls in a china shop, they left empty-handed. Ricky came later to the house out of concern for his mother and to assure her that he would take care of what had happened at her home that day while, at the same time, clearly looking for the diskettes. He never found them. And Misha would never know what force in the Universe had propelled her directly to their place of concealment before he'd gotten there. The fact that they were hidden let her know that they were important and she dropped the bundle into her purse, took them back to her house, loaded and reviewed every one of them, then immediately took them to the bank.

Misha's mother had a massive heart attack the day after the raid on her house. Two days after that, her mother was dead. Misha never spoke another word to Richard Tresvant after that. He was dead to her and he had died in prison with her still wanting absolutely nothing to do with him. She refused to even attend his funeral, still blaming him solidly for their mother's death.

She flipped open the lid of the box. It was empty. Misha foolishly shook the box as if the diskettes might miraculously, magically appear and she had simply overlooked them. Then the harsh chill of realization hit her. Marcus Means had gotten into her safety deposit box and removed the incriminating diskettes. She was more certain of it than the breath that she breathed. How Marcus Means even knew that she had the diskettes would forever be a mystery. How he'd known where she'd been keeping the diskettes for all of these years was also a baffling mystery. How he'd managed to get the diskettes out of the safety deposit box that belonged solely to her and not another soul on earth even knew about, with the exception of the bank itself, she would never know, but she was certain it had been Marcus Means and she couldn't even confront him about it.

-32-

Once the script for the biopic of Keshari Mitchell's life was complete, because of the extremely high level of secrecy Darian wanted to maintain until the film's release, she immediately took the script over to City National Bank in Century City and placed it in a safety deposit box she kept there. She made a single copy of the script and she put the copy into her laptop bag to place in her wall safe at her Hollywood Hills home. Then she popped a $500 bottle of Cristal Rosé in her office, lit one of her favorite Cuban cigars and celebrated with Terrence, her assistant. No fanfare. No media hype yet. It was just the two of them. That was more than cool with Terrence. He really liked Darian.

Terrence immediately noted the cigar Darian was smoking and remembered that it was the same, expensive brand Keshari Mitchell used to indulge in from time to time. There were more than a few other similarities to Keshari Mitchell that Terrence had been noting about Darian Boudreaux over the short time that they'd worked together. More than once, he'd wanted to comment to

Darian about the funny yet strong similarities that she had to his former and now-deceased boss, but, for some odd reason, he always caught himself.

More than once, Terrence's mind had also taken him to a crazy, crazy place and wondered if…what if…well, ENOUGH of that crazy-assed wondering! He downed the delicious glass of champagne from the bottle he and Darian were sharing and then poured himself another glass. The two of them talked and laughed. Terrence was almost as excited as Darian was to start production on the movie. He'd heard the stories of the romances and the drama that often took place on movie sets and he wanted to be a part of that. He also loved to bask in the tremendous level of energy and drive that was the beautiful Darian Boudreaux. She was SO much like his former boss. *She has no idea how much like Keshari she is,* Terrence thought as he watched her. *If only Terrence Henderson truly knew.*

Darian did not want it revealed to anyone that she had been the one who'd written the script for *LARGE* and she seriously stressed this to Terrence as they drank. Terrence asked her why she would want to go and cover up the fact that she had been the person who'd put so much hard work into composing the script for *LARGE*, particularly when every fiber of his being just kept telling him the movie was going to be a huge success. Darian partially lied and told Terrence that it was a very strategic marketing ploy and he would understand the method behind her madness in a few weeks. For now, her husband Mars and Terrence were the only two people on the face of the planet besides herself who were aware that she was the writer of the script for *LARGE* or even that a biopic of the life of Keshari Mitchell was currently in pre-production.

After having Terrence sign a confidentiality agreement specifically related to the film, Darian skillfully related to Terrence the story she had created that the script for *LARGE* had been sold to her by someone who'd known Keshari Mitchell personally and who had agreed to sell the script to Darian Boudreaux for an undisclosed amount of money only on the condition that they maintain full anonymity and that Darian never, ever divulge their identity. After remitting payment to the mysterious scriptwriter's attorney, the person disappeared back into obscurity and Darian was left to proceed with film production however she saw fit.

Terrence rolled on the floor laughing at Darian's craftiness. He now fully understood her "marketing ploy." There were going to be people who speculated even more than they already were that Keshari Mitchell, like Tupac Shakur, was still alive. They were going to wonder all day and night who the mysterious writer had been who had disappeared like a puff of smoke after turning the script for this blockbuster movie over to Darian Boudreaux. Then people where going to start to wonder if Keshari Mitchell herself had not written the script and sold it anonymously, especially if the rumors turned out to be true and Keshari Mitchell, in fact, was not dead.

The rumors and the speculation surrounding the making and release of the movie *LARGE* would soon swirl like a cyclone, and it would be the caliber of attention that even the very best PR firms, assembled and working together, wouldn't have the fire to create. With that level of industry and public consumer attention, ticket sales at the movie box office would be through the roof and Phoenix Films would become an instant household name. Terrence had no idea the primary reason behind Darian's desire to keep the author of the script for *LARGE* anonymous and he probably wouldn't care if he did. What he did know was that Ms. Darian Boudreaux was definitely a genius…just like his former boss had been.

Eleven o'clock rolled around and the two of them were still kicked back on the sectional in Darian's office, buzzed from the bottle of champagne they'd polished off.

"I've got to hurry up and find you a boyfriend, baby," she joked with Terrence. "Otherwise, I'll be monopolizing all your time all of the time."

Terrence had the feeling that Darian already had someone significant in her life to occupy a good deal of her time, but she never, ever talked about that person. She was a mystery and seemed intent on keeping it that way, and Terrence told himself that he had better not allow himself to get too buzzed or he might start really trying to pry into her personal life.

It was after midnight when Darian finally made it home. She called Mars at his condominium in Marina del Rey.

"Hi, baby. I miss you," was all that she said.

"You miss me?" Mars asked sleepily.

"Yes…I miss you," Darian responded.

"Would you like me to come?" Mars asked.

"I'd love it if you came…right now," Darian answered.

"I'm on my way," Mars said, hanging up.

Less than an hour later he was unlocking the door and she was standing there in the semi-darkness, naked, waiting for him.

He picked her up. He carried her upstairs. He made love to his beautiful wife. She fell asleep in his arms as the sun began to rise. A few hours later, two of them sleepily turned to each other and mutually agreed to take the day off. They made love again, Darian's legs wrapped anxiously around Mars's waist, having missed every thrust of the two of them at their best together. She kissed his face. He kissed her lips. Then it was time for the two of them to have another serious discussion about the movie.

-33-

With the completed script for *LARGE* in hand, it was now time to REALLY get down to business with the arduous construction of the proposal package needed to secure a production and distribution deal at one of the major film studios in Hollywood.

Darian spread her work out on the dining table in her Hollywood Hills home, set up her two laptop computers, put on a pot of coffee, and immediately proceeded to grind out the budget numbers and work on the bones, the foundation, of the proposal package while filling in the more minute details regarding the film project once she was satisfied with the overall strength of the foundation. A distribution deal with a major studio would, essentially, assist Phoenix Films in completion of the production of *LARGE*. This included everything from casting to the actual shoot of the film. A production and distribution deal would defray some of the overall costs of production. Then, once production of the movie was complete, the major studio, through its distribution company, would distribute the movie to theaters all over the country.

Darian worked all night for three days straight, doing research, working and reworking the budget numbers, composing the core terms for the production and distribution deal she was seeking from a major Hollywood studio. She asked her attorney to review and formalize the terms. She wanted to make sure that she dotted all of her "I's" and crossed all of her "T's" from a legal standpoint before she went to the major studios and asked for specific things for her movie under contract. Following her attorney's preliminary review, she went back to the drawing board and began to fill in anything and everything that she may have left out. She hired accountants to help fine tune and make the numbers she'd come up with for the movie's full production budget look "realistic" and plausible on paper. She hired a well-known Los Angeles consulting firm that specialized in business proposals for the film and music industries to assist her in constructing a cohesive and attractive final package. Then she went back to her attorney to have him review the completed proposal to make sure everything was okay.

It took roughly three weeks. If it had been anybody else, it would have, of course, taken longer…substantially longer. But Darian, like Keshari Mitchell, worked day and night as if her life depended upon it to accomplish completion of the task. She wasn't hurting for money even a little bit. She had more money than she would ever be able to spend over the course of the rest of her life, but she worked like she was HUNGRY. She worked like a hip-hop MC who scraped and grinded with sheer determination to get to the top of the game.

She had compared all of the major studios in Hollywood—Paramount, Universal, Warner Bros., Columbia, 20th Century Fox, Sony. After much careful contemplation, she decided to pitch the project to Warner Bros. Pictures. Her gut told her she would not have to pitch the project anywhere else and she trusted that gut instinct because it was rarely wrong. Per current numbers depicting gross revenues and profits for the film companies, Warner Bros. held the top slot in the game and Darian only wanted *LARGE* associated with the companies and the people who held top slots in the film industry game. Darian's only intention was to make a meteoric rise to the top of the film industry food chain, and she wanted to surround herself with the significant business entities who were already there as she had done in her former life when she rose to the top of the music industry game.

Darian wanted Warner Bros. to cover a third of the total film budget to include the actual production of the movie, and construction and advertising for the movie's release. She wanted full use of the Warner Bros. studios for as much of the shoot as possible. She wanted Warner Bros. to handle set design and set building. She wanted Phoenix Films to maintain full creative control of the film, including selection of the film's director, associate producer, line producer, the movie's cast, music, dialogue and locations, and, finally, Darian wanted Warner Bros.

to distribute *LARGE* in movie theaters nationally. In return for all of this, Warner Bros. would take a percentage of the profits from *LARGE* in the form of box office ticket sales, consumer media sales, and international distribution. Because of record mogul Keshari Mitchell's overall popularity and the controversial nature of the film's subject matter, Darian knew that she was putting together a highly viable project, and the fact that Phoenix Films would be picking up two-thirds of the total film budget, Darian felt confident that a deal could quickly be inked between Phoenix Films and Warner Bros. Pictures.

There was not one meeting with Warner Bros. executives. There were six of them. There were what seemed like hundreds of phone calls and lunches. Then it was official. Warner Bros. entered into contract with Phoenix Films to make the movie *LARGE*, and Warner Bros. had agreed to all of Darian Boudreaux's terms. The woman was phenomenal, and the entire film industry immediately stopped in their tracks, wanting to know who she was. She had done what was regularly impossible for other fledgling filmmakers. She had secured a major movie deal with the biggest in the game on her very first time out of the gate. She had barely been back in the United States for a year, and she was quickly becoming a force to be reckoned with just as she had in the music industry.

Only someone with king-size hustle acquired via a lengthy stint of running a serious criminal enterprise, someone who also had an MBA from the Wharton School of Business under her belt, could manage to have accomplished such a lofty feat seemingly so effortlessly. Before the ink could fully dry on the contracts and before she could even get off the lot at Warner Bros. Studios, Darian was blowing up Mars's iPhone, sending him excited text messages from her BlackBerry. He smiled to himself when he got the news.

"I never had any doubt that you would do it. Congratulations, baby."

But, now, Mars thought to himself after having sent the text message to his wife, not wanting to put a damper on her celebratory mood, there was a very real reason for fear. The film project was about to go public...very public.

There was media coverage everywhere from *Film Journal* to *MovieMaker* to *Hollywood Reporter* to *Entertainment Tonight* and, for the very first time, the entire film industry and the public knew that a film was about to be made about the life and times of ultra-private, now-deceased music mogul Keshari Mitchell. Everyone wanted to do interviews with Darian Boudreaux. On the front page of *VARIETY*, there was a photograph of Darian posed with the two executives at Warner Bros. Pictures who'd negotiated and finalized the contract for the movie project. The caption and a brief write-up said: *Phoenix Films and Warner Bros. Will Do Movie on Life of Music Mogul Keshari*

Mitchell. Everyone wanted to know Darian Boudreaux's background—who she was, where she'd gone to school, her film industry experience, etc. etc. More and more people's ears and eyes were perking up to the new executive producer in town and some of them wanted to get the opportunity to work with her. And the speculation immediately took the spot- light again about whether or not Keshari Mitchell was really dead.

-34-

Over the course of Marcus Means bogarting his way into new areas of the drug game, terrorizing and taking over territory that belonged to other organizations and other sets, and working his plan for expansion of The Consortium, he also had been having some increasingly serious disagreements with the head of his own set, Devante "Big D" Johnson, who was now second in command in The Consortium. The two of them had never really been on the best of terms, but Marcus always deferred to him in years past because he was the leader of their set. Once Marcus assumed the position as the new head of The Consortium, he really had no more desire to continue to defer to or bite his tongue with Devante Johnson. Devante "Big D" Johnson was, indeed, the head of R4Crips for now, but Marcus could easily step into position to control their soldiers. He'd thought about that for a long time.

The vote that had taken place immediately following Slim J's murder that would determine whether or not The Consortium should meet with other organizations to attempt to call a truce to the violence that had been recently going down on the streets of Los Angeles had made Marcus livid. Devante's "speech" to the other Consortium members that, ultimately, swayed the vote in favor of discussions for a truce had sealed Devante's fate. Marcus was not arranging any discussions to apologize and back down from what he had been doing to increase the power and the area owned and controlled by The Consortium. Over his dead body would he ever do some shit like that. Marcus was sick and tired of that motherfucker. Marcus had been sick and tired for years of a number of that decisions that Devante "Big D" Johnson had been making on behalf of their set and Marcus had patiently bided his time to deal with it all.

Devante Johnson owned a million-dollar home in Baldwin Hills. He had a wife who had been his girl since high school. He had an adult daughter who his wife had given birth to when she and Devante were both just graduating high school. The daughter lived in Culver City. Devante also had a ten-year-old son who was his pride and joy. It was Saturday, just after noon, and the two of them, "mano y mano," were hanging out at home together.

Marcus had turned thoughts over and over again in his mind before he decided the night before that he should pay Devante a visit so the two of them could hash things out.

"What's up, Marc?" Devante said, escorting Marcus Means into the den where he had been playing *Transformers: War for Cybertron* on a Sony PS3 with his ten-year-old son.

"What's up, Lil D?" Marcus said playfully, walking over and giving the cute little boy a "pound" in the cool way that Black men did. Marcus sat down next to the little boy while Devante sat back casually in the huge, comfortable, leather chair positioned across from the leather sectional. He and his son were both dressed in matching black Adidas sweatpants and white tees. They both held hand controllers that were connected to the PS3 device. Marcus Means was quiet for the most part, seemingly taking an interest in the popular video game that Devante and his beloved son were playing. Jillian, Devante's wife, was clearly not at home because her black Mercedes was not in its usual spot in the drive when Marcus arrived. It was just the three of them—Marcus, Devante, and Devante Jr.—and that was ideal.

There was no sign whatsoever of what would come next, but that was the way it was with Marcus Means. He was as calculating as it could get and he could smile at you, looking you straight in the eye, and you would never have the slightest idea that he was about to murder you. Today was no different.

"I never liked your ass," Marcus said. He said it quietly,

almost as if he was making some solemn, emotion-stirring revelation that might evoke tears. "I should have murdered your ass a long time ago, but Rick always stepped in. The Consortium shall work together as one, cohesive unit and we are going all the way to the top of the food chain. There will be no detractors. You should have consulted with me before you went and influenced our group to move in a direction that we should never even consider."

"What???" Devante said quizzically.

He didn't even have the opportunity to respond to what Marcus was saying, to defend his position, when two of Marcus's men entered the den. Devante had left the front door unlocked.

Marcus held Devante's frantically screaming ten-year-old son in his seat beside him as one of the men swiftly stabbed Devante in his gut. Marcus covered the little boy's mouth with his hand to muffle the child's screams. It was absolutely, abominably despicable what the child was witnessing and Marcus didn't even possess the emotional makeup to consider it. Devante struggled wildly, trying to get out of the deep, comfortable chair that now worked against him like an accomplice in his murder. One of the men held Devante in a chokehold, rammed a rag into his mouth to muffle his screams, while the other stabbed Devante again...and again...and again. Blood splattered everywhere. The man viciously gutted Devante with the thirteen-inch stiletto knife he gripped in a gloved fist and then stepped back. Blood and Devante's entrails went spilling out onto the floor. Devante's head lolled back in the chair, his lifeless eyes looking toward the ceiling. Marcus had so disliked Devante for so long that his murder had been personal. It had little at all to do with Marcus's expansion plans for The Consortium and the gruesome way that Devante "Big D" Johnson had just been murdered was proof of it.

Marcus nodded and the men, like the professionals that they were, quickly and effortlessly went to Devante's bathroom to change clothes, put the bloodied clothes as well as the plastic sleeves that had covered their shoes into a black trash bag that would be burned, backtracked to ensure there was no physical evidence that could be traced back to them, then smoothly and silently departed the bloody scene.

Devante Jr., "Big D's" little boy, had, strangely, stopped his screaming and flailing after having watched every second of his father's extremely vicious murder. In a catatonic state, his glassy eyes, which reflected his defensive detachment from the reality of the horrific scene around him, looked straight ahead as Marcus slipped on gloves, screwed the silencer onto his gun and shot the little boy between the eyes.

If there, indeed, was such a place called Hell, Marcus Means would run it and he would orchestrate a very serious game plan to take out the Devil. Even by gangster standards, Marcus Means was the most ruthless, most self-absorbed shit the city of Los Angeles had ever seen.

He had to be the most godless monster walking the face of the entire earth. The man was a tremendous danger to the most basic parts of what was even remotely decent in humanity. It had been just as the Mexicans had said it would be. Marcus Means did not give a fuck about anyone nor anything except for his own agenda, and he would take out his own mother if she stood in his way.

Marcus stood for a moment and looked around him. His emotions were a flat line as he watched the child he'd just killed slumped over on the sofa as if he'd fallen asleep. The only thing that proved otherwise was the gaping wound in the child's face and the growing pool of the child's blood dripping off the leather sofa and onto the floor. Little D had been the only witness to Devante "Big D" Johnson's murder and he was old enough to be very clear about what he'd seen and what had occurred if he had lived to tell about it. Marcus Means didn't believe in leaving witnesses. He also didn't believe in loose ends. Devante "Big D" Johnson had been a loose end. Marcus had invited Devante into The Consortium for one reason and one reason only—to murder him and to seize all of the set's holdings that he controlled. Marcus would pay a substantial death benefit to Devante's wife, pay his deepest condolences at Devante's funeral, divide profits from Devante's holdings with the rest of The Consortium members, and none of them would ever know what had happened...and Marcus would make sure none of them cared by the time it was ever revealed what had actually happened.

When you were as bad as Marcus Means absolutely was, how long would it be before someone who was as ruthless as he, someone who hated Marcus Means as much as he'd hated Devante Johnson, came along and "pushed his cap back?"

-35-

The news stories on every local television station in Los Angeles were horrible and heart-wrenching. Ten-year-old Devante Johnson, Jr. and his father, Devante "Big D" Johnson, were both brought out of their home in their quiet, upscale, Baldwin Hills neighborhood in body bags. They'd been gruesomely murdered in the middle of the afternoon inside their home and, thus far, there were no witnesses who had seen, heard, or knew anything about what had occurred that day. Neighbors who were interviewed by news reporters expressed shock and sadness. Nothing like what had happened that day had ever happened in their upscale neighborhood of expensive homes. Many neighbors interviewed expressed fear for their own safety. Devante Jr. played regularly and went to school with some of the neighbors' kids.

Devante's wife had discovered her husband, Devante, and her son, Devante Jr., after a trip to the beauty shop. What she found upon coming into her home was more than any human being should be made to try to handle. It was certain that she would never be the same again.

The Consortium immediately met up at Marcus Means's home in Bel Air, just as they had when Slim J was murdered, but the mood was far different than it had been right after Slim J was murdered. There was an almost tangible amount of tension in the room now. There was an unbelievable fury around the room over the murder of the little boy.

"You still want to have a sit-down with anyone to discuss a truce?" Marcus asked the other Consortium members.

He already knew their answers.

There was now no way any one of them could want to hash things out amicably with other sets and organizations when Consortium members were dropping off like flies. They were now prepared to take out whoever it was who had killed Slim J and Big D and Big D's young son and they were thoroughly ready to support any plan that took out the culprits as quickly and as viciously as Slim J and Big D had been taken out. The Consortium members who'd talked compromise before were now ready to send some messages of their own: "The Consortium is NOT to be fucked with!"

Marcus, forever calculating, had already formulated a plan to take out the two men who knew firsthand exactly what had happened to Devante "Big D" Johnson. The other Consortium members truly needed to be careful because there was really no telling who might be taken out next.

-36-

Ever since signing with the Lakers, the press followed Krishawn Webb incessantly, trying to get a story, and Krishawn continuously tried to assure them that there wasn't one. He was a talented, intelligent, very attractive, highly paid, professional athlete who had just joined "The Dynasty," one of the many nicknames for the Los Angeles Lakers. He'd been a bachelor for the entire duration of his career. There was no baby mama drama…he had no children yet…and there were no whispered rumors that he was gay. The cherry on top of all of that was that he was really, really nice. The blinged-out, basketball-dunkin' ego monster had never been a part of his repertoire. He was one of the hottest commodities in town at the moment and what you saw was what you got. The public had every reason to adore him. None-theless, the media could smell that a drama was brewing somewhere right along the fringes of his life…maybe not directly within the confines of his personal sphere yet, but very, very close…and getting closer, particularly as the press began to capture more and more photographs of Krishawn with his former fiancée, Misha Tierney. They were no longer even attempting to hide from media scrutiny. They kissed, they held hands, they went out, they laughed, they looked good and they were most definitely TOGETHER. That alone was bound to go into a full-blown drama, particularly when you considered who Misha Tierney was still married to, even if she had filed for divorce.

The new Los Angeles Laker in town had opted not to sell his very chic loft apartment in the SoHo district of New York City when he went shopping for a new, more permanent residence in Los Angeles. After weeks of searching for the ideal property, Krishawn Webb selected an $8 million, six-bedroom, seven-bathroom, Mediterranean home in an ultra-exclusive, gated community in Pacific Palisades. It was definitely not a bachelor pad, and Krishawn wanted a quick closing.

Through his representatives, Krishawn then acquired from South African diamond dealers a near-flawless, three-carat, radiant-cut, BLUE diamond set in a fine, platinum band. It was rumored that Krishawn dropped a million dollars for the ring. After stealing Misha away from the offices at Larger Than Lyfe Entertainment for the day, the couple picnicked on the floor in the empty master suite of the spectacular, Pacific Palisades home on which Krishawn had just closed escrow and, at the bottom of a glass of Cristal Rosé sparkled the magnificent symbol of Krishawn's love and affection and proposal of marriage. Misha happily and tearfully accepted Krishawn's proposal. The happy couple set a wedding date for New Year's Eve that year. Less than one week later, Krishawn's publicist released details of his engagement...the second time around...to record company mogul and celebrity event planner Misha Tierney.

A soap opera writer could not compose better drama, and reporters and paparazzi were hot on their trails, poised to capture every new outbreak of notable news.

When Darian Boudreaux heard the news of the engagement, she was both happy and afraid for her best friend. She had no idea what exactly was up Marcus Means's sleeve when he graciously agreed to give Misha the divorce she wanted, especially after he had forced her into marriage in the first place. Darian also had no idea what had occurred that had driven Misha to her breaking point where she didn't give a fuck anymore about the dangers, the threats nor anything else that had to do with Marcus Means. She filed for divorce from this man she absolutely despised, and then promptly accepted the marriage proposal from the man she truly loved, Krishawn Webb. The thing was that whenever Marcus Means bowed out gracefully from a situation was precisely the time when you had the most to worry about. Misha could be sure that she had not heard the last from him yet.

-37-

Portia had compromised her happiness for long enough and, once and for all, she made a decision. She was done with average-ass, regular men who undervalued her and their relationships with her. She was tired of not being satisfied. She was tired of watching a man she'd catered to walk away from her to be with some other woman. She was tired of waking up alone. She was tired of starting all over again on what seemed like a never-ending search for Mr. Right. She was tired of being damned tired.

Krishawn Webb, Portia's most recent "paramour," had clearly made the decision to return to his old flame, his former fiancée, Misha Tierney. Stories and photos of the two of them sucking each other's faces in public together were plastered on the covers or inside every entertainment magazine in Los Angeles. Portia hadn't even been hurt by it. Actually, a small part of her had kind of expected it. Her dealings with Krishawn, for the most part, had been casual. He was smart, he was sweet, he was sexy, and he was rich…all qualifying mating factors for a woman like Portia. He'd been lonely, probably aching for the presence of that Misha bitch on the few occasions that they'd dated. And, finally, he'd gotten her back and it appeared to be exactly what he wanted, what he'd been missing.

Portia had been making the rounds and a new man had captured her attention. For all intents and purposes, she had never dated this kind of man before. He was a Los Angeles gallery owner, a successful real estate investor and developer…and he had a…hmmm…reputation. His name was Marcus Means.

He was chocolate and fine like the actor Morris Chestnut with shoulder-length dreadlocks and a chiseled body just dying for her to wrap her legs around, a shrewd businessman, a strong, silent type. Portia had heard the stories, especially since the recent news stories linking him to the gang leader who had been thrown from the 42nd story of 300 South Grand, the very same high-rise building where that attorney Phinnaeus Bernard III had been murdered. Marcus Means was alleged to be one of the most dangerous, Black gangsters in the city of Los Angeles and, for Portia, this was, admittedly, kinda sexy. She was sick and tired of getting fucked over and dismissed by men like Mars Buchanan. As crazy as some people now firmly believed her to be, what was probably craziest of all was the fact that she had no fear about approaching Marcus Means. She had no fear about what he might do to her. She was becoming more and more intrigued by his extremely dangerous reputation. She had no fear of him rejecting her. Shit, she began to say to herself in her very warped mind that she'd look good and BE good as a gangster's wife. And she wasted no time formulating her next plans.

-38-

Now that a deal had been reached with Warner Bros. Pictures, it was time for Darian to put her nose to the grindstone for the next phase of her work. With Warner Bros. offering help to her wherever she needed, Darian was ready to assemble a full crew for the filming and post-production of *LARGE*. The work was intensely grueling, but Darian was enjoying every single moment of it. The very first thing on her agenda was the hiring of an associate producer so that she could divvy up the heavy workload of putting together a film crew and get the task completed as quickly as possible. She was *so* ready to start shooting.

The hiring of an associate producer to work for Phoenix Films was a little different than hiring an executive assistant to work for her. Any producer of any level of substance within the Los Angeles film industry was going to want to join up with a film company that had the potential of adding credible "weight" to their résumés. None of them had interest in becoming involved with some fly-by-night film company that might be here today and gone tomorrow. They wanted to be picked up by a well-known name or they wanted to be sold the idea that they were joining a company that was about to become a very well-known name in the industry. Phoenix Films had yet to earn its stripes and Darian had no real, verifiable background in the industry other than degrees from a couple of the top U.S. film schools that she had purchased through her attorney, so she had to quickly and very, very convincingly sell the idea that Phoenix Films was about to make a very definite mark on the film industry and establish itself for the long-run.

Darian went a step further to ensure the associate producer she wanted signed on with Phoenix Films. She constructed a compensation package that was greater than the current market average, rendering hers an offer that the producer could not refuse. She wanted a producer who would bring a hip, fresh, prolific, innovative, non-conformist edge to Phoenix Films. By using well-known, reputable talent agencies in Los Angeles and carefully researching the backgrounds of many of the up-and-coming, young producers in the Los Angeles film industry, particularly the ones the talent agency suggested, Darian got exactly what she wanted.

Over a little more than a week's time, Darian interviewed and hired new associate producer Michael Chastang, who would assist her in the completion of production on the movie *LARGE*, and then work with her to acquire and produce all of Phoenix Films' subsequent movie, television and documentary projects. He was not being hired solely for the *LARGE* project. The chief qualifying factors for the new associate producer had been that he needed to mesh well with Darian, he needed to possess a level of ambition and drive that were impressive to her, he also had to possess the kind of creative vision that Darian firmly believed was needed in order to acquire and produce other highly successful film projects once *LARGE* was released in theaters. Darian was thoroughly impressed with Michael Chastang. He had a prior background as an associate producer on two other major film projects. He also possessed prior background in script editing as well as a small level of line production. Michael definitely brought something unique and needed to the table. He impressed Darian as possessing the kind of dogged tenacity that was very much in tune with her own dogged tenacity.

With the tremendous asset of a qualified associate producer in place, Darian and Michael Chastang, with Terrence bringing up the rear, got busy working the lengthy list of other very significant items that needed to be handled in the pre-production process. Darian needed to hire a casting company for actors. Central Casting in Burbank, the largest and most well-known casting agency in Los Angeles, was quickly hired to recruit the cast for *LARGE*. Darian already had specific actors and actresses in mind for many of the principal and supporting character roles. She wanted Boris Kodjoe to play "Mars Buchanan." She wanted Lisa Raye for the role of "Misha Tierney." She wanted Mel Jackson from the movie *Soul Food* to play the role of "Richard Lawrence Tresvant." She wanted Morris Chestnut to play "Marcus Means." Chenoa Maxwell would be perfect for the role of "Portia Foster." And, for the life of her, she could not decide who would be most ideal for the leading role of "Keshari Mitchell." It was terrifically ironic that she was quickly able to visualize actors in every role except for the person who would play her. She turned that role over and over and over again in her mind and could not visualize a single person who would be ideal to play her. She looked forward to seeing what Central Casting came up with. Over the next few days, Central Casting would be contacting the agents of the specific actors that Darian did want for the film to determine their current availability.

Next, a permanent accounting department for Phoenix Films needed to be put into place. Thus far, Darian had been using a reputable firm with offices in Downtown Los Angeles on a case-by-case basis, because she had not yet moved into any sizeable business transactions that would require the consistent input of an in-house accounting team. As Phoenix Films got ready to go full swing into the production of *LARGE* as well as subsequent film projects, the film company was definitely going to need a proficient and permanent in-house accounting team to handle all of Phoenix Films' financial needs around the clock, from payroll to film budgets to taxes to basic expense reports for Phoenix Films employees.

—39—

omething happened that had never, ever happened while Rick Tresvant controlled The Consortium. One of The Consortium's stash houses was robbed and the robbery was a MAJOR hit. The stash house, located in Bree-Z's territory in Compton, had just received a sizeable delivery. At the time of the hit, the stash house contained a little over $1 million worth of uncut cocaine. It was some of the very same cocaine with the marked-up price tag that had been sold to The Consortium by "The Colombian."

Whenever a delivery was made to any stash house owned by The Consortium, security was doubled, sometimes tripled, until the product was safely processed and moved around the country. Whoever robbed the stash house knew too much about too much, making it seem like an inside job. But it wasn't an inside job...or so The Consortium initially believed. Two Consortium soldiers died at that stash house. Four others were seriously wounded. Three more shot it out against the robbers and managed to go unharmed.

All of the cocaine in the stash house at the time of the robbery was taken. The thugs also got away from the scene with a safe that contained, at the most, approximately $7,000 in cash. Also in the safe was the missing security surveillance videotape that had been taken from 300 South Grand when corporate attorney Phinnaeus Bernard III had been murdered.

Things were about to get WAY extra for somebody.

-40-

Darian had her cameramen and, of course, one camerawoman. She had gaffers and lighting techs. Misha Tierney and Larger Than Lyfe Entertainment's A & R director were coming to Phoenix Films' offices in a couple of days to finalize an agreement for the music for *LARGE*. Darian had a costume designer and hair stylist. She had sound techs and a location manager. She had ALL of the actors that she'd wanted and the pièce de résistance was the actress who would play the leading role. Darian had never, ever even considered her, but she could not have been happier once she viewed the actress's head shots and the actress read for the role.

Now Darian wanted to CELEBRATE. She wanted to celebrate the humongous feat that she had accomplished of writing an amazing script and then securing a production and distribution deal with Warner Bros. Pictures to make the movie *LARGE* on her terms. She wanted to celebrate hiring a very talented associate producer who worked extremely well with her. She wanted to celebrate the fact that she and her associate producer had pulled out all of the stops, did the research, made the calls, and pretty quickly assembled a cast and crew for the film. Darian wanted to celebrate that her fledgling film company was about to go fully into production of its first major film project. She didn't want to do anything over-the-top yet. There were going to be lots of parties over the coming weeks and months. There was the film's "wrap party" for the cast and crew once the shooting of the movie was complete. There was also the film's premiere party where Hollywood's elite would come out to show their support for the film. Darian definitely intended to go over-the-top with that event. For now, she wanted to have a chic and intimate "get-together" at her home for the cast and crew of *LARGE* to get to know each other since they would all be working intensively together for the next two to three months. She got with Terrence and discussed with him what she wanted to do and Terrence immediately got with Misha Tierney's event planning firm to streamline the details and set it in motion.

One week later at seven in the evening, Darian's terrace had been turned into the intimate gathering place she'd wanted. The party was invitation only, and special arrangements were made with a valet service to park the guests' cars in an ideal location down the hill from Darian's amazing hilltop home. There was a full-service, open bar stocked with premium wines and liquors, there were exotic fruit platters, jazz music, and a sit-down dinner catered by Spago. She had a full wait staff to serve the food and drinks. She'd even had a signature, frothy, rum and mango drink called "LARGE" custom-made by Spago especially for the party that night. It was the very first party Darian had thrown in her new home, and, so far, things had been carried out beautifully without a hitch. There was lots of mingling, interesting conversation and laughter, allowing everyone to become better acquainted. Yet another of Darian's missions had been accomplished that evening. She'd brought her cast and crew together to begin to establish, at least temporarily, that bond required to successfully shoot her film and, most hopefully, stay within budget. Darian only wished her beloved husband could be there with her that night.

-41-

The night before the start of filming of *LARGE*, Darian had one of her nightmares. It was a really bad one, and Mars had not been there. They'd been keeping their distance from each other a lot more as the media began to track her movements more and more. It was patently ridiculous. They were married, but it had to be done.

Darian had snapped up in bed, her sheets and pajamas completely drenched in sweat. Her heart beat as if it was going to beat itself right out of her chest. She could remember segments of the nightmare VIVIDLY...because parts of the nightmare had actually occurred. In the dream, Darian was still residing at the W Hotel, setting things in motion to launch her film company. She was at the front desk of the hotel and saw a familiar face across the lobby who turned out to be none other than Marcus Means...and he had noticed a "familiar" face too. He was staring directly at her intently while he sat waiting for the group he was about to meet with. Beyond all of the radical plastic surgery that she'd undergone to completely change her physical identity, Marcus recognized her. He knew precisely who she was. She felt it and he felt it too.

While she slept, Marcus Means and two of his men gained entry into her hotel suite, viciously beat her, and then slit her throat. Darian snapped out of her sleep right at the moment that she'd probably died in the nightmare. She had attempted to scream and the scream seemed caught in her aching throat. She turned over in bed to reach for Mars and remembered he was not there. She'd been having nightmares like this one since the first night that she had been able to fall asleep in Sao Paulo, Brazil. So many nights before this one, she had woken up drenched in sweat and her heart feeling as if it was about to beat itself right out of her chest. In the wee hours of the morning as she lay in bed by herself, she cried herself back to sleep. A couple of hours later, she got up to shower and dress and a car picked her up to take her over to Warner Bros. Studios. She knew the nightmare had everything to do with the nervous tension she felt about the start of the shooting of the film. At least, she hoped that was all the nightmare had been about.

Today was finally the day. Darian was excited and nervous and, maybe, a little bit apprehensive, and then she was excited all over again. She was the geeky girl all over again who didn't know how absolutely beautiful she was on her first day of high school. She was more of a bundle of nerves than she had been back in those very first days of Larger Than Lyfe Entertainment opening its doors, right before Rasheed the Refugee's first album dropped.

Darian and Michael Chastang, Phoenix Films' new associate producer, had taken an intensive tour of Warner Bros. Studios the week before the beginning of the shoot. Representatives from Warner Bros. had fielded Darian's and Michael's lengthy list of questions. Darian took notes like a prize pupil, and the excitement welled up in her even then. Her location manager as well as the film's director, Hype Williams, met with her and Michael Chastang at Phoenix Films' offices as well as at Darian's home. A few times, the executives from Warner Bros. sat in and offered valuable input. They carefully went over the breakdown of the scenes and the scene locations. Hype Williams had read the entire script from cover to cover several times, making notes, asking questions, and using his genius creative mind to map out the film's flow, from opening to closing credits. Darian just adored him. He was hip. He was fly. Darian loved the work he had done as director of *Belly* and she was confident he would do an amazing job with *LARGE*. He had just the right level of edge and creativity that Darian wanted to see in *LARGE*. He seemed to have a "feel" for what she wanted to convey immediately.

The set designer and his team had meetings and walkthroughs with Darian and Michael Chastang and the Warner Bros. executives. The goal of the set design team was to make sure that everything on set, every physical area the actresses slept in, worked in, fought in, and fucked in that would be captured in the filming of the movie, met with the producers' approval and gave absolute realism to the storyline of the film.

After all of that was done and the what seemed like hundreds of meetings had been conducted with lighting, set design, construction, and the rest of the production crew and the production manager, covering all of the ground they could possibly cover excluding the shoot itself, Darian met with Warner Bros. executives on her own to carefully go over EVERYTHING with them, to ensure that all involved were on the same page, to revisit the budget and discuss any questions that were in the air, and to make sure that Warner Bros. was in agreement with all that had been done thus far with the film project.

Making a movie was a humongous task, far greater than Darian had ever imagined, even after more than a year of extremely intensive study of virtually every facet of the workings of the film industry while she was still in Brazil. What looked so effortless in a finished product on screen in theaters literally took hundreds of around-the-clock man-hours, fitting the pieces of a movie production together, bit by bit, like a complex jigsaw puzzle. Making a movie was an even greater challenge, Darian believed, than the music business had been for her, and she had not yet generated a profit from movie-making or even gotten through her very first day of shooting of her current film project to come to this conclusion.

Warner Bros. had taken a HUGE risk with her. Over the process of negotiations, Warner Bros. had completed the standard background checks and knew that Darian had no significant back- ground to manage a multimillion-dollar movie project. What Darian did have was the savvy to show them she had studied and knew the ins and outs of the business side of the film industry probably better than some of them did. She showed them that, in addition, to her strong business acumen, she possessed a high level of creativity that positively flowed through her ideas for the film, *LARGE*, that she'd wanted to do with them.

Darian held film degrees that her attorney had purchased for her prior to her death and she had a string of "investors" who she'd brought together to finance two-thirds of the budget for *LARGE*. The "investors" were nothing more than dummy corporations strategically set up well before Darian's death that were now being used to move her own money around in the film industry. It would blow the average person's mind what a heavy hand organized crime money has in Los Angeles' entertainment industry. Even "A" list stars are sometimes made to jump when some faction of organized crime, operating behind a sophisticated yet bogus corporate entity, are telling them how high.

Warner Bros. had even run a number of intensive background checks to determine the source of the funds from the group of "investors" that Darian was using to cover two-thirds of the financing for the film project. Darian had been trained by some of the best in the game—the Wharton School of Business in Pennsylvania and Richard Lawrence Tresvant, founder of The Consortium. Obviously, she had passed all of Warner Bros.' tests, and, because she had compiled such a detailed, highly professional, and captivating proposal, Warner Bros. had been willing, with little reluctance, to go out on a limb with her.

Today was not a test drive. If there had been any doubt before, there definitely was no doubt now. Darian Boudreaux was officially in the film business. She rode in a golf cart over to the first film set that was an exact replica of Larger Than Lyfe Entertainment's offices. She couldn't help smiling to herself at the memory of it as she went over to sit with Hype Williams, *LARGE's* director. At the very same moment, her BlackBerry jingled.

"If that film reaches the theaters, you're a DEAD bitch!" the caller said in a mechanically disguised voice.

Then the caller hung up.

-42-

Marcus Means had not been happy at all when he'd heard about Misha's pending nuptials to her former fiancé, Krishawn Webb, and he decided to teach her a very valuable lesson. It would thoroughly boggle the average human mind to even try to conceive of what exactly went on in Marcus Means's psychopathic mind that would drive him to get completely bent out of shape at this woman, who hated his fucking guts, finally growing the balls to reclaim her life after he had forced her into marrying him. Marcus's twisted thoughts went a mile a minute, and he was constantly two steps ahead of the game, formulating some new plan to further his ruthless personal agenda. You see, Marcus had something of a "Godfather" complex. In all of his machinations to expand the power, profits and territory of The Consortium, he also had plans on a more personal level where it came to Misha Tierney. This crazy fool had actually been nursing a plan in his mind that he would somehow, over time, make Misha Tierney, this woman who hated him to his core, hated the very ground that would hold his despicable ass up, the very same woman who he had forced into their soon-to-be-defunct, loveless, farcical prison of a marriage, ultimately, become his REAL wife… in a fully consummated marriage. Misha was incredibly smart, he'd thought. She was beautiful and she would be a good mother, ideal to bear the children who would one day assume his position and control The Consortium and continue to expand the empire he was currently building.

Misha would have told Marcus where Keshari was before she ever went along with some shit like that. It was still the "Eighth Wonder of the World" that she had gone along with his forced marriage, particularly for as long as she did, in the first place.

In a black Hugo Boss suit, Cartier sunglasses, with his beautiful, dark dreadlocks pulled back in a sexy knot, Marcus Means, accompanied by his attorney and two of his bodyguards, strode into Larger Than Lyfe Entertainment. He didn't even acknowledge the receptionist as he bypassed her station. She quickly proceeded to call security, and he entered, without knocking, the closed double doors to Misha Tierney's office.

"Good morning to you, my beautiful, soon-to-be former wife. How is life treating you?"

"Marcus, what in the fuck are you doing barging into my office like this? I really don't have time for this shit today."

"Oh, sweetheart," Marcus said kindly, "this won't take long at all."

Marcus was seriously up to something. Misha could feel it.

"There's going to be a changing of the guard, so to speak, today. Effective immediately, I will be taking over Larger Than Lyfe Entertainment."

"What the FUCK?!" Misha exclaimed, getting up from her desk.

At the same time, the office of the building's security arrived to escort Marcus Means and his "entourage" off the premises. Marcus quickly flashed to them a small stack of paperwork provided to him by his attorney that gave him every right to be there. Misha went as white as a ghost. She rushed over to the phone and called David Weisberg's law office. Marcus gave a small chuckle as she dialed the number.

"I need you to get here immediately!" she snapped into the line.

She hung up and immediately rang the office of Larger Than Lyfe Entertainment's new general legal counsel. She was frantic. She and Marcus Means stood in a stand-off in the doorway of her office until David Weisberg arrived. The office of the building's security officers stayed put, still unsure whether or not they would need to radio ahead for the assistance of LAPD. Things were definitely looking as if they were going to get very ugly.

The outer office where the receptionist's station was located was quickly growing into "ground zero" as Larger

Than Lyfe employees didn't want to miss a second of the quickly unfolding melodrama. In a huddle, they peered around the corner at Misha's office, trying to see and hear whatever they could. They knew that whatever was happening was serious, but none of them could catch any specific details, so they stood at the receptionist's station whispering and speculating and waiting to see what would happen next.

"Why don't we all go into the main conference room to try and discuss all of this rationally," LTL's general counsel said as courteously as he could, his deeply furrowed brow completely contradicting his attempts at magnanimity.

The crowd at the receptionist's station quickly scattered.

Misha, Marcus Means, and the attorneys all went into the main conference room, closed the doors and drew the blinds. Mostly, there was a rustling and review of papers by opposing attorneys as Misha defensively crossed her arms over her chest and silently fumed, waiting for some explanation for this massive ass-fuck she was currently getting. Marcus relished the moment.

"Are these your signatures?" Larger Than Lyfe's general counsel asked her.

Misha stared down at all of the signatures incredulously, unable to place in her mind when she had signed away her sister's record company to this monster.

"Yes," she answered finally, "but I swear to God that I do not remember signing a single one of these. He had to have drugged me to get me to sign some shit like this in the presence of a notary. This is all very, very wrong."

It was determined that Marcus Means did, in fact, now hold majority ownership of Larger Than Lyfe Entertainment…all 80 percent that had belonged to Misha Tierney, to be exact. A very underhanded "bargaining agreement" that he had orchestrated had accomplished this unimaginable feat. Misha wanted to grab the letter opener lying on the conference room table and plant it squarely in his jugular. Even for him, she could not believe what this asshole had gone and done.

Through God only knows what sources, Marcus Means had found out the full terms of Keshari Mitchell's will. He knew that 80 percent of the ownership of Larger Than Lyfe Entertainment was left to Misha and the remaining 20 percent were left to two other people who were executives at Larger Than Lyfe Entertainment, 10 percent for each of them respectively. This was pretty much public news and had been released by virtually all of entertainment media following Keshari Mitchell's death. Marcus had originally used this knowledge to coerce Misha into paying him ten points every month from Larger Than Lyfe Entertainment's revenues. Because Misha didn't want to have to answer to accounting for the regular, unexplained, and questionable payments, she'd simply been paying Marcus directly out of her own salary.

Since Keshari Mitchell had been the sole owner of Larger Than Lyfe Entertainment prior to her death, she'd had to do some restructuring on the financial/account-ing end so the breakdown of the company's worth could clearly be identified in "shares" that could be divided among the specifically named heirs in her will. Per the explicit terms in a special clause of her will, all of the shares of ownership of her company that she left to Misha Tierney, Andre DeJesus and Sharonda Richards were non-transferable. This was NOT public knowledge. If, at any time, any one or all of the heirs made the decision that they wanted to sell all or a portion of their shares, they could only sell these shares to David Weisberg. The shares could not be sold or transferred away to anyone except David Weisberg, which had been an extremely strange prospect to Marcus Means. It instantly sent up a red flag, one more confirmation for him that Keshari Mitchell was alive and well.

Now knowing the FULL terms of Keshari Mitchell's will, Marcus Means began to pay David Weisberg visits… increasingly regular visits…at his office, at his home and sometimes when he was out with his wife and friends… and, of course, Marcus brought his typical "Marcus Means swagger" with him when he came. Marcus Means coerced David Weisberg into drafting contracts that sold all of Misha Tierney's shares to David Weisberg. It was a single, mind-blowing transaction that could only be described as ROBBERY. Marcus got Misha to sign all of the needed contracts and no one would ever be able to understand how he'd managed to make that happen, but he had.

Unbeknownst to Misha, he'd given her a little "something" at the time of the contract signing to help coax things along in the right direction. When all was said and done, Marcus Means had wrangled 80 percent ownership of Larger Than Lyfe Entertainment right from under his soon-to-be ex-wife, and she never even knew what hit her. Per the signed contracts and official court documents, Marcus Means purchased majority ownership, all 80 percent of Misha Tierney's shares for only $35 million. Eighty percent of a $475 million record label had been sold for $35 million! It was the jack move of the millennium! And Marcus Means's people had handled all of the fine details to make sure everything fell nicely into place, including putting the transaction before a judge who would not heavily scrutinize the questions clearly present in this highly questionable deal.

David Weisberg would never be the same. He loved Keshari Mitchell like a daughter. Larger Than Lyfe Entertainment had been her life's blood, but Marcus Means had assured him that he would kill his entire family if he did not get what Marcus needed done quickly. It was all completely outrageous.

"How…how did this happen?" Misha asked in confusion.

"You helped him to do this?" Misha asked as she turned to stare down David Weisberg.

David Weisberg bowed his head in shame.

In all of her strategic planning, over all of the years that Keshari Mitchell had painstakingly researched and formulated a step-by-step "exit strategy" should things become too hot for her in L.A., perhaps Keshari had placed too much of her trust in David Weisberg because there was very little he could do now that Keshari was gone other than turn to law enforcement when a very real and very powerful gangster approached him with a list of "demands."

"I had absolutely no choice in this matter," he told Misha and Misha already knew before he said a thing that he didn't.

"Misha, I'm not attempting to overhaul this record label nor sabotage its success," Marcus said. "I would like for you to remain here as president. This decision to take over the record label was a financial one only. For now, everything will remain exactly as it currently is. The only thing that changes today is ownership. This is a thriving company and I would like to keep it that way. If it's any consolation, you, more than ever before, are a very rich woman. Thirty-five million dollars...completely liquid...have been deposited into your account at City National Bank as completion of this sales agreement."

The mention of City National Bank made Misha think briefly of the stolen diskettes. She was so livid that she was visibly shaking. Then she thought about it.

"But, wait a minute," she said. "We're still married. I am certain that there are laws in place in regard to married couples, property within a marriage and acquisitions of this kind."

Marcus chuckled. Marcus's attorney opened his brief-case and presented Misha with their prenuptial agreement.

"I think that it was YOU who absolutely insisted upon this thing," Marcus said. "In simple terms, it essentially says that what's mine is mine in this marriage and what's yours is yours, regardless of what is acquired or disposed of over the course of the marriage. You, for whatever reason that you did, sold your shares of Larger Than Lyfe Entertainment ownership to David Weisberg, who is the only person, per Keshari Mitchell's will, to whom the shares for Larger Than Lyfe Entertainment could be transferred or sold. Mr. Weisberg here agreed to sell the shares to me."

Misha was speechless. It didn't even surprise her that the very people representing well-known, perceived-to-be reputable business and financial entities had aided and abetted Marcus Means in carrying out this colossal stunt. People everywhere had a price and once that price was named, they'd do anything to collect payment.

"You can contest this," Larger Than Lyfe's general counsel quickly interjected. "I can get into court within an hour to get an immediate injunction keeping…uh… Mr. Means and his people out of here until we can clear this whole matter up…and I assure you, Misha, this mess is only temporary and can be set right. The mountain of questions shrouding this shady deal is sufficient enough to get an immediate injunction."

Marcus looked consolingly at Misha. Misha watched

him, reveling in his overwhelming self-importance and an arrogance so extreme that it was far worse than her brother's had ever been. Marcus had wanted to tell her that while she had been downing Silver Patrón like water for the entire two-year period of their marriage, trying to self-medicate the misery of having to be with him, he had been paving the way to accomplish a few goals of his own. He'd put the contracts in front of her, told her to sign them, and she had signed them…clearly without reading a single word of a single one of the documents that had been positioned underneath her pen. She could definitely contest the sale and a JUST judge would surely hear her case…and more than likely reverse the sale. But Marcus Means could tie her ass up in court on a whole host of technicalities for years if he so chose and do the shit just for fun, liking the tidy sum that he stood to make from ownership of Larger Than Lyfe Entertainment, but knowing full well he would be more than okay if he didn't make a thing off the record label and ownership was reverted right back to Misha…and Misha definitely knew this as well.

"I hate you!!!" Misha exclaimed, tears streaming down her face. "With every fiber of my soul, I hate you!"

She hopped up and, on four-and-a-half-inch Jimmy Choo heels, stormed out of the conference room with Larger Than Lyfe Entertainment's general counsel and David Weisberg chasing after her. She took the private elevator down to the garage to get to her car. She could barely breathe and she felt sure that she was about to hyperventilate or have some kind of panic attack. When she got into the car, she had to sit there for nearly an hour trying to get her bearings. She didn't even have the strength to try and make sense of what had just happened. Angry tears trickled down her cheeks as she started her Mercedes and drove away.

=43=

From another phone booth in Santa Monica, Misha contacted Thomas Hencken. She tried to inform him as best she could why she, unfortunately, would not be able to help him after all with his investigation. It was all entirely too dangerous and he, like she was about to do, should strongly consider leaving Marcus Means and The Consortium alone. Men like the men in The Consortium would continue to exist and conduct their business and traffic their drugs and make and launder their money no matter how many law enforcement agencies got involved to bring them down and no matter how many of them law enforcement killed or put behind bars. For every criminal enterprise taken down, Misha said, there would be two or three to replace it. Basically, Misha told Thomas Hencken, she just wanted her life back. She was sick and tired of having to live her life out on eggshells.

Misha told Thomas Hencken that she'd had something that she'd kept in a safety deposit box at the bank for years, diskettes that were highly incriminating to The Consortium's business and to other criminal organizations.

She told Thomas Hencken that she'd gone to the bank to retrieve these diskettes to give them to him and found that they were gone. She told Thomas Hencken that she knew beyond a shadow of a doubt that Marcus Means or someone in his employ had taken the diskettes. She didn't even know how he'd come to know she had them or how he'd discovered WHERE she had them. Misha then went on to tell Thomas Hencken about Marcus Means just taking over Larger Than Lyfe Entertainment.

"I know that what you continue to do comes from a good, benevolent place in your spirit, but Marcus Means is a very, very dangerous man. Surely, through your work with the DEA, you are abundantly aware by now of this man's track record. My brother was bad. It was you who told me yourself that Marcus Means is ten times worse.

"You're no longer with the DEA," Misha continued. "I know you are working alone. I'm sure that you have a family...children. Please let this whole thing go before you get yourself killed."

Thomas Hencken was solemnly quiet at the other end of the line for several moments before he responded.

"I am going to track that bastard until I put him behind bars for the rest of his life."

"Goodbye, Mr. Hencken," Misha said and hung up.

-44-

Misha went AWOL for more than a week after the sensational hostile takeover of Larger Than Lyfe Entertainment. Following the closed-door meeting in which Marcus Means had revealed how he had skillfully found a loophole to work through the special clauses in Keshari Mitchell's will to purchase all of the shares of stock that Misha Tierney owned, Misha grabbed her purse, stormed out of the offices, and disappeared. After the one, final call that she made to Thomas Hencken, she caught the first flight out of L.A. and went to Krishawn Webb's apartment in SoHo. She curled up in his huge bed and cried for days and days. Krishawn flew in as soon as he could after she called him. He was at her side doing all he could to console her. Whatever she wanted, he said, just tell him and he would get it for her. He, like everyone else in L.A., had watched the news and knew what had just gone down at Larger Than Lyfe Entertainment. The shit was crazy unreal…but much crazy unreal shit had certainly gone down behind the scenes in Larger Than Lyfe Entertainment's history. Now that Krishawn knew the secret about Larger Than Lyfe

Entertainment's founder and original owner, what Marcus Means had done was nothing in comparison. What he had done was done every single day by the average corporate raider.

The media coverage back in L.A. was ridiculous. There were discussions of Larger Than Lyfe Entertainment's future. There were news stories with captions noting "the end of an era in music history." There was discussion and speculation about whether or not Larger Than Lyfe Entertainment's superstar artists, Ntozake in particular, would leave the record label. Then, of course, there was discussion and massive speculation regarding why Misha had sold her shares of the record label. Most believed that she had been forced into the sale by her increasingly notorious, soon-to-be ex-husband, and that it had been as strategically orchestrated as their bizarre, almost three-year marriage.

"Keshari Mitchell must be turning over in her grave right about now," one news reporter on BET said.

Over the time that Misha hid away in Krishawn's loft in New York, she and Krishawn had long and very, very serious discussions about EVERYTHING. They talked for hours, sometimes late into the night. Krishawn provided an extremely objective point of view regarding her current predicament. They talked about the future and the future of the two of them together and how Misha's current situation with Marcus Means and Larger Than Lyfe Entertainment hinged so greatly on their future together. They talked about Krishawn's physical attack back in Los

Angeles when the two of them had hooked up at Ntozake's album release party. They even seriously discussed their wedding plans and what they wanted to do in that regard.

Krishawn truly, truly cared about what happened to Misha, and he listened to her and advised her in a way that was always in her best interest. Misha carefully digested all that was said over the days she spent with Krishawn away from the public, away from Marcus Means, away from Larger Than Lyfe Entertainment, away from the parasitic tentacles of media, and she ultimately decided what she would do next.

As much as Misha loved her best friend, Misha was now gladly giving up her position and role at Larger Than Lyfe Entertainment. She'd put her own company, her event planning firm, in second priority to run Keshari's record label because, for as long as she could remember, she had so loved her friend. She'd placed her own life on the line and in second priority to help and honor her best friend. Now it was time, just as Kris had suggested, to LET GO. She had done enough. No one anywhere could possibly question her undying friendship for Keshari Mitchell. No one could possibly blame her when she walked away.

When she returned to Los Angeles the following week, she was going back to her offices at MISHA TIERNEY and she was going to put her heart fully back into the work she positively loved at the company she herself had built from the ground up. Then she was going to get married.

-45-

Over the course of their days-long discussion, the one major issue that Krishawn and Misha seriously wondered about more than once was Marcus Means and what was under his sadistic sleeve that he had plans to do next. The one thing that was really, really crazy and more than a bit scary was the angle he had been taking in regard to Keshari Mitchell. Now that Krishawn knew that Keshari was still alive, he and Misha talked a lot more openly about her and what could potentially happen to her if she was still in the United States. What Krishawn and Misha absolutely could not understand was why Marcus Means had threatened to murder David Weisberg and, likely, his entire family in order to take control of Larger Than Lyfe Entertainment. He had threatened David Weisberg so seriously and to such a degree that David Weisberg had quickly complied with all of Marcus's demands, but Marcus had NOT used the same tactics over the last three years to find out the whereabouts of Keshari Mitchell, who he had made crystal clear to Misha he knew was still alive. Part of the reason he had forced

Misha into marrying him was so he could keep the closest possible tabs on her in hopes of locating Keshari Mitchell through her…or perhaps that was just what he had been leading Misha to believe while he machinated to take over Larger Than Lyfe Entertainment.

Something was up. That was for sure. What was he waiting for? Why hadn't Marcus Means gone after her yet? And, because it was clear she wanted absolutely nothing else to do with The Consortium and was not looking to blow the whistle on any of its players or associates, why was Marcus so hell-bent on finding Keshari Mitchell?

The truth was, if Marcus Means or any other gangster of any serious level of substance wanted to find Keshari, no matter how smart she was, Keshari would have been found by now and she would be very, very dead.

Sick fuck that Marcus Means was, perhaps he was toying with them all and saving the best for last…locating Keshari Mitchell and craftily eliminating her…and there was no doubt that there was something in it that Marcus Means intended to gain by NOT locating and killing Keshari Mitchell right now.

-46-

The production of *LARGE* was now three weeks into filming, and all was progressing very nicely. There had been some "strategic" leaks made to the press and there was already some positive buzz around the film industry regarding the shooting of the movie. The lead actress was performing phenomenally. She had talked to people who'd known Keshari Mitchell, both personally and professionally, so that she could get a better feel for her role. She talked to Misha Tierney. She talked to Mars Buchanan. She had studied everything she could about Keshari Mitchell, even the amazing photo spread of Keshari in *Vogue* magazine, and she nailed the complex mix of softness, refinement, femininity, a woman who was intensely private and possessed an almost masculine level of sheer drive and aggressiveness in the business arena that were all part of the makeup that was Keshari Mitchell.

The on-screen chemistry between the lead actress and Boris Kodjoe made you BELIEVE the love was real watching the footage of the two of them together in the dailies. They terrifically "put down the job" in their love scenes as well as when they were alone together in scenes, being close with one another. Every touch, every glance—that "something" you cannot even begin to explain that powerfully links two people together in love—was all there. It was as if the two actors had spent time with the real Keshari Mitchell and Mars Buchanan to get a feel for what their romantic relationship had been like.

Lisa Raye had definitely been a shoo-in for the role of Misha Tierney. Their physical resemblance was very strong, and then Lisa Raye also had the same fierce combination of "hot girl from the 'hood" mixed with the no-nonsense regality, poise and refinement of a contemporary queen that was definitely, definitely Misha Tierney. All of the actors who had been cast in the film production were the most ideal selections.

Overall, Darian was absolutely loving the filmmaking process. She loved viewing the dailies after a day of shooting and knowing what elements needed to be addressed in editing. After more than two years of isolation in Brazil, she loved the overall interaction with the actors, with her director, with her new associate producer, with the rest of the production crew, and with her associates at Warner Bros. Pictures.

In the very beginning, it felt weird as she watched the dailies containing very real segments of what had once been her life. What she was revealing in *LARGE* was that, while she was in Pennsylvania acquiring a Masters degree with honors in Business Administration from the Wharton School of Business, she had been flying back and forth to the West Coast regularly, helping to pay for her very expensive advanced degree by moving million-dollar shipments of cocaine. *LARGE* would blow the minds of people because it vividly depicted how diligently Keshari Mitchell worked all day every day to keep her two lives completely separate from each other—her life as a record executive at a record label that she started and grew into a major multimillion-dollar enterprise and the life she eventually wanted to walk completely away from as a powerful figure in organized crime. She even showed how Keshari Mitchell had made the media back down toward the beginning of her career when some renegade reporters asserted that Larger Than Lyfe Entertainment was a front for drug money. Her attorneys threatened several well-known news and entertainment magazine entities with massive lawsuits if they did not put an end to their nasty speculations. Then Rick Tresvant had someone in his employ pay a "special visit" to someone in a power position in media and it had been sufficient enough to establish an immediate media "gag rule" all around Keshari. There'd be no more talk in the press about Keshari Mitchell and organized crime…and there hadn't been.

Darian knew that Keshari Mitchell could never come back from the death that she'd faked, so Darian could put it all out there in regards to what Keshari Mitchell's life had been like...the TRUTH of it all. *LARGE* was highly revealing in more ways than one and was bound to be a topic of discussion for a long time.

Darian had not received any more threatening calls following that single call she'd received on her Black-Berry on the first day of filming, but she should have expected that this was the calm before the storm because things went awry immediately after that twenty-first day of filming.

First, it was the news stories that were virtually every-where regarding the takeover of Larger Than Lyfe Enter-tainment by Marcus Means. When Darian heard the news regarding the sale of Larger Than Lyfe Entertainment to Marcus Means, she passed out on the set and shooting stopped momentarily while medics worked to revive her. When she came to, the on-set medics strongly advised her to go home and take it easy for the rest of the day. They also advised her to make an appointment as soon as possible to see her primary care physician to make sure that she was okay. She could answer that question for herself. She was for damned sure NOT okay. What in the fuck was going on?!

When Mars heard the shocking news regarding the majority share of Larger Than Lyfe Entertainment being sold to Marcus Means, his mind went reeling like everyone else's in the entertainment industry. How had Misha allowed this to happen? What was going on? He also quickly went into damage control mode, because he had clients who were currently under contract with Larger Than Lyfe and his firm's job was to protect their interests. Grabbing his laptop, pair of briefcases and iPhone, he told Chris Winters, his assistant, that he was taking the rest of the day off and he went directly to Darian's Hollywood Hills home to wait for her, regardless of how late it was going to be before she got home.

Knowing Darian as well as he did, he already knew she had not taken the news well at all about the changes at her record label. Sure enough, she arrived home shortly after he arrived and she looked like the end of the world had hit her.

"THAT's why that bastard forced Misha into marrying him!" Darian exploded angrily.

"Just be glad his central focus does not appear to be on YOU right now. But, you do know that it is only a matter of time before you are the central focus, right? You need to have your game plan in place for when that time comes around. I'm with you…whatever you want to do."

"I know," Darian responded.

Darian returned to the set of filming the following day and threw herself into the production of *LARGE* like never before. She had always been a workaholic, but she kicked it up a notch after finding out that her beloved record label had been sold to Marcus Means. She was on set from the start of filming until the very end every single day. When shooting wrapped for the day, she often conducted meetings that accompanied the viewing of the dailies to go over notes she'd made over the course of the day's shoot. She made Hype Williams as well as the rest of the production crew and actors earn every penny of their money. It was as if throwing herself deeper into her work at Phoenix Films would somehow drown out her thoughts of Larger Than Lyfe. And, of course, her over-zealous immersion in her work pulled her farther away from her husband…as if their regular schedules had not done enough of that already. Mars began to find it harder and harder to make contact with Darian, and Darian, most of the time, seemed oblivious to the fact that she was grossly neglecting her husband. He would call her BlackBerry and she wouldn't answer. He would text her repeatedly and sometimes it would be hours or even the next day before she responded. Where Darian and Mars had previously been committed since their return to the United States and the starting of their new and separate careers to setting aside at least two days out of every week to be together with their phones turned off and no work to interrupt, they now were lucky when the two of them could successfully coordinate a few minutes together once a week on the telephone. It was bound to be a recipe for disaster. Mars knew that her recent behavior, throwing herself into her work the way that she was, was in direct response to the takeover of Larger Than Lyfe so that she did not have to think about it, but they could NOT continue to go on in this way.

On one particular day after Mars had tried on as much patience and understanding as he could stand, he finally decided that enough was enough, and it was beyond time that both he and Darian made time in their schedules to address the fact that they had both routed their marriage to second priority for their careers, and a change was needed IMMEDIATELY. Mars called Darian's cell phone. No answer. He hung up and called her number again. He still got no answer, only her voicemail.

Mars called Darian's assistant at Phoenix Films. He still laughed at the fact that she had brazenly gone and hired the same executive assistant who had been her assistant at Larger Than Lyfe Entertainment. How she'd managed that feat, Mars would never know. Terrence Henderson had just left for lunch, and the receptionist didn't know any of the details regarding Darian's whereabouts, nor why she would rush to help to locate Darian for the abrasive, frustrated man on the other end of the line. Mars was so fucking tired of having to constantly go on scavenger hunts to find his goddamned wife! He slammed down the phone.

When Mars composed himself enough, he called Darian's

BlackBerry one final time and left a message: "You had better decide right away what is most important to you, or you're going to lose the very thing you said meant the world to you."

At the same time that that voicemail message was being left, Darian received three back-to-back text messages with threats. Then she received another of those threatening phone calls, both on her BlackBerry and at the offices of Phoenix Films—"BITCH, I'm tellin' you for the last time, if that movie makes it to theaters, you are a DEAD BITCH!" Right after that, an electrical fire broke out on the set. What the fuck was going on?!

-47-

Word on the street had it that Marcus Means was behind the murders of both Jermaine "Slim J" Jackson and Devante "Big D" Johnson. True enough, Marcus had definitely killed Big D, but he'd had nothing at all to do with Slim J's murder. It was intensely ironic that Marcus Means was now being pinned with a body that he didn't really lay down, accused of a murder that he did not commit. Word on the street had it that Marcus Means had had an ulterior motive for inviting other set leaders into The Consortium. Word on the street had it that Marcus Means had had intentions of taking all of the set leaders out, one by one, in order to make it easier to move into and take over their territory in his mission to expand The Consortium.

Leon "Big Bree-Z" Poussant was the first person to open his ears and give some credence to the information that was circulating on the streets. He called an unofficial side meeting with the other Consortium members to find out if they'd heard any of what he'd been hearing.

"Dread," leader of R3Crips, had been hearing similar

stories.

"I'm about ready to collect a prorated payout on my $1.5 million and chock this shit up as a hard knocks education for a G," Big Bree-Z said candidly.

Bree-Z had been feeling that something was "off" with Marcus for weeks and he'd been seriously thinking about cutting his losses with the new Consortium and going back to running his set the old-fashioned way. The word had been out on Marcus's shady ass for a long time, but the money that they all stood to make as members of The Consortium momentarily overshadowed all of that… until shit started happening.

"Hold up," Dread said philosophically. "Don't make any final decisions yet. Chill for a minute…and WATCH. I've got a feeling that Marc's luck is about to run out."

"How you know that?" Bree-Z asked.

"Come on. You can't make shit get this deep out here in these streets and not have to pay the price for it. What Marcus outlined for us to get us seriously interested in joining The Consortium is exactly the shit we can have. Right now, we just have to be patient."

-48-

A total of three unexplained fires broke out on the set, one of the supporting actors came down with a violent case of food poisoning, a very expensive camera had somehow been stolen from the set, and the threatening phone calls and text messages increased. Darian discussed the matter with Warner Bros. executives, and security was immediately tripled on the set. A security team was also hired for Darian, accompanying her to Warner Bros. and all other locations of the shoot, and accompanying her home. For a few days, the increased security made things extremely tense on the set and time was lost as segments of the filming had to be reshot again and again. Darian finally called a meeting of the full production crew and all of the actors following shooting on the last day of their sixth week. She was very candid with all of them, expressing her thanks for them working so hard on the production. She also expressed to them that they remember the controversy of the subject matter with which the film dealt. There were very likely specific entities in Los Angeles and elsewhere who did not want to see the movie reach completion in filming nor get released in theaters. Darian assured all of them that Phoenix Films and Warner Bros. Pictures were doing everything in their power to ensure their safety.

The next day, shooting resumed and the air was cleared and they got back on schedule. Darian was glad. Off schedule meant over budget, and she was definitely not having that. She'd listened to the voicemail that her husband had left for her. Unfortunately, with all of the calamity and unexpected problems occurring on the set, she had been so overwhelmed with work that three days had passed since he'd left the message. She decided she would surprise him, make a small sacrifice where work was concerned, and give him her undivided attention.

The last and most important meeting on the agenda for the day was Mars's and Kevin Sperrington's meeting with Ntozake to decide whether or not she would stay on at Larger Than Lyfe Entertainment now that Marcus Means was at the helm. With the drastic recent change in ownership and management over at the record label, they needed to carefully discuss what Ntozake wanted to do, and if it was in her best interest to stay on at Larger Than Lyfe Entertainment. Mars, of course, had his personal feelings about the situation. He felt that Ntozake should immediately begin considering other record labels. Marcus Means was the scum of the fucking earth, and eventually everyone who remained at the record label once he fully took over was going to wind up dirty too. Nonetheless, from a professional standpoint, he had to consider ALL of the factors above and beyond his personal perspective about the matter.

There was much in the works for Ntozake over at LTL. That was for sure. She had a major concert tour kicking off early the next year. They would soon be shooting a mini-movie music video for her new album, which was also very major—no female artist had ever done it. LTL was pulling out all the stops both financially and creatively in terms of producers and songwriters for her much-anticipated second album, and the record label, because she was their premier artist, would definitely do the same with the third. She was moving a very notable number of units and held the number one slot at the record label. With the way she was being catered to, it was a hard thing to just pick up and walk away from because she may not receive the same high level of catering at another record label.

Regardless of the sadistic criminal asshole that rumors around Los Angeles painted Marcus Means out to be, he had taken over Larger Than Lyfe Entertainment to turn a profit, and catering to the needs and career of its premier artist would certainly help to keep Larger Than Lyfe Entertainment in a very profitable position. Ntozake decided to stay at LTL, and a brief statement regarding her decision was immediately released via her publicist to the media.

"Man, you okay?" Kevin Sperrington asked after they'd wrapped the meeting and he'd gotten Ntozake off to the airport. She was laying a track with "The Hova," Jay-Z, for her new album, *Life and Times of a Superstar.*

Mars had been completely distracted throughout their meeting and that was completely out of character for him.

"Yeah, I'm good," Mars said unconvincingly.

"If you wanna talk about it, I got a full bar in my office," Kevin joked.

Mars chuckled.

"Yeah, okay, man," he said, then agitatedly went back to checking the messages on his iPhone.

Kevin Sperrington packed up and left for the day.

Chris Winters had noticed how distracted Mars had seemed all day as well, and he was still there in his office when virtually everyone else was gone, attempting to focus and get some work accomplished.

"Mars," Chris said, leaning her head into his office.

No response.

"Mars!" Chris said again, finally jarring Mars's attention.

"Are you okay?" she asked, coming into the office and taking a seat on the corner of his desk.

Mars rubbed his bald head in frustration.

"Yeah," he lied. "Just got a lot on my mind. Probably need to be heading home to get some sleep."

"You want to talk about it? All that's on your mind, I mean. I might be able to help."

A woman with a plan can manipulate a man like nobody's business. She'll say what he needs to hear with the most impeccable timing. She'll appear to be exactly the support that he needs when he feels that his needs are being neglected by everybody else. She'll do every one of those little, seemingly insignificant things that make him feel special, particularly at a moment when he's not feeling so special, and then BAM! Mars didn't even know what hit him until it was too late. Chris Winters had been into him from the very beginning and she had been biding her time. She knew Mars was romantically involved with someone…obviously, quite seriously…but she, like everyone else, had no idea that he was married, and she knew that whoever it was who was in his life was clearly slipping lately…which was all the better for her.

Mars looked up at her. She had that look in her eye. He felt a whole complicated mix of feelings. Mostly, he felt lonely for a woman who couldn't seem to find it within herself to give him her undivided attention for a few fucking minutes of her day. He unbuttoned her blouse and, before he could fully wrap his mind around the whole concept of restraint and honoring the vows of his marriage, he was fucking Chris Winters from behind. Her skirt was pushed up high around her waist and the tiny thong that he had ripped off of her lay like a broken rubber band on the corner of his desk. He pounded her like a man who was thirsty and she was ice-cold water. Just as he was about to climax, the double doors to his office swung open.

"Oh," was all that Darian could muster as she stood there, mortified, staring at her beloved husband with an over-amplified look of shock registered on his face, his expensive trousers around his ankles, and his dick still inside some woman who most definitely was not his wife in the dimly-lit office.

Darian slammed the doors shut again and rushed for the elevators, tears streaming down her face. Mars didn't even come after her.

-49-

Darian didn't even know how she made it home. Everything was a blur after that. She sat in her dark bedroom for hours smoking a cigar and thinking. She wondered if she had been placing entirely too much pressure on Mars, demanding entirely too much from this man who loved her. I mean, think about it. The two of them were MARRIED, but they both had to act as if they were NOT married. They both had to act as if they didn't really know each other when they knew each other better than anyone else had ever known them. It was all so ridiculous. There was absolutely nothing normal or healthy about it. It was absurd, as absurd as the double life she had tried to live as Keshari Mitchell.

The clocked ticked away and Darian got up, having not gotten a single wink of sleep, and mechanically showered, dressed, had coffee, and then waited for her car to arrive to take her to the studio. She was quiet and seemingly highly distracted the entire day, which was completely out of character for the woman who the production crew had been getting to know. To them, she was typically tough as nails, a workhorse, enjoying her job and giving her input all day. Today, she just felt numb and could not wait for shooting to wrap for the day so she could go home and crawl into bed. Fortunately, it was the weekend, so the film crew would have the next two days off.

Back at the office, Terrence was finalizing travel arrangements for Darian and her associate producer to attend the Sundance, Tribeca, and Cannes Film Festivals the following year. Even though it was months away, both Darian and Michael Chastang, her associate producer, had been tremendously excited about the film festivals. They'd sat in the Craft Services area during the first couple of weeks of filming, sharing coffee, turkey bacon and croissants, and discussing the festivals and the tremendous potential there was for them to acquire Phoenix Films' next movie projects.

Terrence contacted Darian once all the trip plans were finalized to give her a heads-up. He immediately sensed Darian's mood and knew instantly that it had something to do with a man.

"You wanna talk about it, babe?"

"Not right now," Darian responded.

"Well, I'm letting you know that I'm here whenever

you need me…and you can talk about it and cry about for as long as you want."

"Thank you, T.," Darian said quietly.

Terrence hung up the phone with an extremely quizzical expression on his face. No one had called him "T." since Keshari Mitchell's passing. As a matter of fact, Keshari Mitchell had been the only person to regularly call him "T."

-50-

The very first day of the following week of shooting, there was another bizarre occurrence that had a connection to the filming of *LARGE*. As was typical of the production schedule, the entire production crew and actors took the weekend off. Then, on Monday, when everyone returned to work, one of the cameramen didn't show up on the set. He had been reported missing by his family the day before. He'd left the set on Friday and never came home. On the local ABC News, his family appealed to the public for help in finding him. There was a number to the police department for the public to call in with any information they had about his whereabouts or where they had last seen him. Everyone who knew him stated that it was completely out of character for him to be gone even for a few hours without someone, usually his wife, knowing where he was. He wasn't currently going through any kind of personal problems that would cause him to disappear. He didn't abuse alcohol or drugs. He had no enemies to the best of his family's knowledge.

The difficult part about the situation was that production had to continue despite the fact that one of their people was missing. They had to continue to work to maintain schedule and stay within budget. A new cameraman was quickly put into place and shooting continued. Darian personally contacted the family of the missing cameraman to let them know that they and the cameraman were in her thoughts and prayers. She told them that if they needed any assistance whatsoever, even financial assistance, to help locate the missing cameraman, to contact her directly.

The cameraman was eventually located two weeks after the search for him commenced, a week after the filming of *LARGE* had wrapped. He was on the Las Vegas strip sitting at a city bus stop, and he'd had some kind of mental breakdown. How he'd gotten to Las Vegas was a mystery. What happened to him from the time he had been reported missing until he was found was also a mystery. Police attempted to question him once he had been located, and he could not seem to remember a thing, not even the fact that he had been working on the film production of *LARGE* immediately before he disappeared.

-51-

Two weeks passed from that fateful night when Mars had been discovered by his wife in a very…um… compromising position, and Mars called every single day throughout the day in an attempt to talk to Darian. High-powered attorney that he was, representing some of the biggest names in the music and film industries, he had no idea what he was going to say to her. I mean, what exactly could he say when he'd been caught, literally, with his pants down? Whatever the case, even if he did know what he wanted to say, Darian refused to take a single one of his calls. Mars even courageously rode the elevator downstairs to Darian's office a couple of times to try and see her, and Terrence, her assistant, politely told him she was not there or she was unavailable both times that he'd come.

Mars texted Darian's BlackBerry time and time again. It felt like he must have sent her a thousand messages. He sent her e-mail. But, over the course of all of that, he did not receive a single response. He drove up to the Hollywood Hills house. He let himself in. She was not there…even when he waited all night. NOTHING.

Then, out of the blue, she called him.

"Do you want a divorce?" she asked plainly.

"Is that what you want?" Mars responded.

There was silence for a very long time at the other end of the line.

"I don't know," Darian said finally and hung up the phone.

A few days passed and Mars called Darian on her Black-Berry.

"Do you want a divorce?" he asked.

"No," Darian responded.

"Can I see you?"

"Yes."

"I'll come up to the house...seven this evening. Is that okay?"

"Yes," Darian answered.

-52-

That first night when Mars came up to the house, the two of them sat in silence across from one another in their contemporary living room, so close to one another physically, but a million miles apart. Never in a million years would Darian have ever believed that the kind of love that she shared with Mars Buchanan would ever come to infidelity. She knew how special what the two of them shared was, and Mars certainly knew too. What the two of them had been through together in a relatively short period of time, most people would NEVER go through, even if they'd been together for years and years. Theirs was definitely no ordinary love. But, if she knew how special it was, how had she so easily taken it for granted? She'd compromised it all for the sake of her career. She was in no need for money. Why did she still drive herself so damned hard? It was just as both she and Mars said time and time again. She still had more money after escaping her former life than she would ever need in this lifetime and the next, and she could more than afford to live well in both. Perhaps she had been self-sabotaging, throwing herself relentlessly and recklessly into her work at the expense of her marriage to punish herself. It had nothing to do with Mars. She loved him more than anything or anyone else in the world. It had everything to do with her. She was frequently having nightmares about or contemplating privately about the whole construct of "redemption." Perhaps, subconsciously, she didn't feel like she deserved the kind of happiness that was possible with Mars after the life that she'd lived before.

A single tear trickled down her cheek and she got up, went upstairs, and got into her bed. Mars followed her. Without undressing, he kicked off his shoes and climbed into bed with her. He wrapped his arms around her and Darian did not fight him. Moments later, he felt her shaking as she sobbed. He held her tighter. They fell asleep in this way. There were no clear-cut answers yet as to whether they'd stay together.

The next day, the filming of *LARGE* wrapped.

-53-

When you've got $1 million worth of 80 percent pure cocaine that just got jacked from one of your processing houses, you can be absolutely sure of one thing: SOMEBODY'S GOT TO PAY!

Marcus Means didn't even consult the other Consortium members when he put up a $1 million bounty for every one of the motherfuckers who bomb-rushed the Compton processing house. That is, he put up $1 million for each head directly involved in the robbery of The Consortium's cocaine. If six people were directly involved, $6 million would be paid for ALL of their heads. Marcus wanted to know who they were and where they were, and he himself would take care of the rest.

Because of the unheard of size of the bounty, Marcus thought he'd receive an almost instantaneous response, but nobody was biting. Even more important than the gigantic sum of cocaine that had been stolen, which would be valued at well over $1 million once it was cut and processed to The Consortium's clients' specifications, Marcus needed to quickly take care of this problem looming over his head before that videotape made it into the wrong hands.

While Marcus Means had been constantly bad-mouthing Rick Tresvant, saying Rick had gone "soft" and "corporate" and had died because of it, the one thing Marcus needed to recognize was that Richard Tresvant had come into the game smarter than most and he had carefully "studied" and gotten smarter and smarter over the course of his career. Never had The Consortium ever had the level of financial loss…product loss…as when the Compton processing house was robbed… not when Richard Tresvant ran The Consortium. Nobody disrespected Richard Tresvant in a way that they robbed Consortium stash houses.

Where Marcus believed in ruling the streets with intimidation and bloodshed, Rick Tresvant was, in a lot of ways, a "gentleman's gangster," the end of a dying breed. He ruled with the unparalleled intelligence of his mind and strong alliances with some of the most powerful men in the nation. When a "blueblood" White man from a highly revered, Camelot-like family background testified in court in his defense during his murder trial, you came to know the kind of respect that Richard Lawrence Tresvant got and the kind that he gave. Marcus didn't have anything close to that. Marcus had been quickly burning bridges Rick Tresvant had maintained for years all over town. Sure, there were a few people who knew exactly who had robbed the Compton stash house, but they weren't telling Marcus Means shit, and they didn't care if he doubled the bounty that he currently had out. The rules of the streets were funny like that. Even drug dealers and assassins had a code. It was like the code that was always enforced when a rapist or child molester went to prison— you rape a woman or a child, you're gonna get raped. Street code was being enforced against Marcus Means.

-54-

If an asshole like Marcus Means had in his possession the surveillance tape that had been taken from the security office of 300 South Grand on the night of Phinnaeus Bernard III's murder, where would said asshole keep this possibly incriminating tape? That was the question that Thomas Hencken asked himself over and over again.

If someone wanted to find out the identity of the mystery person who had, from a pay phone in South Central Los Angeles, supplied LAPD with valuable information that had led them to secure a warrant to find the murder weapon that had killed Phinnaeus Bernard III in Richard Tresvant's home and, later, secure a first-degree murder conviction, how would someone go about doing that?

Also, suppose the murder weapon had been a plant? Was that even possible? And who would have access to Richard Tresvant's home to plant the murder weapon if it had been a plant? And why would someone work so diligently to set Richard Tresvant up? And HOW had Richard Tresvant's fingerprints wound up all over the murder weapon, if, indeed, it had been a plant? It would have taken a very highly sophisticated "set-up" campaign to accomplish that.

Thomas Hencken received partial answer to some of his pressing questions when a padded envelope with no return address was hand delivered to his home by a courier service owned by the entity that had specifically chosen to send the very incriminating contents of the package to him. He turned the package over in his hands a couple of times to inspect it before he opened it. Inside the envelope was a videotape and, for a moment, Thomas Hencken held it suspiciously in his hands as if it was a bomb.

He went over to his VCR and plugged in the videotape and pressed play.

At the bottom of the screen, was the caption "300 SOUTH GRAND SECURITY." Thomas Hencken could absolutely NOT believe what he was seeing.

The male figure strolling across the garage to Phinnaeus Bernard's Mercedes was undeniable. It was Marcus Means. His shoulder-length, dreadlocked hair was pulled back in a knot, but after zooming in and fixing the quality of the picture, there was no doubt about the identity of the person captured in the footage. Marcus Means got into the rear of the car directly behind Phinnaeus Bernard's driver seat. After zooming in and fixing the picture quality, a positive identification could be made of corporate attorney Phinnaeus Bernard III in the driver's seat. You looked even closer and there appeared to be something held near Phinnaeus Bernard III's head. Thomas Hencken had no doubt that it was a gun. Once he got with the police, they would be able to enlarge and greatly improve the picture quality with their far more sophisticated equipment. The video footage showed the silver Mercedes backing out of its regular, reserved parking space, and, apparently, driving to a lower level in the parking structure…to Phinnaeus Bernard III's death. The time stamps on the video footage placed Marcus Means inside Phinnaeus Bernard III's car at the time of Phinnaeus Bernard III's murder.

If there was such a thing as justice and fairness in the universe, the wheels of that justice must have been turning rapidly right at that very moment. Finally, Marcus Means was about to be taken down.

-55-

For the past couple weeks, media rumors had it that Misha Tierney was putting a stop to her "ginormous" wedding plans to NBA star Krishawn Webb to make a strategically orchestrated escape from L.A., just the two of them, to get married in complete privacy. Darian smiled to herself when she read a small piece online about Misha's supposed plans to elope. If the celebrity news story was true, Darian fully understood the way that Misha must be feeling right now, particularly after the hostile takeover of Larger Than Lyfe Entertainment.

True enough, Misha absolutely wanted a much-needed break from "CelebrityVille." She was sick of having every part of her personal business tracked, disseminated, and analyzed by some highly invasive motherfucker in media, and then served up to the public. She wanted to go someplace exclusive and secluded, just her and her man, and get married before God and a pack of seagulls or sea turtles and no damned body else. She didn't need one second of media coverage to validate her getting married to the man she loved. She wanted a beautiful dress, and she wanted to see her gorgeous, soon-to-be husband in a beautiful tuxedo. She wanted some sunshine, some sand, a lotta water, some wedding cake, and some good champagne. She wanted to "slow wine" with Kris someplace tropical under the stars with the waves of tropical water lapping against the shore and the sheer peace of privacy all around them, and she didn't need anything else. And what she wanted, Krishawn Webb quickly made happen.

Marcus, of course, had now made the decision to prolong the proceedings toward finalizing their divorce for as much as he could. He avoided calls from her attorney. He lagged on needed paperwork to the courts. He loved the idea of toying with Misha just because he could… and because he knew that she wanted to immediately get married to Krishawn Webb.

That son of a bitch was going to drive Misha completely fucking insane. While Misha made calls to her attorney to find some loophole to immediately finalize the divorce to this asshole she despised, Krishawn called in some attorneys of his own and he made it crystal clear that Misha needed a finalized divorce from this monster who had forced her into marriage in the first place YESTERDAY! It was all easier than they had assumed. Misha's and Marcus's marriage had never been consummated, and Krishawn said he did not care if he had to pay off the judge. They needed a prompt annulment, and they needed it right now. And it was done…without Krishawn having to pay off anyone except his attorneys. Misha was ecstatic. Krishawn wanted her happy.

The very next day, Misha had personal shoppers come to the Pacific Palisades house. From sunglasses to sandals to swimsuits to her beautiful wedding gown, she got all of the things she liked and wanted to take on their trip. Krishawn didn't even tell her where they were going. He told her to pack for the tropics. She trusted him implicitly, and the two of them loaded onto a private plane headed for their secret destination.

Paparazzi and entertainment media could smell that something was brewing. They had been watching the comings and goings of one delivery van after another heading through the gates of the ultra-exclusive community where Misha and Krishawn now resided together, their destination Misha and Krishawn's home. They'd captured photographs of Misha going into celebrity cake maker Sylvia Weinstock's in New York, where she spent approximately three hours with Sylvia Weinstock herself designing her wedding cake. Just prior to the two of them leaving Los Angeles on their top-secret trip, Krishawn had gifted Misha with a customized 2011 Bentley Continental GTC Speed in aquamarine. Clearly, LOVE was in the air, and the million-dollar engagement ring had not been enough. Press contacted Krishawn's as well as Misha's publicists to see if they could get an official comment, any new information regarding Krishawn's and Misha's pending nuptials. They came up empty. Both Krishawn and Misha were absolutely determined they were going to keep their plans private, and everyone in both their camps were working around the clock to help the two of them maintain complete secrecy. When their private plane took off from LAX, though, there was a band of paparazzi boarding a plane too. It was crazy what the media would do to be the FIRST to put juicy photos or a story in front of the public. And one of the very first stories that hit the covers of all of the major tabloids was the fact that, against the advice of legal counsel, Krishawn Webb was marrying the woman he loved without a pre-nuptial agreement.

Two weeks later, the couple returned to Los Angeles from Turtle Island in Fiji. They'd spent two magnificent weeks in "Vonu Point," a premium *bure* or traditional Fijian hut-like cottage, where there was no one within 500 yards of them all around. They were treated to some of the very best tropical amenities in the world. They snorkeled, they went horseback riding, they got massages, they talked and talked and talked, and they made love. There was lots of lovemaking.

Misha had wanted to get away from it ALL for a minute with the one person in the world who meant everything to her, and just take a bit of time to BREATHE without the press breathing down her back while she did it. Krishawn had taken care of everything else, and the time away had been exactly what she had needed. She could not wait for the opportunity to do it again, perhaps after basketball season wrapped.

Upon their return to Los Angeles, photos were released to the media by Krishawn's and Misha's public relations representatives that they'd had professionally taken while on the island, and the couple looked absolutely amazing. They were married on the sand at Turtle Island just as Mars and Darian had been, and that irony certainly didn't get past Darian as she smiled and cried at all of the beautiful photos that were displayed in *People* magazine and *Ebony*.

Misha wore an absolutely exquisite Vera Wang "Francesca" mermaid gown and Krishawn wore a custom Ozwald Boateng tux. They were both tanned and smiling and HAPPY. Darian was so, so glad for them. She had complicated Misha's life enough and she would probably never get completely past the guilt of having done so.

The first major project on Misha's agenda upon her return to Los Angeles from Fiji was the after-party for the movie premiere of *LARGE*. Misha was looking forward to it. She was glad to be back full-time, doing the work she absolutely loved at her company, MISHA TIERNEY. Darian had hired Misha Tierney's event planning firm to coordinate all of the arrangements for the fabulous, no-expense-spared after-party, and she had specified that she work only with Misha Tierney herself for this particular event. A few weeks before, representatives at Misha's firm had put together all of the arrangements for the spectacular "wrap" party that Phoenix Films had thrown at the renowned "The Backyard" at the W Hotel in Westwood for all of *LARGE*'s production crew and cast, and the party had been off the hook. Darian carried a hangover for nearly two days after she and Terrence got falling-down drunk on tequila shots and "Blow Jobs." The fun they all had that night was unreal. They unwound after more than two and a half months of filming like college kids after final exams.

This time around, the after-party, immediately following the premiere of *LARGE*, was taking place at Drai's Hollywood located at the W Hotel in Hollywood. For two days, Darian and Misha sat together, laughing and chatting amiably, going over details and menus, and the entire time Darian had wanted to say something, some small thing that only she and Misha had shared that might reveal to Misha who she was. But that was such a selfish notion, she thought, every time she had the urge to do it. Hadn't she placed her best friend in the face of enough danger, enough stress, enough sadness and enough pain? Misha had just gotten married. She looked so, so happy. The energy coming from her was happy and light and peaceful. There was not a single day of any week that went by that Darian didn't think of her sister, her best friend, in some way and pray that she was okay, and she wondered if Misha ever thought about her. Of course, she did, and Darian knew that Misha hurt for her best friend in the same way that she hurt for Misha.

NO, she was not going to do anything to divulge to Misha who she was. It was probably best that Misha believed she was a world away, in another country, someplace safe. But her heart broke more than once as she sat there, wanting to reach out and hug her best friend, and couldn't.

-56-

As the new president and controlling interest of Larger Than Lyfe Entertainment, Marcus decided to make use of one of the perks of his job. It was time that he got out and matriculated with other movers and shakers in the music and film industries. He needed to do a bit of self-promotion to clean up the negative image that he'd been painted with around town. He was just a businessman trying to turn a profit. He decided to attend the red-carpet premiere of *LARGE*, that movie about Keshari Mitchell that was being advertised all over the place.

Marcus's secretary secured a pair of VIP passes for him to attend the premiere, and the passes had been delivered to Marcus's office that morning. He was going to walk the red carpet alongside the likes of Lisa Rayc, Will Smith, Samuel L. Jackson and his wife, and all of those other "Hollywood" types. Marcus chuckled to himself at the thought of it—lots of hand-shaking, fake-ass grinning by plastic-ass people, and the flashbulbs of too many cameras. It would make for a nice little field trip.

He suited up, his secretary ordered him a limo, and the limousine arrived to pick him up from Larger Than Lyfe Entertainment's offices in Century City on the evening of the premiere. The traffic was going to be horrible along Hollywood Boulevard because of the premiere, so they were getting an early start.

Portia was seated in the rear of the chauffeured Maybach, her Narciso Rodriguez wrap dress hiked up over her amazing, mile-high legs, her legs spread open, and her pantyless crotch on full and tantalizing display for Marcus when he got into the car.

He chuckled to himself and shook his head. He knew who she was. He'd heard stories about the crazy bitch she was. He could vividly remember the news story about her sneaking onto Keshari Mitchell's highly secured, private property in an attempt to break into Keshari's home over some dude.

With a remote control, Marcus rolled open the curtained and glass-walled partition that separated him from his driver.

"Who is this bitch?" Marcus asked the driver.

"She said she was your date, sir," the driver responded.

Marcus closed the partition again. He was mildly impressed that Portia had, however she'd done it, managed to maneuver herself into HIS car. That took a certain level of courage, gumption and skill. He liked that.

"How did you get into my car?" Marcus asked.

"I have my ways," Portia said in her sultry voice.

"Oh, I bet you do," Marcus responded. "And how exactly did you know where I was going to be and that this was my car?"

"I have my ways," Portia answered unabashedly, almost matter- of-factly.

"Do you know who I am?" Marcus asked, a slightly ominous undertone to his words.

"Definitely," Portia smiled coyly, opening her legs a little bit wider. "Which is why I'm here. We're going to the movie premiere for *LARGE*, right?"

Marcus had to admit that he kinda liked her style. She was also fine as hell. He could hang with her tonight.

"Right," he responded smoothly.

-57-

It was the night of the premiere. "Sheri" had just left the house after doing Darian's makeup. Now Darian and Mars were getting dressed, moving around each other in their currently messy bedroom, trying to get ready, not as playful as they typically were in moments like this, but the mood was light, lighter than it had been for weeks. Mars had permanently moved out of the Marina Del Rey condo and into the Hollywood Hills house. It was the first step they'd made in the right direction for their marriage. No one knew about it yet, but it was likely to make the news soon. The two had mutually agreed that that was okay.

"I forgive you," Darian said almost matter-of-factly, initiating a dialogue the two of them had been skirting around since that first night that Mars had come up to the house. "How could I NOT forgive you? Look at all you've given up and compromised in your life for me. I love you. And I do not ever want to even have to think about living the rest of my life without you."

"Remember our wedding?" Darian asked quietly.

"Of course, I remember our wedding," Mars answered.

"Let's do something to reclaim us," Darian said. "I don't ever want the two of us to grow as far apart as we have allowed ourselves to grow since coming back here. Let's go somewhere…like we did years ago…in that other life… when we were trying to get to know one another in the beginning of our relationship without interference of media or our careers or anything."

Mars liked that idea.

"Okay," Mars said.

"Look at a map of the world, pick a place, and that's where we'll go."

Mars chuckled at his beautiful wife's typical, larger than life way of doing things. It was so much a part of what had made him fall in love with her in the first place.

"Next weekend, we leave."

"Okay," Mars responded.

There were helicopters above. There were spotlights shining into the night sky. Entertainment news reporters worked the crowd, asking questions. Photographers crowded the sidewalk, setting up their equipment in preparation for the event. It was the red-carpet premiere for *LARGE* at Grauman's Chinese Theatre in Hollywood, and there was a buzz of excitement all around.

Darian was a bundle of nerves as their limousine pulled

up in front of the Grauman's Chinese Theatre, and she and Mars stepped out. He held her hand to calm her. It was still so funny to him how vastly different her personal and business personalities were. They were like night and day.

It was the very first public appearance Darian and Mars were making together as a couple, and the media absolutely ate it up. The cameras absolutely loved the two of them together. They looked really, really good together.

"How is it that Mars Buchanan always seems to have the luck of the gods and becomes romantically linked to these amazingly beautiful, very powerful women? I'd like to take a walk in his shoes for a day," one entertainment news reporter said with a laugh.

"I'd like to take a walk in his shoes for a whole year," another reporter joked.

Both Darian and Mars smiled and said hello to business associates and others they knew in the crowd who were working their way into the theater. Marcus Means, of all people, was there. When Darian caught a glimpse of him in the crowd with that crazy bitch Portia Foster on his arm, she felt hot nausea overcome her as if she was going to throw up. The two filed inside the theater with the others and found their seats. Terrence was already seated with his date, and he reached over and squeezed Darian's hand.

"You did it, babe! You are about to become as large as my former boss, Keshari Mitchell herself!"

Darian smiled at the comment for more reasons than one.

The film opened with a woman sitting in the darkness of some undisclosed location smoking a cigar and thinking back over her life. There only thing that gave away some indication of where she was were the waves of the sea crashing against the shore. There were flashes of the woman's childhood...her and Misha Tierney, neighbors growing up together and calling each other sisters. Hip-hop became popular and Keshari Mitchell fell in love with it. Then her mother became very ill with cancer, and her whole life changed. From that point, Richard Tresvant was introduced and it was shown how he craftily manipulated his way into the most powerful role in Keshari's life at a time when she was deeply troubled following the passing of her mother and was little more than an impressionable teenager. She was highly intelligent, which was a large part of the reason that Richard Tresvant took her under his wing. Keshari went off to college and graduated with high honors from UCLA with Misha at her side, and Richard Tresvant footed the bill. All the while, Keshari was getting deeper and deeper into "the game" while Misha tried desperately for a long time to pull her away from it.

Keshari left Los Angeles for Pennsylvania to attend the Wharton School of Business for her MBA, and it was revealed how she began flying back and forth to Los Angeles very regularly to move work for The Consortium. It was mind-boggling to most how she had managed to go for years, becoming more and more powerful and well-known within the music industry, and did not once get indicted for her criminal activities. And, all the while, the media steered cautiously clear of composing stories about her rumored affiliations to organized crime.

Throughout the movie, Keshari was increasingly riddled with turmoil about the part of her life she worked so ferociously to keep private and completely separate from her life and her business as a record label executive. She seemed to be constantly overwhelmed with a huge and unshakable moral dilemma that ultimately led her to want to completely extricate herself from The Consortium, a decision that, in most organized crime rings, is both unacceptable and deadly. When she met and fell in love with then-West Coast general counsel for ASCAP (American Society of Composers, Authors and Publishers), Mars Buchanan, she had reached a point of conclusion in regard to her membership in The Consortium. She no longer cared about the repercussions, she wanted out and there would be nothing to keep her from that.

In the darkness of the movie theater, Darian attempted to sneak a peek at some of the viewers' faces, hoping to gauge from their expressions whether or not she had hit her mark with the film, if they were liking it, if they were talking as they watched, if what the film conveyed was shattering a lot of the assumptions about the Keshari Mitchell many of them had known. Mars could feel her anxiously squirming in her seat, overwhelmingly concerned about people's reaction to the film, and he squeezed her hand reassuringly. There was no other perfectionist like her.

As horrendous as the decision had been to ever become involved in what she had been a part of, Keshari Mitchell, nonetheless, evoked the sympathy and some level of understanding of her movie-viewing audience that night. "She was an extremely talented woman," one well-known actor said. "I can't judge her. There are quite a few of us here tonight, myself included, who are fortunate that our own lives did not take a similar path. We're all human... and we're all flawed. None of us can say what we would never do until we have walked that proverbial mile in her shoes."

Toward the end of the film, several families were interviewed whose children were put through college by Keshari Mitchell. One young man proudly held up the Bachelor's degree in Mathematics that he had acquired from Keshari Mitchell's alma mater, UCLA, and that she had funded 100 percent. An AIDS support organization in South Central Los Angeles was funded very largely by Keshari Mitchell's philanthropy. Long before her death, she had left significant sums of money to well-known cancer organizations for both research and for cancer patients who were unable to pay for all of their expensive treatments. In total, it was revealed that Keshari Mitchell had given well over a million dollars to cancer organizations during her lifetime in memoriam of her now-deceased mother who had lost her battle to cancer when Keshari was still a child.

As mysterious as the indomitable business mind who had been Keshari Mitchell had been, whether she held strong connections to organized crime or not, she had done numerous very, very positive things for people who truly needed it within disadvantaged communities around Los Angeles, and there were people who STILL looked up to her even in death.

As the movie moved from Keshari Mitchell's charitable and philanthropic contributions to its end, viewers were briskly taken over to LAX where a woman of Keshari Mitchell's stature, with physical characteristics very similar to Keshari Mitchell's from a distance, handed her passport to a customs officer before walking through the security checkpoint, obviously to board her international flight to some unknown locale. In this instance, Darian had taken creative license when writing the script for *LARGE* because Keshari Mitchell had been in disguise when she left the United States, a disguise that she had perfected and also used on her new passport. The credits began to roll as she disappeared into the crowds of people moving about, gone…possibly…forever.

The movie had been UNBELIEVABLE! It was equal parts drama, documentary and the amazing hip-hop music that had turned Keshari Mitchell and Larger Than Lyfe Entertainment into icons in the music industry. No matter who had sat down to watch the movie that night, whether they had been Keshari Mitchell's friends or foes, you could not help but be in admiration and awe at the sheer tenacity and genius business acumen that had propelled her to the very top of the music game before she was even forty years old.

The lights in the movie theater slowly came up again, and mouths were gaping open. There was animated chatter everywhere. That had been Darian's goal. She had wanted to get them all talking, thinking. There was bound to be talk about Keshari Mitchell and *LARGE* for a long time to come.

Darian looked over at Terrence, and he had the most peculiar expression on his face. He and Darian held eye contact for one moment too long and then she knew and he knew and there was an understanding that passed quickly between the two of them. Terrence would keep her secret to the grave.

Back outside on the red carpet, paparazzi were taking full advantage of the camera ops. A very attractive Jada Pinkett Smith and Will Smith posed with Darian Boudreaux and Mars Buchanan. Darian posed for photographs by herself. Then she posed for photographs with Lisa Raye and with Kerry Washington, who had played the hell out of the role of Keshari Mitchell. She posed for photos with Rasheed the Refugee, and, for a split second, he had the most peculiar look on his face. The energy coming from the woman taking the photographs with him felt... familiar.

Rasheed the Refugee had done exceedingly well in the film. He had been working hard with his acting coach and it showed. He was determined that he would be taken seriously in the film industry. His role had been fairly small but significant, because he had been the first and most successful artist ever signed to Keshari Mitchell's record label. Darian smiled proudly every single time that she had watched footage of him in the dailies for the film shooting. She still loved him. His unbelievable talent had put her on the map.

Darian was so excited about the reaction the movie had gotten, and she was ready to head to the after-party at Drai's Hollywood. A chilled glass of Cristal and a bit of time to bask in the shine of her hard work sounded like just the prescription she needed. It had been a long, hard and eventful journey…both her life as Keshari Mitchell and the making of the film about Keshari Mitchell's "larger than life" life.

Marcus Means watched her intently from a distance. A feeling of "familiarity" flashed through Marcus's mind. He'd seen this woman before, and he could not place where. He had no idea why he got such a strong feeling that he knew her. Then, he suddenly remembered. He had seen her at the W Hotel once.

LARGE would be opening nationally in theaters everywhere the next day.

–58–

Following the premiere of *LARGE*, Marcus and Portia had mutually decided to skip the after-party to engage in a little "playtime" by themselves. That movie had left a lot of shit on Marcus's mind. Only someone on the INSIDE could have provided some of the details that were revealed in that movie, and he only hoped it didn't put a whole host of new problems on his plate, particularly causing the feds to start sniffing around him any more than they already were, believing the shit that had been revealed in that movie. Many of the names had been changed in the movie, of course, but that wouldn't stop the feds from digging. Nonetheless, he would investigate further and deal with that matter later. Add it to the already-long list of other shit that was trying to take him out. It had been a long time since he had indulged in some much-needed R & R.

Marcus leaned over and bit Portia's beautiful apple of an ass, perched up in the air waiting for him to fuck her. He bit hard. The bite left teeth marks and drew a small amount of blood.

"Ow-w-w-w-w!" she yelped angrily, then whirled around on Marcus's huge bed to slap the shit out of him.

Marcus grabbed her hand. He smiled.

"You're mine now. That's what you wanted. Right?"

Slowly, an angry and disheveled Portia smiled back.

"Yeah," she said. "That's right."

"Then, there it is."

Two, more twisted people could not ever, ever have gotten together.

Marcus fucked her like she'd never been fucked before, and she fell fast asleep in the down pillows all around them on a bed of a size that matched his ego. He woke her up a couple hours later, flipped her over and fucked her again, loving the feel of her positively perfect ass slapping his groin.

The police burst into the bedroom and placed a naked and nearly climaxed Marcus Means under arrest. Portia, once again, had landed herself right in the epicenter of some completely outlandish shit.

"Sorry to break up your party," the police officer said, "but we're gonna need to take you downtown."

The drama going down in Los Angeles was now WHITE-HOT!

—59—

O pening weekend at the box office for *LARGE* was a HUGE success. *LARGE* was Number One at the box office in ticket sales on its premiere weekend. Every major film studio in Hollywood now wanted to work with Phoenix Films on upcoming projects. In the days following the premiere, there were significant political and legal discussions on several cable and local news shows about America's "war on drugs" and the trouble that was almost completely out of control at Mexico's and the United States' borders involving Mexican drug cartels. The movie *LARGE* was mentioned more than once in these discussions.

Everyone from Anderson Cooper to Larry King to Bill Maher invited Darian Boudreaux to appear on their shows to talk about her perspective on the "war on drugs" and the double life that record mogul/major trafficker Keshari Mitchell had led as depicted in the movie *LARGE*. Phoenix Films' new PR department had to construct a schedule for Darian to coordinate all of the interviews and talk shows and magazine stories that were now on her plate. Darian had known that she would instantly become in much greater demand following the release of *LARGE*. Nonetheless, she instructed the PR department to coordinate all of the interviews and talk shows around the two-week break she was taking beginning the following week. She and her husband were going to get some much-needed alone time together.

Much research had been done in regard to the numerous threatening telephone calls and text messages Darian received during the filming of *LARGE*. After weeks of work and phone calls and follow-ups by Darian's cellular service provider, the wireless company informed Darian that the messages appeared to have come from some sort of computer hacker who had used a rather sophisticated spoofing system each time that they sent her the text messages or called her so that they could not be traced. Therefore, the wireless company had been unsuccessful at locating the identity of the perpetrators. They apologized profusely and offered up some free services and accessories. Darian had figured in advance that they were likely to come up empty-handed. From prior experience, she knew the technology that people from the life she'd walked away from had access to. The movie was released in theaters, and the threatening phone calls and text messages ended as strangely as they had started. It was another of those mysteries, like the strange fires that had broken out on the set during filming and the cameraman who went missing for two weeks and then was found at a bus stop on the Las Vegas strip with amnesia, that would go forever unanswered and be forever connected to the overwhelming mystique of *LARGE*.

Immediately prior to her departure, Darian sat down with her associate producer Michael Chastang to discuss what was next on Phoenix Films' roster. First, there was Larger Than Lyfe Entertainment artist Ntozake's mini-movie music video project. Even though Marcus means was now at the helm of the record label, Darian had contracted to do the project, and she had to admit she was excited about doing it. Keshari Mitchell had hand-picked Ntozake herself to groom her for superstardom, and it would be something else for Darian to work with her now that Ntozake was actually realizing that super-stardom that Keshari Mitchell foresaw for her. The story-line and script for the project were already complete. Darian had hired a pair of writers to get that job accomplished during the filming of *LARGE*.

Next, there was the project that Darian and Michael had excitedly discussed while they were on the set during the filming of *LARGE*. Darian and Michael both wanted to do an African-American version of *Sex and the City* that was based in Los Angeles. Popular Black actresses, great clothes, great dialogue and relationships that were relatable filmed all over Los Angeles at some of L.A.'s hottest locales. Michael Chastang's job while Darian was traveling was to begin laying the development and pre-production groundwork for the film project, including a rough play at the budget numbers to do the project.

After that, there was a very special project that Darian believed she could take to tremendous commercial success. It was an African-American short film that had been submitted to Phoenix Films and Terrence had weeded it out and strongly suggested that Darian take a serious look at it when the Phoenix Films began receiving its first treatments and film reel submissions from all over the country. It was a sexy, very current love story about a woman who'd always identified herself as heterosexual falling in love with another woman. Darian wanted to further develop the storyline, give it mainstream appeal and take the story to a full movie length. She asked Michael Chastang to get the particulars together and make contact with the filmmaker, who was based in New York, so they could talk negotiations once she returned from her trip. Darian was definitely moving into develop-ment with this project.

Next, Darian did two television interviews, one on *Access Hollywood* and the other on *Entertainment Tonight*. She discussed *LARGE* and how happy she was about the tremendous success the film was having, and she briefly talked her plans for Phoenix Films' next movie projects. Then Shaun Robinson, the interviewer on *Access Hollywood*, branched over to a question that was more personal.

"We all saw you at the red-carpet premiere with gorgeous entertainment attorney Mars Buchanan. Anything serious there? Any wedding bells in the near future?"

Darian smiled demurely.

"No comment," she responded.

At Mars's office, Mars had arranged for the other partners to take care of all of his clients' needs while he travelled. To the day, no one knew that he was married, not even his family. They believed that his relationship with Darian Boudreaux was one that had grown more serious over the course of them dating. No one knew how long the two had been dating. No one questioned it. The media was loving the two of them together. And Mars's best friend, Jason Payne, was just glad he had finally made a connection with someone. Jason and his wife had gone out with Mars and Darian a couple of times and Darian was very likeable.

The one thing Mars knew he needed to take care of before he left that had yet to be addressed was what had happened between him and Chris Winters. So far, the two had been awkwardly attempting to work around each other as if nothing had happened. That was not working, at least, for Mars, it wasn't. He'd had a discussion with his friend Jason Payne about what had happened, and Jason could only laugh and shake his head.

"Awwwwww, man," he said. "What the fuck?! You trying to catch a sexual harassment suit?!"

The options were that Mars could pay Chris Winters off and send her on her way, which was unethical but an easy fix for the situation, or he could continue trying unsuccessfully to act as if nothing had happened…up until it potentially blew up in their faces.

Mars opted to have a serious conversation with Chris and pay her off if she was amenable to it. She wasn't open to a pay-off.

"Mars," she said rationally, "I was feelin' you, an opportunity presented itself, I leapt at the opportunity, we both crossed the line. No harm, no foul. I'd like to continue to work and grow here at The Buchanan Group if that's okay with you. What happened that night is PAST."

It wasn't like he was in a position where he could force the issue…without facing litigation, so Mars bid good-bye to Chris and his partners and headed to Hollywood to meet his wife. They had a car coming to take them to the airport. They were flying to Florida that evening.

-60-

As things very quickly turned out, the videotape that had been delivered to Thomas Hencken really didn't mean one whole helluva lot...at least, not as far as the murder of corporate attorney Phinnaeus Bernard III was concerned. Why?

DOUBLE JEOPARDY.

Marcus Means could go and make a music video at Larger Than Lyfe Entertainment, using Ntozake as a back-up dancer, and rap about how, blow-by-blow, he murdered attorney Phinnaeus Bernard III, and he would never spend one hour in jail for it, because the California court system had already wrongfully convicted Richard Lawrence Tresvant for the murder. The criminal case regarding the murder of Phinnaeus Bernard III could never be tried again in any court in the United States due to the restrictions regarding double jeopardy.

Marcus Means had literally gotten away with murder. He had gotten away scot-free with the brutal, execution-style slaying of an "upstanding," high-profile corporate attorney, a White dude, no less, who had helped The

Consortium for years to set up and operate completely legitimate corporations that laundered millions of Consortium dollars, and he had gotten away with this murder on a technicality. All the time that Richard Tresvant had been vehemently proclaiming his innocence, Steve Cooley had been nursing some sort of vendetta to take him down and had succeeded in doing so and, at the same time, had allowed the true murderer to walk away.

Thomas Hencken had taken days to try to decide what to do with the videotape after viewing it. He invited a trusted, longtime friend, a detective with the LAPD to come to his house to view the tape and to get his perspective. After viewing the tape, Thomas Hencken's friend engaged him in a long, serious discussion that he truly hoped would have an impact on Thomas Hencken. It didn't.

"You know the law has become a crap shoot, and the bad guys are typically winning. You've been on this Consortium thing for a long time…maybe TOO long. We all have. We, the LAPD, have had some wins against The Consortium and against other major organizations like them. So has the FBI. So has the Justice Department. So has the DEA. You know that. We've had far more losses. We, at least, have some strength in our numbers. You are now working alone. That is a very, very dangerous position to be in against these thugs, and you know it. I don't care how covertly you think you're working. They are ALWAYS payin' somebody to watch their backs, including some of our own men.

"I think the question you need to ask yourself at this point is WHY you're still doing this. With as much money as there is being generated in major organized crime throughout the day every day of every year, do you think that you single-handedly have the possibility of putting even a dent of a hurting on what these thugs do? They've got some of our own people on their payrolls. We will NEVER eliminate organized crime. We just try to control it enough so that average citizens like you and me can have, at least, a running chance at surviving. It's time for you to try to get as much of your life back as you can before it's too late. Your boys need you. Take some time off. Take a trip. Go and spend some time with them."

The next day after that conversation, Thomas Hencken went to have a discussion with Steve Cooley, the district attorney of Los Angeles. He showed him the videotape he had received from an anonymous source. Steve Cooley asked Thomas Hencken if he had followed up with the courier company to try and find out the identity of the sender. Thomas Hencken expressed that he had, and had come up empty. The courier company claimed to have no record at all of a delivery made to Thomas Hencken's address at any time that entire month. Steve Cooley also questioned, just as Thomas Hencken had, why the videotape had been sent to him instead of directly to the police. All of it opened up far more unanswered and unanswerable questions than there already were floating around on the desktops of Los Angeles law enforcement.

Steve Cooley was in a very bad place. He could play the political game and leave things as they currently stood, with the world believing that Richard Tresvant had murdered Phinnaeus Bernard III. It would certainly save face for him and the D.A.'s office. Or he could do the right thing and come up with a solid case to take down Marcus Means…because there was no way that he could be a high-ranking official in the halls of justice and let this vicious thug get completely away with what he had done. That placed all of the citizens of Los Angeles in danger. He had taken an oath to protect and uphold justice.

What was ultimately decided since they could not go after Marcus Means for Phinnaeus Bernard's murder was that the D.A.'s office would go after Marcus Means for conspiracy to commit murder and murder-for-hire in the murder of Richard Lawrence Tresvant, the very same charges that Keshari Mitchell had been made to face years before, immediately prior to her death. They'd implemented deductive reasoning in their review of the irrefutable facts established by the videotape to begin constructing their case of conspiracy to commit murder and murder-for-hire against Marcus Means. It was a long shot, but, once again, Steve Cooley was willing to take the crap shoot to try and make a significant hit against The Consortium, seemingly as recklessly obsessed as Thomas Hencken was.

In order for the charges to stick and not be based solely

on circumstantial evidence, the D.A. needed a solid, reliable witness or someone who had been directly involved in the successful hit against Richard Tresvant who could corroborate the charges being lodged against Marcus Means. There were some folks in prison who would do anything to have lengthy prison sentences shortened or eliminated altogether. Some prisoners were even willing cooperate with the law if it meant they could gain their freedom.

Because Steve Cooley knew Thomas Hencken and his lengthy work history with the DEA, he agreed to work with Thomas Hencken on an "unofficial" basis to assemble a solid case against Marcus Means. Thomas Hencken immediately began touching base with some old contacts and prison informants who had been acquired over his time in the DEA. Steve Cooley and the district attorney's office did the same. Thomas Hencken did some checks to determine who was currently locked up and who specifically had been locked up at the very same time and at the very same prison where Richard Tresvant had been locked up and murdered. It didn't take long at all for a fish to bite. The "fish" in question was currently in prison doing a twenty-five year bid and covertly told a very convincing story of being the cell mate of the man, a gang member from Marcus Means's own set, who had been hired "from the outside in" by Marcus Means himself to take out Richard Tresvant. The informant even spoke of substantial payments that had been made to his cellmate's family as payment for the "job." Because the cellmate was currently in jail on a second murder conviction, serving life without parole, his family regularly put the maximum amount of money on his commissary "books" every single month. Marcus Means then pulled strings for this hired "enforcer" to receive other "benefits" like sex visits, a color television for his cell, a cell phone, which was illegal contraband in most prison systems, and a job moving Consortium "work" in the prison. Marcus had most definitely laced the cellmate for the very significant job that he'd done taking out Richard Tresvant, the informant said. He'd seen the proof of it with his own eyes. He had no idea how the cellmate had managed to get to Richard Tresvant. Because of who he was, Richard Tresvant had been under maximum security from the time that he got to the prison up until the time that he was killed. Nevertheless, major hits against "high-profile" individuals were successfully carried out all the time, regardless of how high the security levels were around the target.

Steve Cooley, Los Angeles' district attorney, the Los Angeles Police Department, and Thomas Hencken were now all working frantically together. They quickly checked, cross-checked, and checked again all of the facts of the informant's story. They knew how slippery characters like Marcus Means with enough money to pay $1,000-an-hour attorneys could be, and they did not want to chance a thing.

In return for the informant's testimony at Marcus

Means's trial, he would be scheduled for an immediate parole and release from prison. With fifteen years already served on his twenty-five-year sentence, the State of California seemed to believe that it was a fair trade for the information he was providing, and they immediately started the wheels turning for his release. The prison informant was quickly moved by the Los Angeles district attorney into protective custody at another prison and would be kept in protective custody until his release and then, after his release, be placed in "civilian" protective custody until Marcus Means's trial.

Perhaps the past fifteen years of his life behind bars had snuffed out the better portion of the informant's brain cells. There was a code in the streets and there for damned sure was a code in the prison system, and he had violated the fuck out of it. I guess wanting to go home had made him forget or compelled him not to care.

With all ducks in a row, a warrant was secured and LAPD went to get Marcus Means. Ironically, it had been on the same night of the red-carpet premiere of the movie *LARGE*, the biopic of Keshari Mitchell's life. Marcus was as mad as hell when he was arrested, but he laughed in the faces of the police and made them a promise that he would walk on the trumped-up charges against him within a week.

The case that Los Angeles was building against Marcus Means was hinging almost solely upon the prison witness who claimed to be the cell mate to Richard Tresvant's killer, and the videotape that showed who Phinnaeus Bernard III's true murderer was and that Richard Tresvant had, in fact, been set up just as he had relentlessly declared throughout his murder trial by the man who stood to gain the most if Richard Tresvant was permanently out of the way. With the information they received from the informant, the district attorney also went and attempted to "persuade" the alleged killer to offer up his testimony in exchange for a sentence reduction.

A major political game was starting. Steve Cooley had something to prove. He'd put the wrong man behind bars. The murderer was still on the streets and still controlling millions of dollars made mainly from the trafficking of cocaine. And there were constituents in the top tax tiers who were mad as hell at him. Now Steve Cooley was compelled for more reasons than one to make Marcus Means fry, and he was going work every available angle he could, call in every available favor that would assist his case, and find every additional charge that he could pin on Marcus Means at his arraignment.

-61-

Marcus Means was quickly arraigned in Los Angeles Superior Court in Downtown Los Angeles and bail was promptly denied regardless of how valiantly Marcus's overpriced attorney argued for a bail amount to be set.

"Are you out of your mind?!" the judge snapped at the attorney. "This Marcus Means thug is Public Enemy Number One! I'm sure if we hold him long enough, there's a whole host of charges to add to these current ones. BAIL IS DENIED!"

The local Los Angeles news networks were all over the story and Darian, Misha, Mars, Krishawn and even Portia Foster along with all the rest of Los Angeles were closely following all of it, blow by blow, as it quickly unfolded. Because of the tremendous level of sensationalism surrounding the story, including the allegations that Marcus Means was one of the most powerful gangsters on the West Coast, the story quickly became national news. Footage from the now-infamous videotape that had been stolen from the security office at 300 South Grand that identified Marcus Means as the true killer of corporate attorney Phinnaeus Bernard III was made public and Marcus Means, of course, was portrayed via every available media source as Los Angeles' ultimate villain, which made people begin discussing again the future of Larger Than Lyfe Entertainment now that Marcus Means was at the helm.

Marcus Means controlled many completely legitimate, profit-making business enterprises in and around Los Angeles, and what was transpiring now was a PR nightmare that could be costly, if not lethal, to all of them, but, somehow, Marcus Means was not even shaken by the karmic demons that appeared to be trying to eat his ass alive. The wheels of his sadistic mind were well-oiled and were turning and calculating his next moves just as they had before he'd been arrested. What was happening right now was nothing more than a rude interruption to Marcus's typical day-to-day business, but Marcus was assured he would soon return to what he'd been doing exactly where he'd left off. And even if the case did go all the way to trial, and by some highly unlikely turn of events, Marcus was convicted and sent to prison, he would still continue to run The Consortium with an iron fist and not lose a single step in doing so.

Once Darian and Mars arrived in Florida, where they'd gone to finish getting ready for their trip together, they both continued to follow the Marcus Means situation via television and the internet. They discussed the case and the likely outcome, but they mutually refused to become so engrossed in it that it took away from the private time they had carefully orchestrated to spend together. Mars was very concerned about Ntozake remaining at Larger Than Lyfe Entertainment and the effect all of what was currently happening could potentially have on her career. Darian had a feeling Marcus Means would soon be getting the last laugh on this entire saga. No one knew the sick fuck he was like she and Misha did. Misha was hoping the D.A. skinned that son of a bitch alive and let her and the rest of the city watch, but, like Darian, she strongly suspected Marcus would find some way to walk from the charges and leave the entire city of L.A. with their collective jaws on the floor in shock.

As the days began to tick by, Marcus Means was on a slow simmer, growing increasingly angry in his restricted cell away from the general population at Twin Towers Jail in Downtown Los Angeles, threatening his attorney throughout the day that he had better hurry up and get him out. Marcus knew who was behind all of this shit. He knew the motherfucker who had been watching him, tracking him, photographing him and trying to find a way to take him down…to take The Consortium down… for far too long now. You would have thought enough would have been enough when the motherfucker was forced to resign from the DEA. But, clearly, it hadn't been.

The first thing that happened while Marcus waited to go before a judge again for a new bail hearing was the prison informant died while in prison protective custody in northern California. Someone had laced one of his meals with cyanide, and he died before he could get the medical treatment he needed. Marcus didn't even blink an eye, and the D.A. and LAPD certainly couldn't look sideways at him and try to pin the murder on him. He'd been placed in high-security incarceration since the night of his arrest and they were up his ass, watching his every fucking move and listening to every phone call he made. He was one-hundred-percent INNOCENT.

One thing was for sure, though. Snitches really do get stitches. This one got his in the form of a pine box. With no primary witness, the likelihood of a successful case against Marcus Means was very quickly becoming very slim. The man who had successfully carried out the hit on Richard Tresvant would never testify, whether the D.A. and the State of California subpoenaed him to do so or not. He respected the code.

Next down was Thomas Hencken. Not even days after the primary witness died from cyanide poisoning, Thomas Hencken was found dead at his computer desk in his ranch-style Torrance home. His throat had been slit in "Colombian necklace" fashion, from one ear to the other, and his tongue had been viciously yanked through the gaping slit in his throat. It was a message that told those in the know that he had said too much, had gotten too involved in the wrong people's affairs, or that he was a snitch. It was a strong warning to anyone who might venture the idea of picking up where Thomas Hencken had left off. It let them know that that was absolutely the wrong decision to make.

Thomas Hencken's laptop and desktop computers along with every incriminating file he had painstakingly compiled for years had been taken. Physical evidence, photographs, video footage, court transcripts, lists of significant contacts were all gone. Thomas Hencken's lifeless body had sat in his desk chair positioned at his desk in front of the window looking out onto his neighborhood street for two days as if nothing at all was wrong. Steve Cooley had been attempting to reach him for two days and finally sent a squad car out to his house. Thomas Hencken's car was in his driveway. Nothing seemed untoward…at least, not from the street. When police peered into the front window of the house, something clearly was not right. They broke into the house and immediately made the grisly discovery.

As Denzel Washington in *Training Day* said, "It's not what you know. It's what you can prove." Bodies were dropping all over the place, but Los Angeles police had no proof to stick a charge on Marcus Means and where they did have irrefutable proof, they couldn't even touch him. Now how was that for justice?

On the same day that Los Angeles police found Thomas Hencken murdered in his home, before breaking news reports of the gruesome scene of the murder were on television sets all over the city, Marcus Means's case was taken early that morning by his attorney before a new judge and the attorney was, again, seeking bail and his client's immediate release until Marcus Means's pretrial hearing. There was much angry wrangling back and forth between the defense attorney and the district attorney's office. The D.A.'s office firmly believed that Marcus Means's attorney had slithered around until he was able to get the case put before a judge that Marcus Means could pay off. Because the State's primary witness, the prison informant, was now dead, Marcus Means's attorney promptly asserted that there was not very much of a case against his client anyway. Most of the evidence against Marcus Means was circumstantial, Marcus's attorney said, and he dramatically drilled this point home again and again as he pleaded with the court to set bail for his client. Marcus Means's attorney then went on to assess that he believed that the district attorney was under-handedly trying to retry the Phinnaeus Bernard murder case under the umbrella of these new charges against his client in a political ball game set up to save his own face. The assistant D.A. who was present that morning representing the district attorney's office glared angrily at the overpaid snake of a lawyer who stood next to him defending this scum of the earth gangster who should have been behind bars for the rest of his natural life years ago or dead.

Ultimately, bail was set at an unheard of $5 million, and Marcus Means was required to turn over his passport to the court as well as wear a monitoring device until his next court date. Marcus gladly agreed. The pretrial hearing was scheduled exactly one month from that day.

When the news quickly became public, it was like a massive explosion had hit the city. The citizens of Los Angeles could already feel the winds turning in Marcus Means's favor and that he, probably with the help of a suitcase full of bloody, organized crime money to bribe everybody, was about to get away with yet another extremely heinous set of crimes. When breaking news regarding the murder of former DEA operative Thomas Hencken hit the airwaves an hour later, the news had come too late to have any impact on Marcus Means's bail hearing. Marcus Means was already being processed out of jail.

Marcus Means was released from police custody later that day and he, his attorney, and his sizeable team of security literally had to press through the throng of reporters attempting to secure answers to questions to this unbelievable breaking news story of his release on bail… right after a DEA agent who had been in pursuit of him and The Consortium for years had just been viciously murdered. Right before Marcus exited the courthouse, a dejected Steve Cooley declined to answer the reporters' questions, promising there would be a press conference in a couple of hours. He clearly would be rushing over to his offices to attempt to do some speedy and futile damage control because some very, very wrong shit had just occurred. When the next elections came before the citizens of Los Angeles and Steve Cooley was on the ballot, it wasn't too hard to tell what would likely happen. Marcus Means's case hadn't even gone to pretrial yet, and the whole situation was already smelling like a grotesque waste of taxpayer money and court time.

As Marcus squeezed through the throng of reporters, he turned to them and flashed his most confident, sparkling smile, a smile as bright as the sun and that screamed victory before he slid into a big, black Suburban that waited for him and his people at the curb and sped away.

"That man is the DEVIL!" one reporter snapped.

Nah, the Devil had nothing on Marcus Means.

The first thing on Marcus's agenda was a meeting with the other Consortium members. Things were already being put into place at his home. When the Suburban pulled through the crowd of news trucks outside Marcus's Bel Air home and delivered him to his front door, he showered, put on a fresh suit, then headed into the library, the very same room where the murder weapon that had been used to set up Richard Tresvant had been found by police officers right before Richard Tresvant was arrested and charged with the murder of Phinnaeus Bernard III. One of the Consortium members was already there. Shortly thereafter, the remaining Consortium members arrived.

The room was quiet for a long time. They all stared at "Dread," leader of R3Crips, bound and gagged in a chair in the center of the room.

Bree-Z was the first person who finally spoke up.

"Marc, man, what the fuck?! What's up here?"

Marcus stood up, loaded the clip into the gun from his desk drawer and screwed on the silencer. He walked over to Dread.

"This is the motherfucker who robbed the Compton house! I've got a million dollars worth of cocaine that is still missing…and a little something else that this sneaky bitch saw fit to do."

"WHAT?!" the other members said.

Marcus yanked Dread's dreadlocked head back and put the gun under his chin. The blood spatter was wide when he pulled the trigger. Keep in mind there were news vans right outside his house. Marcus had a way of doing things that made you instantly understand he was one of the most ruthless motherfuckers walking the face of the earth. He would dispose of Dread's dead body and it wouldn't turn up for years, and not one of the men in the room would say a word about it to anyone…if they truly understood the importance of silence and truly liked the breath of living.

"Any questions?" he said, stepping back from Dread as he slumped from the chair and fell to the floor.

"This is the new Consortium," Marcus said, "and you're either for it or you're against it. It's time to grind. There are millions and millions of dollars to be made. We are going to become the richest, most powerful, Black men on the planet."

-62-

The yacht crew was in place, the boat was fully stocked with everything from orange juice to caviar to DVD movies to meet all of their wants and needs, Mars and Darian were completely packed and smiling and excited, and they were set to sail out for two weeks on "Larger Than Lyfe," the yacht that Keshari Mitchell had left to Mars in her will. Their goal was to fall in love all over again…not that they were not in love with each other now, but they hoped to rekindle what had existed between the two of them when it was just the two of them in Brazil and on Turtle Island on their wedding day. When it had been just the two of them, before they made the trek back to the United States, there'd been an understanding, an intimacy, a closeness and privacy that excluded all others, a continuously open line of communication with no secrets and no judgments, a love so profound that the first priority on both of their agendas during that unbelievable time was each other.

"Do you love me?" Mars asked as the two of them rode to the private wharf in Palm Beach where the yacht was docked.

"I LOVE you," Darian said with every fiber of her being. "Do you love me?"

"Uh-uh," Mars joked and Darian slapped him playfully. "Woman, you are far more trouble than you're worth."

He planted a kiss on her forehead.

"I love you more than anything else in the world, Mrs. Mars Buchanan."

They'd brought swimsuits and other very casual weekend wear, several very good bottles of wine, a few books both of them wanted to read, their iPods, both loaded with new music selected especially for their trip, their laptops and BlackBerrys with the mutual promise to each other that they would only take or make business-related phone calls when it was an absolute emergency and under no other circumstances, the two set out on their very special excursion. They both smiled at each other and slipped on sunglasses as the hired crew lifted the yacht's anchor and slowly moved the boat out of its dock space and into the open water. They would sail for ten days, stopping at island ports here and there for the day. They'd stay on land for a couple of days when they got to Santo Domingo in the Dominican Republic. They'd do some shopping, purchase some of the Dominican Republic's renowned cigars, and tour the sights. The sun was shining. There was a steady breeze. All was perfect for new beginnings.

Five days into their trip, Mars's yacht, "Larger Than Lyfe," exploded. Mars and Darian were on the boat, to the best of everyone's knowledge. The Coast Guard Search and Rescue (SAR) team searched for days for the bodies and found both Mars's and Darian's remains off the coast of the Dominican Republic. Darian had just revealed to Mars that she was pregnant.

Following Darian Boudreaux's untimely death, a small corporation purchased Phoenix Films. The corporation was ultimately owned by The Consortium. There was no way to know for sure if Marcus Means was responsible for the deaths of Darian Boudreaux and Mars Buchanan, but he did have a new meeting with the Mexicans immediately after the national news stories confirming the deaths.

Marcus's upcoming trial was not even close to being a major priority for him.

The game goes on. The game changes…and never changes. And the only thing "with teeth" that American government has come up with so far in an attempt to win the so-called "war on drugs" is legalization. Legalization didn't substantially lower crime rates nor deter the problems associated with the use and abuse of alcohol. Think it'll have any real impact on cocaine? Heroin? Crystal meth? When you think about it, gangsters have been here in the United States successfully and profitably working their angle, even in the face of detrimental legislation such as the RICO Act, since this great nation cut its first baby teeth, and gangsters will probably be the one faction still standing even after the imminent collapse of all as we currently know it here in the United States.

EPILOGUE

Some people will probably ask why I made the decision to kill Keshari Mitchell/Darian Boudreaux in my second manuscript. It needs to be made very, very clear. NO gangster lives into ripe old age to reminisce about his dangerous exploits...NONE. Both Keshari Mitchell and Darian Boudreaux lived life, materially speaking, that was FABULOUS, ENVIABLE, LARGER THAN LIFE. But, in Biblical terms, "No good can come from ill-gotten gain." In metaphysical terms, LIKE attracts LIKE. There was no possible way that anything so ensconced in negativity could continue indefinitely without some tragic end. That is Universal law.

While Keshari Mitchell developed something within her conscience that demanded that she walk away from "the game," the cutthroat enterprise of cocaine trafficking and sale, no matter the consequences, she, interestingly enough, had no qualms about continuing to live on the tremendous amount of wealth that she had amassed from this very same trafficking and sale. She kept very large quantities of very dirty money secreted away in Swiss and other offshore bank accounts, safe from the possibility of government seizure, and she used this money to, literally, recreate herself, start a new life and continue to indulge in and enjoy the extravagant lifestyle and manner to which she had become accustomed as one of the most powerful, female organized criminals in the United States.

It would never sit right with me morally, ethically to represent only part of the story of the gangster's life, the seemingly "good" part without the very real reality of the bad parts...many times, the tragically FINAL bad parts... that virtually always accompany the conscious choice to be in the game...because I believe that that is part of what pulls more and more of our young people into "the game," people not getting a full taste of the harsh reality of the game because they are so mesmerized and distracted by the "spoils" of the game. They watch the music videos and the movies and listen to rap music telling stories that are nothing more than a PR campaign for luring the young, the foolish, the desperate, the disenfranchised and the impressionable into "the game"—fast money, fast women, fast, shiny cars, a little taste of power and the adrenaline-rushing danger to which so many are attracted.

There are HEAVY repercussions for getting into the game and the ultimate climax for EVERY player who makes the conscious decision to be "in the game" is either prison or death...without exception. Keshari Mitchell/ Darian Boudreaux met the fate of a person who made the conscious decision to be "in the game." And, many times, the people who love people like Keshari Mitchell/ Darian Boudreaux most, the people who have no involvement in the game whatsoever, but care about someone who IS in the game, the innocent bystanders, also get hurt.

RISE OF THE PHOENIX: Larger than Lyfe II is the last gangster's story from me as a writer...I think.

HOLD UP...WAIT A MINUTE
(THE TRUE FINAL CHAPTER)

Darian snapped awake in bed. She was drenched in sweat. She sat up and sipped the water that sat on her bedside table. She looked over at her gorgeous husband sleeping beside her in bed. Mars Buchanan was the glue that held it all together for her. He had given up everything, sacrificed everything for his love for her. After all that she had done in her life, she might never be able to fully embrace the fact that she deserved that kind of love. Since arriving in Brazil, she had been regularly battling a complex mix of very troubling emotions…and nightmares. Sometimes she found herself almost incapable of differentiating her bad dreams from reality.

She had just had yet another of the many unbelievably far-fetched dreams she had been having since fleeing the United States and landing in Brazil. In this particular dream, she had finally made the decision to go back to the U.S. and she had started a film company and Marcus Means had, somehow, found out who she really was…and murdered her.

Mars sat up in bed. He stroked Darian's hair. He was

becoming more and more accustomed to her nightmares and, considering the circumstances, he understood. He often wondered if the nightmares were karma…karma for the life she'd led and the things that she'd done before she did the unthinkable and faked her own death to flee from the wrong path that she had chosen in her former life.

ABOUT THE AUTHOR

Cynthia Diane Thornton is the author of *Larger Than Lyfe*. She divides her time between Los Angeles, CA and Memphis, TN. Cynthia is currently completing her third novel.

INTRIGUED BY DARIAN'S STORY?
FIND OUT HOW IT ALL BEGAN IN

LARGER
than
LYFE

BY CYNTHIA DIANE THORNTON
AVAILABLE FROM STREBOR BOOKS

PROLOGUE

Misha had given Keshari all of the fucking space that she intended to give to her. Enough was e-goddamned-nough. Misha knew that Keshari had been going through a lot over the past few weeks. Nix that. The past year had been a long one for Keshari. Keshari had some major, life-altering decisions to make. She had a mountain of demands to shoulder from one day to the next and it was a wonder that she hadn't burnt out or collapsed from stress and exhaustion a long time ago. She kept so much bottled up inside herself. Misha was closer to Keshari and knew her better than anybody else, but even she often glimpsed that solemn, distant look in her best friend's eyes and said to herself, "She's right here in front of me, yet she's so, so damned far away...like she's all alone in the world. I wonder what she's thinking about because I know she'll never tell me."

The last time that the two of them spoke, Keshari had told Misha that she was going to take a bit of time to herself to try and get her head together. She started working from home. She was taking very few, if any, calls. She wasn't accepting any visitors either. For the past week, Misha had called Keshari's house more times than she could count and, although Keshari's damned housekeeper could barely speak English, she could definitely crank out that "Mees Mitchell es unavailable," and then promptly hang up.

That morning, however, Misha had firmly decided to bypass the futile phone calls. She was going straight to Keshari's house and she was NOT leaving until she saw Keshari, made sure that her best friend was okay, and gave her a piece of her mind. If Keshari dedicated more time to her personal needs on a regular basis instead of putting everything she had into work, Misha planned to tell Keshari, she wouldn't be all holed up in that big ass house like she was Howard fucking Hughes! She knew that there was so much more to Keshari's situation than a constantly gargantuan workload, but she didn't even know how to begin to touch upon those things. So Misha would do what she had always done with Keshari. She would scold Keshari in the way that best girlfriends often did, in the trademark fashion that only Misha could do; she would act as if Keshari's situation was almost a normal one, with a solution as simple as Keshari "taking personal time for herself, chilling out, and getting some rest." Then she would end her admonishments by letting Keshari know that she loved her and that she would always be there for her in whatever way that she needed her to be…for ANYTHING. Keshari would come through her current situation just as she had courageously, miraculously come through so much else.

Misha got dressed and was preparing to leave when a messenger rang her doorbell. Misha quickly signed for the envelope the messenger held on his clipboard and ripped it open. It was a letter from Keshari. Misha read it as quickly as she could while juggling files from her office, invitation samples for an upcoming party that she was throwing, her purse, sunglasses, BlackBerry, and keys.

"WHAT THE FUCK?!" Misha exclaimed, realizing what was being conveyed in Keshari's letter to her.

Everything she held went all over the floor as she went racing frantically out to her car.

♪ 🎧 ♪

Mars was in his office when his secretary came to the door escorting a messenger delivering a package that could only be signed for by Mars Buchanan himself. Mars opened the messenger envelope and instantly recognized the pink parchment stationery inside. He closed the door to his office and sat down to carefully read Keshari's communication to him in privacy. He hadn't seen her in weeks, not since their break-up, and he had to admit to himself that he really, really missed her.

"Shit!" Mars exclaimed in shock, dropping the letter to the floor.

He told his secretary to cancel his schedule for the day, saying quickly that he had an emergency, as he went running for the elevator. A moment later, his Mercedes was speeding at 100 miles per hour up the 405 freeway to Keshari's Palos Verdes home.

♫ 🎧 ♫

Mars arrived at Paradiso Drive to a scene of utter chaos. Emergency vehicles were everywhere and emergency workers contended with television news crews arriving on the scene. Mars could barely get through the pandemonium as he pulled up outside the gates at Keshari's home. A reporter recognized him and rushed over to the car.

"Get the FUCK away from me!" Mars yelled, rolling up his window.

Sam Perkins, head of Keshari's security team, opened the gates and Mars's car sped inside.

"Sam, what's going on?" Mars asked anxiously, hopping out of the car.

Sam Perkins bowed his head and Mars took off running up the drive.

Misha was standing on the lawn, emitting the most chilling scream that Mars had ever heard, as a pair of police officers attempted to calm her. Mars went to her and she collapsed in his arms. Cold, frozen fear took hold of his heart.

"What's happened, Misha? Come on. What's happened?" Mars asked, hugging Misha and attempting to console her.

"She's…she's…she's…dead!" Misha garbled through her hysterical sobbing. "She's GONE!"

–1–

A caravan of black, customized Suburbans coasted swiftly up Alameda Street, across Broadway, and into Long Beach's deserted industrial section near the waterfront. It was almost 2 a.m. and virtually all of the shipping and manufacturing facilities in the area were closed down for the night, scheduled to reopen for their daily business around 6 a.m.

The caravan of expensive SUVs pulled onto the graveled lot of a white brick warehouse at the darkened end of Third Street. The driver in the first truck pressed the buzzer at the warehouse entrance. The warehouse's tall, steel doors rolled open. The caravan of trucks pulled smoothly inside. The doors rolled shut again behind them.

Four armed men, with the kind of muscular bulk acquired during lengthy stints in state and federal prison systems, hopped out of the front and rear vehicles and checked the warehouse's perimeter. After confirmation that the warehouse was secure, one of the men gave a signal to the middle truck's driver. The driver hopped out and held open the Suburban's rear door and out stepped Keshari Mitchell, tall, brown, exotic-looking, clad in black leather Chanel, with a long, sleek, braided ponytail and striking, almond-shaped green eyes. She strode with refined confidence over to the center of the warehouse where her business associates awaited her, her bodyguards watching everything around them as if they were protecting the President.

"Ms. Mitchell," Javier Sandovar said graciously, taking Keshari's hand, "so good to see you again. Why don't we get right down to business?"

Mario Jimenez and Oso Suarez, two of the bulky, tattooed men who'd accompanied Javier Sandovar, whipped five, large utility cases onto the table and clicked them open. Inside each of the utility cases were fifteen kilograms of 80 percent pure, Colombian cocaine. With smooth precision, Oso Suarez cut a small slit in one of the large, plastic packages of white powder. With the blade of his knife, he scooped out a small amount of the powder and dropped it into a tiny test tube. He added solution with a dropper to confirm that the product he'd brought was exactly what Keshari had come to buy. The mixture of the solution and white powder turned a bright blue.

"Very nice," Keshari said, removing a gold, Cartier cigar holder and lighter from her clutch. She clipped the cigar's end and lit it, exhaling a pungent cloud of the expensive, Cuban cigar smoke into the air. Javier smiled at her and nodded, pleased with her approval.

"Two million?" Keshari asked.

"Two million," Javier answered.

Keshari nodded to one of the bodyguards, who pulled two large duffle bags from the rear of the middle Suburban and brought them over to the table, unzipping them to display crisp, new hundred-dollar bills bound together in ten thousand-dollar stacks. Oso Suarez carefully went through each of the duffle bags to confirm that all of the money was there. He nodded to Javier.

"Very good, then," Javier said. "We'll see each other again in one month. The offshore accounts will be in place. Payment is expected upon confirmation of completion of each delivery."

"Of course." Keshari smiled, Javier kissing her on both cheeks.

"By the way, we have been following Mr. Tresvant's upcoming trial," Javier said. "Tell him that we send our regards and support. It is all most unfortunate. My family hopes that his current situation will not interfere in any way with our business relationship. Murder charges against powerful, Black men tend to draw federal attention."

"I assure you, Javier, and I ask that you pass my assurances on to the rest of your family. All bases are covered. We look forward to Richard's exoneration on all charges and a very prosperous future between our two organizations."

"Let us hope so." Javier smiled.

Keshari strode over to her waiting car and slid inside

while her bodyguards kept a watchful eye on Keshari's business associates and the product that their organization had just purchased. Two of them loaded the cases of cocaine into the front and middle SUVs. The warehouse doors rolled open. Keshari's bodyguards all loaded into the three trucks. A moment later, the caravan of black automobiles disappeared back into the early morning darkness.